Anthology of
Splatterpunk
Volume 2

curated by

Samantha Hawkins

A HellBound Books® LLC Publication

CONTENTS:

HellBound Books
Anthology of
Splatterpunk
Volume 2

The Starving Artist Type

Shannon Blake Skelton

The man who could eat himself was never an "official" attraction on the sideshow circuit. If you visited a carnival, you would never see a bill advertising "The Starving Artist." You would never catch a talker bellowing to the rubes to "come see the man who devours his own digits, gnaws at his own nose" in "acts of depravity not seen since the days of the Ro-mans." None of that. Rather, awareness of the Starving Artist carried through whispers and carefully coded notes palmed to passersby. Awareness of the Artist's intimate performance pivoted on careful coordination with a few townsfolk, and some roustabouts rousties striking up conversations with locals to entice them to a "special" type of show, located back behind the trucks and joints. It was a tactic that was once used to attract single men – usually military types – to kootch shows that risked being raided by local lawmen. But this was no kootch show. This was something much more "unique."

I first saw a Starving Artist performance when I was with Bill Hamand Amusements. Hamand ran the carnie circuit in East Texas. Basically, from Dallas to the Louisiana line, Hamand lorded over the region's midways, sideshows, and attractions. I came on as a roustabout to his territory somewhere in the spring of 1978. After giving up on college, trying my hand at oil rig work, and having my heart broken by an almond-eyed girl down in Juarez, I fell in with a group of carnies in Beaumont. Next thing I knew, I was working day in and day out with a crew who termed themselves the "losers, boozers, and coozers." I ran with a rough crew and had an equally tough life, especially for a college boy, but it was what I needed at that time.

It was my first year with the show, and I was still learning the ropes, but Gentleman Jack had taken me on as his special project. He had been a showman for decades and still retained those peculiar particulars of his chosen profession. Bits and pieces of slang, and outlandish tales from the road found their way into all our conversations. Always dressed in a black bowler cap, checkered tie and crimson vest, sporting a gigantic, curled moustache waxed to absolute precision, Jack appeared to be a character out of children's vision of the carnival. Most of us others wore filthy T-shirts, greasy long hair, unkempt sideburns, and ratty jeans – nothing too presentable, really. We were just trying to disappear or forget. Not Jack. He wanted to remember. Jack still held onto that vision of the old show business days. Vaudeville. Dancing dog acts. Phony geek shows. Everybody always laughing and having a grand old time; even the rubes enjoyed being swindled back then. It was all part of the fun in those olden days. But by 1978, the life of the typical showman was characterized less by glamour and glitz and more by bumps of speed and the occasional case of drip dick caught from a local show whore.

We had just set up in Nacogdoches, which is "full of roaches" as Groucho said, and after waking up with about 12 cicadas in my sleeping bag, I tend to agree. I was walking the midway and old Jack came up to me with a playful gleam in his eye and slapped me on the shoulder. "My boy, it is time that you see one of our more interesting attractions."

I glanced at him. He curled the edges of his moustache in self-satisfaction.

"I've already seen the kootch show. It's not bad. I saw better down in Juarez, but-"

He stopped me. "I'm talking about another attraction only a few know about."

"What do you mean?"

"Well, meet me in 15 minutes back behind the floss booth."

As I waited and the sun set, I heard the revving of the generators and the whirring of "The Zipper" flipping end over end punctuated by cries of joy. The funnel cake's oily sweetness permeated the air as the spinning glow from the "Gravitron" turned the surrounding area into a swirl of red and green.

I heard Jack's voice behind me. "Come on," he said, leading the way with his cane.

We maneuvered by all the trucks and trailers, and he guided me over to a large, square grey tent. Unlike the other show tents, out on the midway with all their garish hues and screeching music, this solemn tent drew no attention. Indeed, its ordinariness was a key feature. On first appearance, this unremarkable ashen canvas structure looked like some sort of prep area for one of the grease booths, perhaps a station for cutting potatoes or dipping corn dogs.

Jack lifted the edge of the tent with his cane and ushered me in. Immediately, about 20 seated men in the dimly lit tent glanced my way. From the way they pulled up their collars and lowered their hats, I recognized this space as one of anonymity, one of shame. Something akin to sneaking into a porno theatre. I sat amongst the others on a folding chair and gazed toward a makeshift stage about 20 feet in front of us. Jack pulled up a chair next to me and whispered, "You are not gonna believe your eyes, my boy."

I heard a small drumroll from a snare off stage right; a cymbal crash and a weak spotlight opened. On the stage stood a portly, elderly man with a long, impeccably coiffed silver beard. In a 3-piece suit of indigo velvet, adorned with an elongated chain from his pocket watch running the perimeter of his belly, he stood in complete stillness. The man's eyes shot back and forth, scanning the crowd, yet he remained frozen. He reached to his side and pulled up an ancient, chrome microphone.

Then in a monotone, humming voice he commanded: "Listen!"

Silence.

Jack leaned over to me. "That's Georgie. I've known him since our days back in the Dust Bowl."

Georgie's eyes noted the small disruption and shot a disapproving glance our way.

Then, Georgie began. "Now, there is little introduction needed. You have gathered to witness the spellbinding, the grotesque, the mesmerizing, the vomit-inducing . . . in the annals of all that is decent and humane, you have never seen anything quite like 'The Starving Artist.'"

A gong rang out. I applauded in anticipation, but the looks and stares from the small audience indicated to me that this was not that type of show. Georgie disappeared behind the shabby curtain at the back of the mini stage. Then, the Artist emerged.

Enveloped in a billowy, snowy robe of what appeared to be angora, the figure shambled onto the stage. Perhaps 6 feet in height, the performer hid his identity behind a black leather mask with only 4 openings: two for his eyes, one for his nose and a large gash for his mouth. Only his cold grey eyes, flaring nostrils, and twisted mouth could be seen. All his other features remained concealed under the skintight head wrapping.

Though frail in posture, the Artist projected an air of haughtiness and contempt, even as he looked out over us. Behind him, two stagehands — heads concealed by executioner's hoods — wheeled out a high-backed wooden chair covered with maroon velvet. At first glance it appeared to be a piece of furniture stolen from a cathedral. If it had once been in the possession of a priest, it had long since been debased, profaned, and desecrated. Along its sides of stained wood, where there had presumably once been carvings of Christian symbols, there now existed chiseled images of dismembered feet, plucked eyes, sliced ears and extracted tongues.

The stagehands pushed the throne right behind the Artist. The hooded attendants approached the Artist, and with a theatrical flair, peeled off his robe to reveal a bony body clad only in a pair of black, leather briefs. I sensed the audience inspecting his pale, knobby form. The Artist's appearance could best be described as if someone had taken a skeleton and tightly wrapped it in a translucent, bleached animal hide. The eyes behind the mask stared out in a mournful awfulness, while the mouth loosened, and his tongue ran over his lips.

Like some sort of protein deprived body sculptor, the hobbling Artist began to pose so that we could observe all the aspects of his form. His neck was a twisted conglomeration of blue blood vessels, red arteries and striated tendons wrapped into a pretzel of desiccated muscle and rice paper flesh. Where his neck met his torso, the Artist's clavicles protruded like that of a malnourished baby bird. The Artist's bony shoulders jutted upwards, while his arms were impossibly long, like those of an extraterrestrial. His bony brittleness made the swollen elbows look gargantuan and his wrists particularly frail. The fingers stretched in a way that reminded me of the elongated digits of a missing link marsupial. The Artist's ribs were visible, poking out, as were certain propulsions of blood just under the skin. He had no discernable stomach, but rather we simply saw his vertebrae. There were no sizeable genitalia to speak of, while his thighs were twigs that quivered as he posed. The knees popped out while his tibia and fibula, at first glance, seemed simply to be bare bones. The feet themselves had no padding or muscle and strained under the Artist's slightest movements. He concluded his poses, nodded in recognition of the audience, and sat in the regal chair.

We could see his heart pumping as it rattled his ribcage. Then his lungs began to heave in a rapid, then manic progression of breaths. At first, I thought that the small exertion had taxed him, but then I realized the Artist was readying himself, preparing himself. He stared ahead, not acknowledging us. We – the observers, the viewers, the spectators – were witnessing something not intended for us. We were interlopers on a private ritual. A ceremony of unknown origin whose purpose remained mysterious. The Artist's breathing increased to an inhuman speed and his chest heaved while his weakened frame rocked in the chair. The rhythm of these movements struck me as a self-induced trance.

I leaned over to Jack and whispered, "I think I should leave."

A firm hand grasped my thigh, and Jack shook his head back and forth. Apparently, I was a witness to whatever was to come next.

I looked back at the Artist. His breathing was so rapid, I felt that his chest would burst from exertion. His eyes wiggled behind the mask and the mouth began jabbering, his tongue lolled, and saliva spilled from the corners of his mouth. The Artist raised his quivering right arm as it vibrated in violent spasms. He brought the bony finger up to his mouth and his darting tongue licked its tip. Then, he slowly slid the vibrating finger into his mouth and with a wet snap, he bit into it. The Artist pushed the finger in as his jaw grinded on it. Blood, now mixed with the spit, began to ooze from his mouth as the gnawing commenced. Then, with more vigor, he moved to the middle finger and chomped down. This time, blood sprayed into his right eye, and he blinked it away so as to continue his gruesome affair. Then the ring finger. Now a fever set in his eyes, and I could see a smile swelling under the mask. The cheeks protruded, dancing as his cuspids came down on the fingers, slashing through skin, tendon, and bone. With increased speed, the Artist moved to the smallest finger, and with a self-satisfied smirk and a single bite, it was in his mouth.

I wanted to turn away, yet this profanity was enticing, hypnotic. I recall wondering if this was an elaborate illusion. Regardless of its authenticity, the performance itself was entrancing. With all his bony fingers now in his maw, I could see his neck muscles pulsating, rippling as he tried to swallow the pieces. The audience stared in complete silence as we saw him work the fingers down his throat. Once the pieces were down, we all could see that his once non-existent belly now had a shape to it. Indeed, his torso, his arms, his legs – his whole being – seemed to be reclaiming some life to it. The Artist held up his hand, on which only the thumb remained. Like a boa constrictor, his jaw unlocked and opened to a nauseating, gaping size. He stuck his right hand in his mouth and began to push it in, gnashing like a creature, as he drove his hand, then the forearm further, further into his mouth. Then, the mouth, reanimated and strengthened by consuming the flesh, began to move in a violent, shaking manner, almost like a power tool, gobbling up the forearm until we faced a masked man who had eaten his way up to his own elbow.

I noticed that the belly was indeed growing, and as his ravenous appetite increased, the color returned to his skin, and a type of strength grew in him. Yet, he did not stop at the elbow, as his chomping bicuspids created a foaming, pink froth that was bubbling down his naked torso. When the entire arm was devoured, and only an empty space remained at his shoulder, I could tell the Artist's confidence had returned. He formed his lips into an "O" and let out a high-pitched whistle. The hooded stage crew appeared holding curved knives of some considerable length in one hand, and a steel rod with hooks in the other. They stood at the Artist's side as he remained seated, his right shoulder spewing blood.

The Artist, still sitting, bent at his waist, exposing his bare back. The attendants leaned over and hooked the rods into his flesh. They held up the skin across his back and began slicing and peeling long pieces with smooth cuts, like one does when skinning a hoisted deer. The Artist, seemingly unaware of the pain, pulled his right foot up to his face and pushed the toes, and then entire foot into his mouth. The crunching of the bony, brittle feet sounded not moist, but dry and hollow. The hooded workers flayed more pieces, each time hanging them from the side of the chair. From the foot the Artist moved to the lower leg and bits of white and pink bone jettisoned across the stage like gruesome popcorn. The cursed attendants, also in a frenzy, sliced more and more from his back. The bent at the waist Artist, almost appearing to be in the act of self-fellatio, began chewing on his right knee, all the way up his thigh to his leather briefs.

Then the Artist paused, the hooded flayers retreated, and the performer sat back to catch his breath. His entire right arm and right leg were now gone, masticated, and deposited into his belly, which had grown to a considerable size. The chair, drenched in thick foamy blood and peppered with small bits of flesh, bone and sinew, seemed to heave under the Artist's new weight. But he had just begun. With his remaining hand, he waved the infernal assistants back over. They continued to labor on his back, while he munched on his left hand, its fingers and thumbs, then palm and wrist. The smell of the blood wafted amongst us, but we all sat, transfixed upon the atrocities before us, though I recall taking deep, calming breaths to keep my own bile from flooding into my mouth.

In minutes, his other arm was consumed, as was the other leg. All that remained was the masked, shirtless figure, rocking back and forth in the chair soaked in blood. No legs. No arms. Only a torso. The extended belly was knobby with its protrusions of ingested bones, while remnants of gristle and sinew littered the stage floor. Puddles of an oily substance had gathered under the chair, no doubt a ghastly runoff of fluids and organic detritus.

Now, the masked demonic minions came to the torso and playfully hovered the strips of the Artist's back flesh above his mouth. Like a great white snapping at a fleeing seal, the Artist lunged at the pieces and greedily sucked them down like one would spaghetti. When the lean fillets extracted from his back were consumed, one hooded assistant positioned himself behind the gory chair, and wrapped his arms around the Artist's neck, holding the performer's head stationary. The other assistant carefully drew out a chrome hand scythe and in one swipe, sliced the Artist's nose off. Blood shot from his nostrils, spraying the attendant as he roughly shoved the snout into the artist's jabbering mouth. Then, he went to the Artist's eyes, drew out a switch blade, and began to dig into his right eye, carving it out and throwing it on the stage floor. Then, the left eye. He jabbed again and again as the clear vitreous fluid ejaculated from the eye socket. Once the eye was completely fished out, he jammed it into the Artist's mouth, who groaned in ecstasy as he chewed the rubbery material. The attendant went to the eye on the stage floor and stomped on it, creating a squealing noise like that of air being pressed from a balloon. Then, in one swift movement, the attendant scooped up the smashed eye and shoved it into the Artist's mouth. Then, stillness. The hooded stage crew exited.

The head sat there, atop its torso, devoid of any and all limbs and appendages, with its masked visage oozing blood from where its eyes and nose had once been. But the heart of the torso was still beating, and the lungs were inhaling and exhaling. In fact, in the eerie silence of the tent, the only sound we could make out were the Artist's exhausted, gasping breaths.

It appeared that the gruesome show had concluded. I sat, curious if we were to applaud, cheer or simply leave. And confused as to what I had just witnessed. Was this a complex illusion, or something more cursed? I looked around at my fellow audience members; their eyes remained fixed on the stage as if they awaited something else to occur. I began to stand, and Jack seized my hand.

"Oh, it's not over, my son."

I sat back down and considered the tableau in front of us. A torso, with a massively engorged belly, shorn of arms and legs, topped by a masked head devoid of eyes and a nose.

Breaking the silence, Georgie reappeared from behind the curtain with a satisfied smile.

"Thank you all for attending this performance. Now, you may believe that this show has concluded. And in some ways, it has. But we have a special coda for you."

He crossed the stage like a professor delivering a lecture on an esoteric topic that he has fully mastered.

"When Bill Hamand entered show business and founded our little amusement enterprise so many years ago, he believed that we – as entertainers, as artists, and providers of joy – should always give back to each and every community we visit."

He paused. "Some amusement organizations raise a little money for a local charity, others give a percentage of their takings to a town scholarship. We here at Bill Hamand Amusements take our dedication to community service very, very seriously."

The Artist's limbless torso remained still, but I noted that his breathing continued.

"And that is precisely why you are here today. All of you were invited. Some of you are from the community, others are from our own organization. And one of you is here for a very special reason."

The spotlight flashed away from the stage and focused on a smallish man 3 seats down from me.

I heard Georgie bellow into the microphone, "Mr. Lawrence Eggert. Could you please stand up."

The squat man of 40 or so flashed a quick smile, adjusted his glasses and got to his feet. Light bounced off his balding head.

"Please, come to the stage." At that moment, Eggert seemed to look for an escape, but a few men from the crowd stood up and seized him.

The men – whom I did not recognize – pushed and pulled him to the stage, while Eggert thrashed and screamed.

Georgie murmured, "It is no use, Mr. Eggert."

Even though Eggert resisted, it was futile. The men threw Eggert upon the stage and from behind the curtain the hooded assistants emerged and clamped a steel hoop around his neck. Eggert began to tug at the device around his neck. The stage crew wrestled his hands together and bound them at his waist with some ancient, rusted manacles.

The hooded crew pushed Eggert to his knees.

Georgie approached him and leaned down, still speaking into the microphone.

"Mr. Eggert. Are you a resident of this town of Nacogdoches?"

The terrified man's eyes flashed, and tears welled in the corners of his eyes.

Eggert nodded.

"Did you at one time operate an ice cream truck?"

He nodded again in agreement.

"Was this business named 'Creamy Goodness'?"

There were a few groans from the crowd. Eggert was beginning to understand what this was about. On his knees, he now stared at the floor in shame.

"WAS IT?" Georgie screamed into the microphone as he leaned right into Eggert's face.

Eggert glanced back up and nodded. Now Eggert appeared to be a wide-eyed dog cowering at his abusive master.

Georgie trod across the stage in self-satisfaction.

"We, Mr. Eggert, we are here as witnesses. Not just to this performance – but also the performance which awaits. I offer you testimony in the form of your peers and fellow community members. Each are in attendance to seek justice. Please, gentleman, stand and proclaim the truth."

Eggert tried to shield the blinding spotlight to see who spoke against him, but it was no use. They were cloaked in darkness.

One voice proclaimed, "You touched my sister, Joanna. Age 6."

Another voice chimed in, "You fondled my brother, Isaac. Age 7. He is still missing. He either ran away or you killed him."

Yet another shouted, "Julia. 12. She threw herself off Riley Bridge because of what you did to her."

And a final, gruff voice stood and said, "Charles. My son. He was 13 but had the mind of an 8-year-old. You gave him ice cream, invited him into your truck and violated him. Because of that he stuck a gun in his mouth."

Then, there was only silence except the weeping of Eggert.

Still, the Artist's head and torso remained, unmoving in the chair.

"You see, Mr. Eggert. We at Bill Hamand Amusements always partner with communities. Sure, we run the midway with smiles. We sell you an experience that takes you out of your humdrum life for a few hours. But this – this extra added attraction — that of the Starving Artist – is one we hold for very special people, such as yourself. We in show business call you a 'Chester' – and I am sure I do not need to explain what that means."

Georgie motioned toward the hooded crew, and they pushed Eggert's face toward the bloodied torso in the chair.

Eggert screamed as the Artist's gaping mouth began jabbering with an intensity as he sensed an approaching meal. The hooded men, as if pushing a wooden plank into the teeth of a saw, pressed Eggerts' face into the mouth of the Artist. The gnashing teeth shredded Eggert's nose. Crimson fluid spurted into the air and Eggert screamed. The hooded minions pulled Eggert's face back from the Artist and turned his face to show the crowd the grisly work.

The predator squealed, blood flinging out of the hole that was once his nose as Georgie thundered, "You see, justice is restorative in so many ways. Look upon the Artist!"

Georgie pointed at the Artist's masked face. There, in the gaping hole that once held his nose, there was movement. A protuberance began to sprout from behind the Artist's nose hole. Within seconds, there was no longer a hole, and the Artist's nose had returned. Even Eggert, through his pure terror, gazed upon this strange reacquisition with awe.

"What you see here is NOT an illusion, but rather justice. Let the regeneration begin!"

And with that, the hooded stage crew disappeared for a moment and returned with a hospital stretcher. They lifted the screeching and bloodied Eggert and slammed him onto the gurney. The blood had stopped jetting from his face, but there was certainly much more pain to come.

Retrieving their tools of agony, the hooded men began flaying Eggert's chest and pushing the bloody ribbons into the Artist's awaiting mouth. Then, with the same switch blade used on the Artist, one assistant made quick work of Eggert's eyes, gouging them out into his palm. He then plopped them into the Artist's mouth. And, like some sort of nightmarish illusion, the Artist's eyes began to reappear.

Eggert's howls of agony reached such a level of intensity that they became a type of background noise for me, like a squeaking cabinet that you grow to ignore. They wheeled the bleeding man over, and like feeding branches into a woodchipper, the masked crew pushed Eggert's right hand toward the Artist's flapping mouth. With great speed the fingers, and then the entire arm, disappeared into the Artist's motoring jaws. We could see the Artist's neck straining, but once the pieces of the limbs made it past his throat, we noticed a small, bony twig poke from the Artist's bloody shoulder. Within seconds, an arm began to grow.

Eggert, now passed out from the pain, could resist no longer and no longer did his screams fill the tent.

With a compliant feast before him, and a newly regenerated arm, the Artist's frenzy increased and he gobbled down the molester's other arm, then hoisted the man's right leg up and consumed it with gargantuan bites, hardly waiting to swallow. He finished off the final leg and threw Eggert's meaty torso to the stage floor. The Artist stood in triumph, covered in the blood of himself and his meal. Satisfied, he began to strike poses that one would see at a body building contest. Flexing, curling, pumping. Under the layer of blood, we could see the Artist had been transformed. He smiled at his muscular arms and admired his powerful legs.

The hooded attendants entered with buckets in hand. With precision, they sponged away the blood and fluids from the Artist's body. The reborn Artist took pleasure in this ghoulish cleansing. Once his well-toned and muscular body was wiped down, the attendants cleaned and polished the black masque that still concealed his identity. They returned with the white angora robe. Previously coated in blood and viscera, the now lean and muscular – no longer bony and frail – Artist smiled as the attendants approached him and respectfully placed him within the robe as if he were a triumphant prizefighter.

And with that, the crowd applauded. They more than applauded; they stood in appreciation, they whooped in celebration and hollered their approval of the performance. The Artist, now smiling, gleaming in the adoration, waved to the fawning spectators. And the spotlight flashed off and we were returned to darkness.

The audience quickly dispersed, retaining their anonymity. Jack stood up and turned to me.

"Well, what did you think?"

I chuckled. I was replaying it all through my mind. I thought to myself that this must have been a gag. "How did they do all that?"

Jack laughed. "Old tricks of the trade. You'll learn them if you stick around long enough." He held the tent open for me as we both exited. We both walked to the midway in silence. Just as we were parting, I turned to him and said, "Hey Jack, how long has he been in the business?"

He moved up to me and whispered, "The Starving Artist has been at it for as long as I can recall. I even remember my grandpa telling me tales of a guy just like him, who did this same kind of service."

And with that, Gentleman Jack tipped his cap in a proper gesture, spun his cane like Charlie Chaplin, and jaunted down the midway.

Onslaught

Juan Ozuna

What's that clambering inside my head,
Can it be the fiend called Dread?
Its talons whisk my brain to bits,
While on the floor I shake in fits.
Please cease! I plead, I PLEAD!
Please stop this painful misery.
But Dread still lashes unabated,
I feel my mind's eviscerated.
I bash my head against the wall,
But still the torment does not stall.
With maddened cries, my fingers maul,
And peel the flesh from off my skull.
My screaming eyes, they look and spot,
A drill, and then I get a thought.
I take the drill and poke my head,
Until I reach that fiend called Dread.

Alex stopped writing. He didn't know how to finish the poem. What would happen after he's drilled a hole in his head? He imagined the drill would soften and stir up a bit of the neural matter and that sludge might pour out after he's withdrawn the tool. But the hole put into his forehead would probably be too narrow. Much too thin for chunks of the blended brain to spew through, much less a creature. Which raised the question of what exactly Dread was? He'd described it as some fiend crawling around his cranium and slashing his brain. But Dread was much more intimate than a creature. Dread was a part of him, entangled in every process of his nervous system. To get rid of Dread, Alex would have to empty out his brain entirely. Everything must go. Until then, Dread will persist.

This was getting much too complicated for Alex. He set the pad and pen down and grabbed the pipe from the coffee table. He lit it up and breathed in the sweet grass, letting it burn his lungs before blowing it out. He bent to set it down but then brought it back to his lips and took an even deeper hit. The immolated weed was thrown onto an ashtray, and another bowl loaded.

Alex soon forgot entirely about Dread, the high affording him a blissful ignorance to everything in the world.

Until his phone buzzed. He lifted it up. His dad left a text message:

Your mother killed herself last night. I'm joining her soon. Just want to finish this one last beer. I know we don't talk much, but I just want you to know I love you, son. You and Aura should think about doing the same, rather than be eaten like wild animals. That's no way to go.

Dread was back like a punch to the gut. Alex's hands trembled, turned purple. He took deep, successive hits of the pipe, then stumbled to the fridge and grabbed an IPA. He downed its innards, then grabbed another bottle and depleted it. The color came back to his hands, and they didn't shake as much.

Alex turned and looked out the window towards his neighbor's house. Their drapes were open, and inside was a creature of twisting limbs and many eyeballs. Upon closer observation, Alex recognized Mrs. and Mr. Gonzalez, who lived a few doors down, and David Barajas, who lived the next block over. There were other faces Alex remembered but couldn't put a name to; faces he'd seen mowing lawns or drinking beer in the front yard by a crackling grill. All those familiar faces were there in that single home as if sucked there by a gravitational force. Their expressions were twisted; open mouths yawned wide, tongues lapped like agitated serpents, and eyes rolled as if lubricated.

They were having an orgy.

Alex felt a warmth in his pants, and his prick twitched with excitement. He considered joining.

On the street, a truck drove by blasting hymns, its sides painted in bright, red letters with the word REPENT. Alex's arousal dissipated.

The truck drove by a group of kids huddled on the sidewalk. They all looked pre-teen. Some were aiming pellet guns at the sky, and those without guns were throwing rocks. All were yelling obscenities. Alex noticed a liquor bottle being passed and chugged, passed and chugged. A couple kids would pause to take drags from a cigarette. The children moved sloppily, but all were fiercely determined, full of liquid courage. They cursed and spit at the sky.

Alex wondered where their parents might be and then realized they were probably participants in the orgy next door. He considered rolling some joints and distributing them to the youths but then remembered he had a limited supply.

Alex sighed. These kids will have to live fast now, he thought. Experience as much as they can before the slaughter.

He looked up at the sky crowded with puffy white clouds. He imagined them opening and dispersing. Bright lights shining through cast from ships of inconceivable mass. A chorus resonates worldwide, the sound of humans and beasts screaming madly. And the sky thunders as a horde of sinister beings descend like dark angels to bring death and anguish.

He stares, waiting for such a scene to occur.

***

Yesterday.

It happened around 4 p.m. Of course, people worldwide saw it in their own time zone, but every human saw it at the exact moment. For Alex and Aura, it was 4 p.m.

They had been watching a show about an air-bending twelve-year-old monk when their television screen flickered and buzzed static. The image then changed to a wide shot of desert land and red sky. There were too many moons in the sky. But the land was just like any other barren landscape, sparsely sprinkled with vegetation. A breeze stirred up clouds of dust, and there were mountains far off in the distance. It looked like the kind of place where breathing felt like breathing in glass.

Slowly, the camera turned. There were sounds before the camera revealed anything, sounds that could have come from Hell. Tortured cries and groaning defeat. The camera panned slowly. The landscape grew unfocused while at the forefront, a grisly picture was revealed...

What was facing Alex and Aura from their television screen was humanoid, but more massive than any being of Earth. The facial features were much too small for how big its head was. It was nude, and its complexion pale. The way it looked directly at the screen with its pinpoint eyes made Alex shiver.

Behind this solitary creature, the scene was blurry. Still, shapes could be made out moving crazily, and things were being tossed around. Fires were blazing and smoke rising.

The thing spoke: "Hello, apes. I am Thrall, leader of the Merci." Its voice was high-pitched, almost a whistle. The lips looked like they barely parted.

"Soon, you'll be right here," and the thing named Thrall pointed at a slim black tongue that darted out.

Because of the alien's technology, the message was understood globally, translated automatically so that each human being could discern its horrible meaning. Its language was, in actuality, hisses and whistles.

Thrall said, "Enjoy your last days, for we, the Merci, will soon arrive." Its black tongue slipped out and licked the air. "But first, I'd like to give you a glimpse of what to expect."

Thrall moved away from the camera. Alex and Aura were left speechless when confronted with the destruction of an alien planet.

"These are the last of the Elcron," Thrall said.

Shown on the screen were little bald beings. Pixies came to Alex's mind when he saw them. The Elcron were screaming and being eaten by the gigantic beings called the Merci.

Thrall stepped back in front of the camera, grinning hideously as the screams reverberated through the air. He closed his eyes and breathed in the agony, inhaling the thick blood swirling in the air. It filled his nostrils which were tiny slits. Saliva spilled from Thrall's quivering lips.

The recording device followed Thrall's movements as he approached a village of mud and wood homes. A third element of fire now also composed those homes, distorted them into flaming heads that cried crackling to a crimson sky. The few trees sprinkled around the land were burned to their cores, leaving blackened dendritic remains that reached like long fingers towards the red sky. Situated at a distance from the village were massive spacecraft with sinister designs—gory scenes of genocide.

But the most captivating image was the feasting. Seated on the ground throughout the village were a herd of Merci, a multitude of humanoid beasts nibbling and chewing the Elcron villagers. The flaming homes could easily have been used as campfires to roast the inhabitants, but these were not used. Instead, it seemed the Merci preferred to eat their victims raw, messily. They showed each other where the most meat was, which seemed difficult since the Elcron were slim beings. They still found pockets of flesh to pull and peel and pluck. Because their mouths were tiny, they had to pull small increments that could fit between their lips.

The Merci dined merrily, and under their merriment, the anguished screams of the Elcron grew dimmer.

The camera zoomed in on Thrall's face. He looked like he was orgasming. The camera then panned to all the dying Elcron crying out to brothers and sisters, mothers and fathers. Death was slow as they watched each other be eaten.

Alex sat horrified in silence. The camera focused on one Elcron female, and her words were translated. She was calling the names of those relatives coming apart before her eyes. Interspersed between these callings were screams as her entrails were pulled from her torso.

The camera then focused on other individuals. Alex ate up every word like he was a hungry, sunken vagrant, and the words were morsels of meat.

"Eat me, leave her alone!" a brother was pleading to a Merci gnawing his sister.

The camera leapt to another.

"Close your eyes; the pain will subside!" a mother comforted her children. The next moment she was reduced to primitive yells that echoed into the thickening atmosphere of smoke and misty crimson. The air reminded Alex of a sauna, but the liquid bathing these alien's bodies was congealed, sticky, and red. It was a grisly scene that made Aura run away and puke in the bathroom. Alex didn't notice her absence. He watched –

As the camera flickered back to Thrall, grinning. The beast scurried across the hot desert floor, camera following. Thrall reached his own meal, a struggling Elcron whose ankles and wrists and knees had been bent in ways not meant to, preventing escape. The Elcron's bony form wriggled as Thrall lifted it up.

With a sick and sadistic smile, Thrall twirled the Elcron until the connective tissues between the head and shoulders snapped. Alex winced at this sound. He thought the untethered body might float up and away towards the sky, but it just sunk to the ground and thumped.

Thrall lifted the dripping head to his nostrils and inhaled with a deep ecstasy that sent his eyes rolling inward. His black tongue vibrated and lapped at the shreds of flesh streaming beneath the young Elcron's head. Blood dripped, painting Thrall in crimson, staining his pale skin.

The body of the Elcron wriggled on the floor, its neurons perhaps still firing, still saying run…run. Even with your broken limbs and severed head, run! The young Elcron wriggled as its relatives watched and moaned as they too were squished between Merci teeth and claws.

"So delectable. So fresh," Thrall said. He bent and lifted the headless body and slung it over the branch of a blackened tree. Thrall then raised the head and brought it down on a large boulder, splitting the skull down the middle. He carefully lifted the two halves, so they remained intact. With an ease that only repeated practice could afford, he separated the two casings. The delicious filling now resided in two separate cerebral bowls.

Thrall offered one cerebral container to a fellow Merci. The comrade must have been nervous, though, because he fumbled the bowl to the ground. It thudded and dispersed a red cloud of dirt. A silence descended as those around watched the neural matter spill out and mix with the dirt. The comrade looked up to Thrall, trembling.

Thrall kicked his fellow Merci to the ground, then grasped for the Elcron body, lifting it off its wooden hanger. He twisted it at the waist, then tore. Dropping the legs, Thrall grasped the upper torso by the collar bone. He then lashed at the Merci mercilessly, all the while bits of flesh flew away from the Elcron whip revealing its underlying spinal column. Sharp, splintered ribs scratched at the howling subordinate.

The foolish Merci's cries accompanied the howls of pain from the Elcron being devoured all around – a choir of misery!

Thrall did not halt but instead lashed harder.

A group of Merci gathered to observe the bloody punishment, their meals still squirming or limp in their grasp.

After a few more lashings, the spine of the Elcron broke, so Thrall threw the remains at a bound Elcron elder writhing in the dirt. The elder trembled, then shifted his position, so the splintered remains of his granddaughter didn't poke him in the face.

"BRAK! VOM NRECTUR MATIS – " "STOP! THIS IS MADNESS – "

Thrall ended the elder's screams with a kick to the ribs. He then proceeded to kick the elder in the face until his features were erased.

Heaving heavily, Thrall looked toward the smaller Merci he beat, still laying in a fetal position on the ground. Then he turned towards the camera, spittle flying onto the lens.

"You see…" Thrall was back to addressing the camera and people of Earth. "We are coming… and we will rip your bodies apart!"

Thrall took the disfigured Elcron elder and plucked an eyeball out. He swirled the eye around in his mouth like a mint, then crunched. Most people of Earth were shitting themselves by this point.

"We will be arriving soon. So please, I ask that these next few days you eat gluttonously. Heap some extra meat on those brittle bones. May your tables be gloriously heaped with your last feasts. Eat up…and wait. Because we are on our way."

Thrall nodded to his cameraman to cut off the transmission. The people on Earth were returned to their regular programming. Families stared wide-eyed in unspoken terror as family comedies resumed playing. Many elderly hearts had given out during the transmission. Their owner's slumped bodies went unnoticed until relatives were snapped from their paralysis. For many lonely men, their porn resumed, but they found that they did not possess the previous enthusiasm to continue, their pricks limp within their grasp.

For Alex and Aura, the air-bending monk and the rest of his gang were back on their flying bison, escaping from fire-benders.

It was a couple more minutes until the emergency broadcasts started blaring on screens worldwide.

***

Present.

Alex stared out the window waiting for their arrival. He turned from the sky back to the inebriated children and contemplated getting out the Ziplock bag of coke he kept in a drawer and showing the kids how to use it. Fuck it. These were their last days, right? He felt terrible because they will miss out on plenty of experiences. Still, maybe he could show them highs they've never experienced and never will again.

The front door slammed open.

"Babe! Come here!"

Alex ran through the living room to the front door where his pregnant girlfriend was lugging a box. She looked like she was having difficulty carrying it. The edge was pressing against her black dress, into her pregnant belly. Alex feared that the corners were piercing the baby's head (but it didn't really matter what happened to the baby since they will all be dead soon anyway). Alex lunged and grabbed the box from her and set it down. The thing must have been fifty pounds.

"What is that?" Alex said.

"You are going to love this." Aura said. "My mom had two, so she let me have one. Apparently, they're giving them away at Target. Seeing as the world is ending, they thought they might as well help assuage people's minds during these times. They're so wonderful. The Feelers, I mean."

She waddled over to the box and produced her car keys to make an incision in the tape. Quick slashes, and then the top opened. Aura tipped the box over until it fell on its side and pink packing popcorn spilled out like a soft sea. Alex just watched. Watched as a thing rolled out of the box and settled on the living room carpet.

To Alex, the thing looked almost like a brain, but it wasn't. It was too round and large. Alex guessed it must have been a couple feet in height. The thing was gray and looked like a bundle of nerves.

"Uh…like I said. What the fuck is that?" Alex said.

He feared – and this fear was probably induced by all the weed and alcohol he'd consumed – that Aura had gone out and loped off the heads of several persons. She then sawed off the tops of the skulls and retrieved the gray matter contained within. With several handfuls of cerebral matter, she then mashed them together, like a kid playing with Play-Doh, creating this amalgamation that now sat in their living room.

Of course, this is not what occurred.

"Uh. Like I said, this is a Feeler," Aura repeated.

"Ok. What does it do?" Alex was trying so hard to hide his disgust, but Aura seemed so excited that he couldn't help but humor her. His instinct was to stomp the bundle in front of him. Still, he ignored this instinct because his whole life – well, the rest of it – was committed to making Aura feel as secure as possible. Even before news was heard of the alien invasion, Alex had started hitting the gym.

He didn't have a gun, but he didn't think that would affect the aliens, even if he had one. Scientists postulated that since these beings walked onto any planet un-equipped with a spacesuit, their bodies must be highly resistant to external factors. This was proven to be true after closer examinations of the transmission: In the background, the insect beasts were seen carrying victims into flames and laughing as the victims charred within their grasp. Also, several attempts were made to blast the insects away with a weapon that seemed to shoot lightning from its muzzle. The shot Merci would just clamber back up and scurry toward their assailant and decapitate them.

So, guns wouldn't have any effect. They might as well be getting attacked by ghosts.

Alex stared at the Feeler on the floor.

"They're supposed to make you feel good." Aura said.

"Supposed to make me feel good…Really? All I feel is buzzed."

"Hold up. It's not on yet." Aura bent over and wriggled her fingers into the Feeler's many folds, squishing around until finally finding the switch, which she flipped.

An electric charge engulfed the room, exciting each individual nerve ending on its human occupants. A gasp escaped Aura's lips, and the lump in her womb gave a nudge. The lump was scheduled for release from its biological abode in two weeks, but for now it kicked with excitement.

"Oh…Ohhhh. Shit, this feels good!" Alex moaned. He clasped his eyes tight and looked up toward an unseen showerhead that bathed him in euphoria. The Feeler broke free from Aura's grasp and wandered the home, casting its sphere of influence.

Thrums of excitement pulsated throughout the room.

Alex and Aura stood in the living room, just enjoying the high. A half-hour later, Aura snapped out of it and said, "Some music would be amazing right now."

Alex smiled, his eyes slits. He went to retrieve his cello from the bedroom, then skipped back to the living room, humming. Alex sat on the sofa, and Aura sat next to him. He then positioned the cello between his legs and bowed a note.

They both gasped. And twitched with excitement. Feeling a high unmatched by weed or sex or heroin, or all three combined.

The stimulation of their brains went unseen as the Feeler rolled through the living room, its intoxicating waves combining with Alex's musical ones. Action potentials were reached, and neurons fired. The string's metallic buzzing tickled gooseflesh onto their skin.

Alex hugged the cello closer, his wood growing between his legs and thumping the cello's dorsal surface. He bowed harder, faster, and the sounds elicited more incredible elation.

Aura twitched beside him and moaned with excitement. Even though she was carrying another human, she felt weightless. She felt as if she were floating off the ground, away through the ceiling, and soaring into the sky until bursting through dense clouds. Breathtaking and terrifying was the high as she flew away in her mind.

Alex came to a vibrato passage, and the waves seemed to fuse the player and instrument into one blurred entity. Flesh joined wood and strings. Everything else in the world and beyond became non-existent. The C-string rang the sound of deep space…

They were traveling. Them and the music. Speeding through a dark expanse, past brightly burning star clusters, then burrowing through black holes. Faster and faster. A galactic journey that rushed past their senses. They would have been frightened had it not been so beautiful—

A phone alarm went off. "Clair de Lune" by Debussy. It startled Alex and Aura back to the world of their living room.

"The performance! Babe, the orchestra is still getting together tonight. Can you imagine? How fantastic the music would be with a Feeler nearby? Do you want to –"

"Of course. Just hearing you alone has been the greatest high of my life. I can't imagine a whole orchestra playing." Aura jumped from the sofa. She hurried upstairs to get ready.

They both had forgotten about aliens.

"Honey, where will you sit? Any seat is available," Alex said. He fastened his cello away like a madman gets bound to the chair he will get fried in.

Aura came back down a few steps. "Any seat? Hmmm? I've always wanted to sit on the balcony. I'll be right up front near the guardrails so I can have a bird's eye view!"

Alex grinned. He'd never been this excited before. He hurried after Aura to change as well.

***

The performance was downtown at Symphony Hall. Many arrived, some trudging like dark, gaunt figures in the night, tears leaking down their faces. But most were accompanied by rolling, brain-like Feelers; they had become an overnight sensation. The people accompanied by Feelers walked straight-backed and talked fast, wide-eyed. They were higher than they'd ever been. The Feeler's sphere of influence differentiated between no persons, though. They lifted the moods of anyone in their vicinity, and so those trudging figures once seated and surrounded by feelers couldn't help but smile and forget about the inevitable end.

Alex was seated amongst his fellow cellists, and the performance began. The strings started singing a low tune—mournful and pained. Sticks gently thumped drums, brass instruments blew softly, carefully, then spit harder, more menacing, every brass instrument joining in one crescendo.

Then silence. A lone violin rang out, crying for the crowd's attention.

The audience was paralyzed with awe. They sat back as the Feelers rolled down aisles, up onto balconies, under seats, and continued rolling until there was a charged atmosphere permeating the entire music hall. The orchestra played to a packed house of over two and a half thousand humans and a hundred feelers. All were being vibrated by the orchestra's many instruments and many timbres.

The symphony crescendoed again, elevating the audience into a state of being previously unattained. Everyone felt weightless as the collective greatness of the orchestra swelled. The music washed upon the audience in waves, drenching them in dense enjoyment, lifting them higher and higher. The musicians plucked and blew and fingered with an intense fervor that was expanding. At some point, senses augmented, minds splintered, thresholds ruptured, and the musicians and audience were…

…Traveling now, ferried by musical waves past stars intensely burning, then past star clusters and through black holes. Guests on a galactic symphonic journey. They would have been frightened had it not been so beautiful.

To Alex, there was only the music. It's all that existed. He bowed frantically, squealing through passages. It's as if he and the sound lived as *one*, and they warped physicality, traveled through time itself. Alex's whole being squirmed, his senses exponentially heightened. He climaxed.

Some moans and grunts accompanied the instruments from all over the hall. Several people forgot where they were, stripped away their clothing with wild gesticulation, and then maneuvered madly at their sexual organs. A few of the older guest's hearts gave out during the performance, and they sagged into themselves, but no one noticed. Everyone was too busy losing their minds.

They were nowhere now. Ringing into a black void. Them and the sound. It carried them to eternity.

A feeler bumped into Aura's legs, but she paid it no mind. She was lost in the waves like a shipwrecked sailor being thrust about. Seated in her balcony seat that overlooked the whole hall, hands gripping the guardrails tightly in front of her. She felt the vibrations like wind on her skin – through her skin! She needed more of it. Don't stop this too good a feeling, she thought. There was no end of the world, for Aura was living in infinity itself. Her body was broken fragments drifting through space and catching on every planet and star, exploding these with great power, great passion. Over and over, she felt herself ascending. When she thought she'd reached her highest potential, the barrier was broken yet again. And she needed more. The intensity too quickly becoming mute. She leaned a bit closer over the railing, so the waves hit her more fully.

But how wonderful would it be to be right next to those colossal sounds that wrung the mind free of all worry, Aura thought? She craved to be closer to the sound's source, near that cello instrument her husband was embracing, to touch it…

Aura leaned a bit further over the guardrail, reaching for the sound, stretching her arms and neck out, ears twitching. She went a bit too far and toppled over the railing. She plunged towards the seats below. Her head struck first, hitting a headrest and receding back into the neck like a turtle. Her whole body crushed and killed the couple in those very seats.

A woman stirred from her reverie, looked down at the collapsed mass on her right, then released a horrific scream that cut through the symphony. People in the nearby seats jolted to alertness and turned back to the spectacle. Like a ripple, audience members awakened from their orgasmic states, and morbid curiosity billowed through the air. Screams scratched and grew, but the orchestra continued playing. Alex kept playing, head bowed, undeterred.

The musicians were lost in the music.

A gray-haired man approached Aura and dragged her into the middle of the aisle. Her head lolled during the transfer, loose from its spine. The gray-haired man dropped Aura after meeting her gaze – her head was twisted backward, revealing a fixed, euphoric grin. She died happy, at least. The man then noticed the bulge of her stomach.

"Someone help me?! I think she's pregnant!" the man pleaded.

But the crowd was too busy rushing to escape the horrible scene. People in various stages of undress ran for the exit doors, of which there were far too few to allow easy passage. Those swarms gathered and piled atop one another. Bodies stacked upon bodies, crushing the fallen underneath.

The gray-haired man nearly gave up until a young male attendant stepped up.

"What do you need?" the young attendant said, eyes all pupils and his skin paled.

"We need to get this baby out now!" the old man gestured to Aura's lump. The gray-haired, formal-dressed man was, in fact, an artist – oil paintings of landscapes being his specialty – but his skull wore the expression of a madman.

"Do you have a knife?!" the gray-haired artist said. The attendant procured a pocketknife and handed it over.

A feeler stumbled onto Aura's corpse, so the artist kicked it away. He got on his knees but then hesitated. He believed the baby didn't have long to survive floating as it was in a dead host. But in his hysterical state of mind and frantic nerves, the image of Aura's tangled form was genuinely horrifying. Time was running out, though. He must save the baby, must! And so, the artist imagined the grotesque scene instead as art:

The knife he clutched, he viewed instead like a paintbrush, and Aura the medium. The image was more merciful towards his sanity. Taking that paintbrush, he cut through Aura's black dress and began to apply hard, purposeful brush strokes to the curve of her stomach. Aura lay diligently, still smiling, as the artist chipped her into pieces that he tossed to the side. His knife worked her large belly, which in his mind took the form of an oil landscape; a mountain, or rather volcano, for openings soon emerged, and magma flowed, crimson poured.

Soon the artist was pulling out a slimy red form. The baby he held opened its mouth and wailed.

On the other side of the symphony hall, a couple trying to leave their seats were shoved back as the turbulent crowd streamed in all directions. The wife tripped and fell into the central aisle and was immediately stomped upon by a burly man, unaware of his surroundings. Others trampled her in their hurried confusion. The flattened wife's husband, in his grief-stricken state, leaped at the burly man, grabbing for his head and pulling back with animalistic intensity. They kicked about and bit at each other, bumping into other people and causing further altercations. Similar acts of animal aggression occurred throughout the music hall, and they only continued to grow in their hideousness. Rage and blood proliferated and expelled into the closed atmosphere, turning it a red haze.

The Feelers kept rolling.

The orchestra members remained in their seats, most with their eyes clasped tight. They continued playing, unbothered by the growing madness.

They wandered away from their physical being. And were blind to the massive crowd that swept onto and behind the stage in search of escape. The desperate crowd ran into the musicians, knocking the instruments from their animated hands. Some of these were cellists who, enraged at being pulled from their ecstatic playing, responded by sticking their cello necks into the sides of human necks. Violinists pounced and used their strings to grate off the dermis of their victims. Brass players used their instruments to bash in the heads of the disruptive audience. Meanwhile, the woodwind players pierced their flutes and clarinets through open, screaming mouths.

The mad musicians laughed and foamed from their mouths with delirious delight, pointing at the frantic guests trying to dislodge the instruments.

They spit on the choked guests – collapsed and pale – then retrieved their instruments, dripping blood and soaking their lips and hands as they resumed playing.

The hysteria grew. The hall was a Bosch painting. Images of Hell everywhere. Torment and anguish and the evilest deeds possible were being performed. This was Hell without a devil. And humans were the demons.

Still holding the newborn pulled from Aura's womb, the artist tried to escape a side exit, but bodies swayed and blocked the way.

"Move the fuck back!" The shout erupted from behind the artist. He swiveled, then stared into the black eye of a gun. The man holding it was red, sweating, and his veins bulged hard against the skin of his face and neck. The artist ducked quickly out of the way, but the young attendant who helped him was too distracted to notice, still focused on the exit.

Thunder erupted, a furious blow to a monstrous drum, and a bullet passed through the young attendant's spinal column. The bullet exited the attendant's gaped mouth, spraying a crimson mist upon departure, then continued to the next person terminating in their skull. The attendant's face quivered and shook, eyes bulged out then shut tightly. Agony was him. The attendant, still alive, collapsed, and all he could do was lay and wait for death as the frenzied mob trampled and disfigured him under their red-stained dress shoes and heels.

The mad artist paid no attention to the attendant while stepping over him, following safely behind the gun-wielder as the maniac parted the crowd around the exit like Moses parted the sea.

Up on stage, the orchestra still played.

Alex played viciously, otherworldly. He continued playing for hours, bowing and fingering without rest, undeterred by the stench of blood. All around him, limbs cracked and bowels released, teeth chittered and bit, throats roared full of intestines, bodies fell, bodies spoiled. Still, Alex played. He played even when the joints of his elbows and shoulders popped, and tendons snapped from their inhuman movement. Still, he played when the bow snapped and broke, and he was forced to use limbs…

***

The wave of madness blanketed the globe in death and decay. The humans dreaded death and did not wish to dwell on it. So, they escaped by plunging their minds in chemical highs provided by the Feelers. But a hunger arose, a primitive lust. Feelings swelled into demonic entities; humans felt less humanly. They ate each other. They tore each other apart, set those loose limbs ablaze, and hollered as the smoke rose. Disputes erupted from the top floors of apartment buildings. Humans soon flung from those high stories and hit the pavement where they sank into themselves. Buildings exploded and crumbled. Bombs descended upon cities, dented them inwards. Countries screamed, collided. Guns shouted and crippled listeners. Fires roared, screeched at a smoky black sky – a sky of ashes like gray and black insects fluttering, falling and dusting the ground, the homes, the people.

The humans had reached the ultimate high. But they'd regressed to a primitive state of mind in the process. Maybe that is where the ultimate high lay hidden.

As this chaos engulfed the world, the Feelers kept rolling. The Feelers couldn't understand what they were doing to their human owners. They were just a drug, abused and overdosed on. The world was breathing its last labored breaths, sweating flames and rubble; its heartbeat trembled by explosions and shock until it took its last breath.

***

When the Merci finally arrived on Earth, they came upon a planet that had already eaten itself, leaving none for them. The world was nothing but rubble and rot.

Thrall grunted his disappointment, then turned to the last humans who managed to stay alive, captured as they were fleeing the carnage. Thrall spotted a gray-bearded man clutching a baby. He hurried over and bit into the man's shoulder. The artist dropped, spewing the newborn from his arms.

Aura's baby girl rolled, stopped, then cried an elegy to the smoke-filled skies.

"Load that one on board. I'll have it for a snack later," Thrall ordered, then returned to his meal.

Once finished, Thrall sighed, then he and the Merci departed the burning planet.

Back on the ground, several Feelers remained. They rolled out of their hiding places, still sending their waves. They tumbled over unrecognizable rubble; could be stone, could be bone. A feeling of loneliness weighed their souls down, down. Their existence was without purpose now as they wandered the Earth endlessly till their dying days.

Hollow Eyes

Sarah Moon

*T*his is fucking stupid, Stephanie thought to herself, grabbing her backpack off the bed. She stopped in front of her floor mirror and checked her appearance. Even though they were just going camping, she never left the house without getting dolled up. She had straightened her brown hair into place and today's choice of eyeshadow was purple, to accentuate her brown eyes. A black tank top hugged her body over a push up bra doing its job to perfection. Ripped jeans had been her M.O. since high school, with chucks, as always, the finishing touch. She loved her chucks and had a pair in every color. Satisfied, she left her room, closing the door behind her with a sigh.

Stephanie didn't mind hiking, but she absolutely hated camping. The dirt and lack of showers were the worst. She hated the fact that, no matter what, dirt would be packed under her nails by the end of the trip. It's one thing she never understood. It's not like she fucking played in it. The thought of her skin feeling grimy, and gross made her shudder. And peeing outside? Ugh! God only knew what could crawl up your shit or bite you while you hovered, bare-assed, over some twigs. But this was Arizona. She'd already had five too many run-ins with rattlesnakes during her "party in the desert" days. Those were some good times: romping through the desert, bonfires, and drunk sex bent over a tailgate. And the best part was by the end of the night, she would still end up in her own bed.

Justin and Jessica honked from the jeep outside. "Could've at least picked somewhere in the woods instead of the fucking desert," she mumbled to herself. Per usual, it was always Jessica's way or the highway. Jess had always had a pull on her. If she didn't get her way, all hell would break loose, and they wouldn't speak for over a week. *Let's go be the third wheel, Steph.* She took a deep breath and slammed the door behind her, walking out towards the Jeep. *Who the fuck?* She could see there was an extra person in the back. Opening the back passenger door, she tossed in her backpack and hopped up onto the seat.

"Heyyy, bitch! This is Dan!" Jess gave her that notorious look of "just go with it."

"Hey, guys."

Lovely

Jessica had a way of picking unheard of places out in the middle of nowhere in an attempt to be adventurous. They had been best friends for years and stacked some pretty badass memories together, even though Stephanie always felt forced to go on these wild adventures. Though if there were drugs, alcohol, and men involved she didn't mind so much. In that aspect of their friendship, they were two peas in a pod and loved to party. Hell…even if getting hammered wasn't an option, they'd make it one. Big tits made it easy to stash shooters and weed. Knowing the unlikelihood of a gas station close by, Steph had stashed a bottle of Tito's vodka in her bag, along with some Purple Kush, to get through the weekend.

"So, what exactly is the plan?" Stephanie asked.

"We are going to camp outside of Crown King; don't worry there's a bar. It will be fun. Then tomorrow, we'll check out some hiking trails about an hour away up in the sticks."

Stephanie sucked in some air and let out a sigh of relief. Maybe this wouldn't be so bad after all, and she could pull the stick out of her ass. Jess cranked up the music as the car pulled away from the curb. Her boyfriend Justin had a habit of listening to his music unapologetically loud every time they went on a trip.

Steph ran her eyes over Dan. *Good enough.* He had long, shaggy brown hair, blue eyes that popped out from behind his locks, a chiseled jawline, and a bad boy look to him. *Perfect, at least she was somewhat considerate.* Her eyes fell to the bulge in his pants. She couldn't help but wonder what he was packing. He tapped his fingers on his leg to the beat of the music and stared out the window.

It was a two-hour drive through the hot desert landscape before they finally pulled into their campground. They were on the border of desert and forest, but if they traveled further up the road, pine would fully take over. That was the funny thing about Arizona, the drastic change in landscape only miles apart. An hour in one direction might lead you deeper into the desert to eventually find another patch of woods. A couple hours in another and you'd be confronted with miles and miles of rolling hills.

As the jeep crawled over the pine riddled soil, before coming to a halt in front of a marked space, Steph was surprised that they weren't alone. Plenty of people had set up camp surrounding their spot, beers already in hand during the middle of the day. A mile back she'd seen a dive bar nestled along a hillside, the dilapidated wooden building still enticing as ever.

Eager to explore, Stephanie was ready to set up the massive two-bedroom tent she knew was stuffed in the luggage container on the roof. Jessica always had top notch camping gear thanks to her father. Steph always assumed that's where her desire to be outdoors came from; she grew up with an avid hunter as a role model.

Jessica outstretched her arms and took in the pleasant scent of fresh air as she watched the guys pull the tent off the jeep. She looked over at Steph, who stood with her arms crossed, rocking back and forth impatiently. "See, I'm not always a selfish ass. I know how much you love camping," Jess said. She bumped her hip into Steph's. "I wanted to surprise you with something a little different."

"I suppose it's the thought that counts." Steph nudged her shoulder with a crooked smile on her face. "It's about that time, beer-thirty, right?"

"I'll light a fire under Justin's ass, and we'll head to the bar. There's a chili festival going on this weekend, which means plenty of people to mingle with." As soon as the words left her lips, Steph's ears perked up like a cat's. The party animal in her wasn't going to contain itself for much longer.

The girls joined the guys in setting up the campsite. Stephanie rushed them at every sluggish moment. Two double inflatable mattresses filled the majority of the tent. Stephanie smirked. *Only two mattresses…fuckin' Jess.* They were smart enough to gather wood before heading to the bar. No one needed to be gathering wood in the middle of the night, drunk off their ass. Steph dumped two cases of water into the ice chest. The girls knew by morning, no matter how much Justin warned them not to drink too much, they wouldn't be able to get enough water to quench their dry mouths.

The Jeep slowly crawled into the dirt lot of the bar and Justin searched for a space to park. It was packed; this festival was no joke. Live music rumbled through their bodies from an outdoor stage. The old log bar had a faded red sign that read: The Waterhole. Justin shot a look to Jess as he shifted into park. "Don't forget, tomorrow we have a long day." He was always the voice of reason, but the girls never listened. The youngest of the group, he was also the most mature.

"I know babe, don't worry. Lighten up, we are going to have fun," she shot back, using her famous innocent smirk and icy blue eyes to subdue his concern.

He furrowed his brow and shook his head, running a hand over his long black beard. He knew exactly what that meant. The girls had a history of going hard in the paint, and once they got going there was no telling them to stop.

The night consisted of drunken shenanigans, sloppy two-stepping, belligerent laughter, out of tune singing, and far too many drinks. Jess and Steph were able to get Justin to loosen up, and Dan said he was all for it. He wasn't opposed to a fun night in a place he had never been, and old musty places didn't bother him much. By the time they'd closed the bar, no one was able to drive. The group stumbled down the road towards the campground. Patrons leaving the bar were ferrying groups back to their sites and they snagged a ride by hopping in the bed of a truck driven by one of the locals. The night air that would normally be quiet and piney was filled with laughter, cigarette smoke, booze seeping from pores, and tires rolling over packed dirt. Having to walk a mile to pick up the Jeep the next morning was the last thing on their minds.

By the time they arrived back at camp, Jess looked like a harlequin doll with her matted blonde hair and smeared makeup. Justin rolled his eyes at the sight of his girlfriend. Steph was a little more together, her hair pulled into a high bun on top of her head.

Dan kept to himself, merely observing the drunken women as he got a fire going. It wasn't long before annoyance took hold and he and Justin left the girls to entertain each other with their sardonic banter. Justin had also reached his limit at that point, so he and Dan tapped out. Someone had to be responsible and make sure things would be good to go for their hike in the morning. Steph and Jess wandered off, making friends before eventually stumbling their way back to the tent. Jessica's flirtatious behavior never seemed to bother Justin. Hell, sometimes she would even bring another girl back for some fun. They were still young in their relationship and not too deep into their commitment. Steph knew he and Jess liked it that way.

Dawn was coming by the time the girls crashed through the tent, crossfaded. The bottle of Tito's was empty and nearly an eighth of the weed had been burnt between the two. Justin and Dan stirred at the commotion. They were clearly sleeping, but the two horny girls wanted to have their way with them. Justin wouldn't have it, not with the way Jess looked. He was pretty pissed she had gone too far yet again. Dan, on the other hand, pretended to be asleep. Stephanie felt rejected but knew she should probably get a little sleep anyway.

A feeling of regret slipped over the girls. With Justin being pissed, and Dan apparently knocked out into another dimension, they exchanged twin 'cringe' expressions, as if caught stealing from a cookie jar. In only a couple of hours they would be hiking up a mountain, and Stephanie knew the entire night would become a blur.

We went hard.

As the morning light began to haze over the campgrounds, the girls slid into the warm sheets and drifted off. Justin wrapped Jess in a bear hug, while Dan and Steph lay back-to-back. It only took seconds before they were loudly snoring, the cease of chatter and the natural sounds of the forest lulling them to sleep.

***

Stephanie woke with her head bent down, chin on her chest. Groggy, she felt a pinching pain on her wrists. She slightly lifted her head and attempted to open her eyes, but they were met with pressure.

What the fuck?

She tried to bring her hands to her face but couldn't. Her hands were tightly bound behind her. The hangover she'd dreaded in those early morning hours had fully set in, making her desperate for water and ibuprofen. A swipe of her dry tongue over filmy teeth made her try to gather saliva under her tongue. She managed to clear some of the brain fog that rested over her like a wet blanket. Realization struck that she was sitting in a seated position, not in a warm bed. She pulled on her arms and tried to shift her feet but couldn't; more restraint.

Is this some sort of joke? What the hell did I do last night? What did Dan and I do?

She could feel a soft fabric over her eyes, wrapping around her head, as she squeezed her eyelids together. Shaking her head was no use; the cloth was too constricting. Stephanie craned her head into awkward positions, trying to see beneath the blindfold. But again, no use.

"Guys! What the fuck? Untie me! Jessica?"

A gurgled response and a feminine groan answered her cry. Twisting her hands, her fumbling encountered braided material. *Rope.* She poked at the knot that ensured she wasn't escaping anytime soon. Her mind began to race, trying to make sense of things. A pang of nausea wrenched her stomach and that familiar shitty feeling of having too many the night before fully set in.

God, I'm still fucked up. This is great.

She tried to stand, only to be met with more restraint across her chest. The pain of the rope digging into her wrists, ankles, and chest began to throb. A canyon would carve into her chest if it was any tighter. She wouldn't be surprised if there was blood on her ankles and hands. Her surroundings gave off a musky, stale scent, like a room closed off for years. The smell of earth and pine was replaced by an odor that reminded her of mold and copper.

"Hey, wake up!" she yelled towards the source of the sound. "WAKE UP!"

She heard footfalls coming from a direction ahead and a little distant. Footfalls against hard ground...as if someone were walking barefoot down a hallway. The steps got closer.

"You guys, what is going on?!" Stephanie shouted.

Her question was answered by a string of childlike giggles. More footsteps swarmed her ears, too many for just one person. A whole damn group...But why were these people so quiet?

"No, no, no! Please don't!"

Stephanie could immediately make out Justin's voice. "No, wait! Please! Get away from her," he cried out.

Stephanie went into a panic. Fight or flight set in, and a feeling of dread washed over her at the realization she couldn't do either.

Unable to see, she knew there was imminent danger lurking. She frantically twisted her hands, trying to find some slack to pull out of the ropes encircling her wrists like handcuffs. A loud slap reverberated from ahead of her, followed by a slurp. Stephanie's heart was pounding inside her ribcage, she wanted to scream but something told her she shouldn't.

"NO! PLEASE STOP!!" Justin cried, screaming hysterically. The sound of a chair bucking off the ground echoed while a terrifying grinding noise bounced off of the walls around her. Stephanie couldn't imagine where it might be coming from. Justin released a sound Steph had never heard come from a human—a roar and scream of disbelieving anger and terror. The loud thud of something big smacking the ground made her soul jump out of her body. The multitude of footsteps grew distant until they could no longer be heard. *Did they leave?*

Stephanie began to hyperventilate. "WHAT THE FUCK IS HAPPENING?!" Her breaths, so fast, made it difficult to breathe.

Two light footsteps moved in front of her, the sound of skin separating from some sort of surface with every step. She could feel strands of hair being pulled away from her head, the lock twirling between someone's fingers. "Please, help me," Stephanie whimpered. The blindfold was jerked from her eyes. Straining, she squinted through the blur, making out the figure of a child standing before her. The child's face had two large black crevices for eyes and black veins stretched over its cheeks.

Black eyes? Does this kid have black, hollow eyes? She rapidly blinked, clearing her vision.

No...it's just a fucking kid. Have I been drugged? Stephanie sucked in deep, slow breaths trying to rid the panic. It hadn't helped.

The child looked at Steph with a wide grin. It was a little girl, no more than nine years old. Her body was covered in dirt and grime. Tangled black hair fell from her head in knotted chunks, her teeth were yellow and rotten.

Blood? Is that fucking blood on her hands? Steph thought.

"Where are your parents? Where am I?" Her voice cracked as the shock ravaged her body. The girl brought her small hands over her mouth and chuckled. She ran her tongue over the wet crimson that bathed her skin and scampered out of the room through a doorway in the corner next to her. The room fell silent except for Justin's hysterical cries.

Stephanie scanned her surroundings, her heart dropping at the scene across the room in front of her. She was falling apart, unable to comprehend what was happening. Justin sat stunned, tied to a chair, his eyes wide and overflowing with tears. Next to him sat Jessica's decapitated body. Her head lay on the ground, mouth slightly agape, a grimace that was almost a mockery of her usual smirk on her face. Blood pooled beneath her head, saturating her blonde hair with coagulating gore. A stream of blood ran in a thin rivulet from her mouth, dripping from her chin in droplets before combining with the puddle beneath. Steph had never seen so much blood. Her corpse was covered in it, not a piece of her clothing visible through the gore. Muscle, veins and ragged skin were crudely displayed upon the stump of her neck and below the chin of her severed head. Steph felt her gorge rise, her mouth falling open.

Stephanie's eyes began to overflow with tears. *There's no way, there's no fucking way this is real,* were her only thoughts. Before she could scream, Justin was quick to stop her.

"Don't scream Steph, don't you fucking scream! They will come back," Justin said in a quiet, quivering voice.

As much as she wanted to belt out a scream, she wasn't sure if her pounding chest would allow it. She could barely breathe, her chest tight with her choked inhalations. There was nothing she could do for Jess, but she knew she would want her to try and survive. "Where's Dan?" she finally managed; her words slow as they struggled past her lips. She had to pull it together, but this was so fucked up.

"I don't know, but we need to figure a way out. There are a lot of them."

"What do you mean, them?"

"Fuckin' children, Steph. Little fuckin' kids. I don't know how we got here, but that one you met just fuckin' killed Jess. Sawed her head off like it was nothing." Tears and snot stained his shirt, glistening on his distraught face.

Steph looked around the room for a source of escape or defense. They were clearly in a house. An old, run-down house falling apart at its seams. Yellowed walls lined the completely empty room. Crumbling, blackened linoleum layered the floor. Sunshine from a window was the only source of light, creating a soft, white glow between Justin and Steph. How the hell were they going to get out of this mess?

A high-pitched squeaking intruded on their ears. *Wheels?*

"Stay quiet, don't bring attention to yourself, no matter how much worse it gets," Justin whispered over the sound. It wasn't his first time seeing so much blood. He'd survived combat in Afghanistan and would make damn sure they'd survive this. His eyes were red and puffy, the usual sparkling green dulled by bloodshot veins.

A silhouette of a wheelchair came into view in the doorway. A small girl pushed the chair into the room, her black hair curtained over her face. A little boy followed behind her, their old clothes equally tattered. In the chair sat an old, shriveled man. Steph and Justin shot each other a look of confusion. The man looked like a corpse; his almost translucent skin clung tightly to bones with little muscle between. He didn't move, his eyes staring forward, his head tilted in a static position, wispy white hair haloed around his head. The children wheeled him next to Justin.

"Sir?" Justin mumbled but got no response from the corpse of a man. He homed in on the man's chest. It barely lifted, but he was clearly alive. Soft, wheezy breaths came from his lips, his nose whistling with each stuttering exhale.

An older pre-teen child entered the room. Tall and scrawny, with knotted brown hair that draped down to his buttocks. He moved in front of Jessica's corpse with a blade in his hand. Kneeling down, he lifted her severed head, skin and tendons wrapping around his hand as he held it in his palm. He slid the blade deep into the socket of one eye, leveraging it out with a pop of broken suction. Justin and Stephanie watched in horror as the nerve trailed behind, the kid grasping and yanking it until it snapped. After handing it off to the little girl, she placed it in the old man's mouth, forcing it to the back of his throat. The old man choked it down, then resumed his motionless position.

They are going to fucking eat us, Steph thought. She and Justin looked at each other with horrified incredulity as continuous salty waterfalls ran down their dirt covered cheeks.

More children began to trickle in, their clothes covered in moth-ridden holes, seams pulling apart. Their faces were dirty, with open sores lining their skin. They had a look of hunger in their eyes, licking their lips as their gazes fell upon Jessica's body. One by one, the children removed pieces of Jessica's skin in flaps, stripping her body of its outer organ, revealing the glistening muscle beneath. Together they sat cross-legged in a group at the center of the room, stuffing the pieces of skin into their faces with revolting enthusiasm.

When they were done feasting on the outer flesh, they came back for more, tearing into the organs with bare, sharp-nailed fingers. The children's arms quickly became drenched in blood, elbow deep. It dripped from their hands as they feasted, juices squeezing from organs between their fingers. They glared at Stephanie and Justin with bloody smiles, viscera dripping down their cheeks and chins. Tendons and veins snapped as they ripped Jessica apart from the inside out. Two chewed on the intestines from opposite ends like a macabre scene from "Lady and the Tramp." Steph and Justin sat motionless, horrified, and in shock. They had to squeeze their eyes shut, no longer able to comprehend the sight unfolding before them. Their hearts shattered as they listened to the sounds of ripping teeth and mouths slurping down the remains of their friend.

Once the room fell silent, Stephanie peeked through slitted eyes. The children were gathered on their knees in front of the old man. They didn't move; she couldn't even hear them breathe.

They are fucking praying.

They sat like statues, not moving a muscle for what seemed like an eternity before they reanimated and began to trickle out of the room, taking the old man with them. A little girl ran back and grabbed Jessica's still intact eyeless head that had dropped from the boy's hands and rolled out of the way before the feast.

Stephanie and Justin met each other's wide, bloodshot eyes, both emotionally and physically drained. They looked at Jessica's leftover body, an emptied carcass, the only thing left a bit of muscle and her bones. Steph could no longer keep the growing soup of bile down. It shot from her lips like a rocket, adding to the smell of copper and death.

"It's now or never Steph," Justin said in an urgent whisper, showing Stephanie his free hands. He had been busy pulling at the restraints while his girlfriend was being devoured piece by piece. With his military background, he was knowledgeable in a variety of knots. Still, freeing himself had to have been no easy feat; the rope a jumbled-up mess with no rhyme or reason, done by a child. To the children's credit, their knots were tight as hell.

Justin ran behind Stephanie, frantically tugging at the tangled puzzle of knots restraining her. "It's time to go. We need to find Dan."

All she could do was nod in return.

"The window is our only shot. As soon as I open it, you fucking run and don't stop until you find Dan or help."

Once freed, Stephanie got up slowly, trying not to make a sound. Together they moved towards the window. The silence was broken when Stephanie's shoe slid out from under her, the blood and gore left behind making for a slick surface.

"Fuck!" She slid on her hands, gliding as if soap were coating the ground, trying to get to her feet. Justin grabbed her under the armpits, trying to pick her up. The thumps from her body hitting the ground were loud, too loud.

A little girl laughed from the doorway. Justin and Stephanie lifted their heads and looked in her direction. The little girl wore Jessica's face. It didn't look real, misshapen, hanging well below her chin, like something from a Halloween store. The girl's eyes were discs of pure black and emptiness beneath the grotesque mask. She wiggled her tongue between the malleable lips. A brutal butcher's blade, still dripping with Jessica's blood, rested in her hand.

"The window, fucking go, now!" Justin yelled at Steph.

Stephanie panicked, fumbling with the window latch. She finally got it open and began to climb out. Behind her she could hear Justin scuffling with the little girl as more footfalls began to trickle into the room. Steph jumped through the window, landing on grassy ground. The sun beat down on her, and the warmth and a feeling of freedom rushed over her. She scrambled to her feet and turned to help Justin. His face was frozen as his eyes met hers, head slightly trembling. Blood dripped from his lips, mixing with saliva as it snaked its way down his chin. The blade of a knife poked its shiny point out from the center of his chest. He coughed, spraying blood across Stephanie's face. That strong man she always saw in Justin was gone, fear and devastation taking over his features.

"Run," Justin mouthed. But Stephanie was frozen in place.

Behind Justin, Steph could see the children gathering around him with black, empty eyes. She could hear the sound of blades entering his body, over and over. The giggles of the children echoed from the dim room. The child wearing Jessica's face appeared from behind Justin, and she reached around and ran her blade across his throat. Slicing it cleanly, she moved it back and forth, tearing deeply towards his spine. Blood poured from around the blade. She pulled his head back, letting it dangle from his torso, held on only by his cervical spine and strands of tissue. Blood from his arteries sprayed like a geyser, painting Stephanie's body red.

Stephanie spun around and began to run through the woods. She had no idea where she was or where she was going, driven only by the need to escape. At full speed, she fled through the forest, her mind in shock, no longer processing her surroundings. Off in the distance she spotted a figure. *Blonde hair? Why does that look like Jess?* As she sprinted forward, her foot caught on something unseen. With a loud snap, it sent Stephanie flying through the air. Trying to land on her feet, she instead came down on her knee with a loud crunch.

"Fuck!" she yelled out in agony.

Steph's knee was snapped, her leg bent in the wrong direction. The back of her knee was torn open, exposing the tissue beneath.

"I'm so fucked!" she screamed.

Pushing herself up onto her one good leg, she grabbed a tree for support. She needed to find help. Stephanie hopped through the forest; the pain so intense she thought she might black out. Hope was beginning to float away. The sun was quickly setting and soon she wouldn't be able to see shit. Who knows how good of hunters those demented fucks back there were? Stephanie's mind and body became numb as she continued to hop through the woods. Panic was no longer present; her mind was no longer present. Nothing was left but an empty shell. The horror of what she had witnessed was too much for her to handle. They were gone, all of them. Maybe even Dan.

Darkness blanketed the earth, crickets chirped, and coyotes howled in the distance. Stephanie sat on a rock to rest. The moon brought little light to the forest around her. When she looked up, she took in the sight of the multitude of stars. She felt so small and so alone, stuck out here in these woods.

Fucking nothing; there's nothing fucking out here.

Stephanie removed her shirt and found a small branch she could use for a brace. As she grabbed her leg, she pinched her eyes shut, hoping the pain couldn't get much worse. Her jeans were soaked around the wound. A loud hollow pop echoed through the trees as she forced her leg straight again. She gritted her teeth, holding back her screams of pain. It hurt so damn bad. She used her shirt to hold the brace in place, tying it off with a knot. Her nerves were overshot, the pain pulsating throughout her entire body. She felt electric.

Taking a deep, shaky breath, she shifted her eyes in all directions. She didn't know if the direction she was going would even lead anywhere. Maybe it would be better to just succumb to nature. A little plop hit the ground ahead of her feet. *What the hell.* She crawled towards the sound and found a little package. A brown wooden box. She grabbed her lighter from her back pocket and sparked a tiny flame.

The cedar box had a metal clasp on the front. Resting the oddity on her lap, she popped it open slowly, nervous about its contents. Inside rested a hand—man's hand. Stephanie flung the box from her lap, letting out a yelp. Was it Dan's? Realization set in that she was being watched. A new wave of panic washed over as she forced her way to her feet. Giggles bounced off the trees in all directions. Without a plan, she moved through the trees as fast as she could. If they really wanted her, it wouldn't be difficult to snatch her now.

What the hell are they doing?

She continued on, listening to the sounds of the children that surrounded her. Twigs snapped with their little movements and bushes rustled. This time, rather than a whole clan, it sounded like only a couple of them. The air was cool, and she was becoming cold. No, she was starting to freeze, she felt it on the tip of her ears and the back of her neck.

"Steph! Help me!"

"Dan!" she yelled back with a little glimmer of hope.

No response. Silence, followed by more giggles.

"STEPHANIE!" This time Dan's voice was louder and more panicked.

She began limping towards the sound. The children's voices seemed far behind, their movements tapering off until the sound vanished completely. A dim flicker pierced through the blackness. *No fucking way.*

Stephanie worked her way towards the light. The pain angered her; she wanted to rest, to sleep. Dan was somewhere out there and now there was potential for help. Another house maybe, and hopefully with a normal fucking human inside.

She closed in on the flickering, the silhouette of a cabin appearing off in the distance. Stephanie dropped to the ground; she couldn't bear the agony any longer, she was seeing stars. How much blood had she lost while hobbling through the woods in the darkness? She crawled her way over the packed earth towards the house, the scent of dirt and pine heavy in her nostrils. The sky began to lighten from black to a dark, deep maroon. She looked up, searching for the moon; it hung bright and red.

What the fuck? Am I dying… from a broken leg? You're kidding me.

Stephanie let her eyes fall back on the house. They widened as she scanned the outside. There it was, the same open window she'd crawled out of. Had she managed to land herself right in the middle of the yard of the same group of psychopaths that killed her friends?

Weakly, she pushed herself up onto her rump. She sat with her legs sprawled out in front of her in defeat. Her homemade tourniquet wasn't enough; her jeans were sopping wet from the waist down on her bad leg. She let her head fall back, and the moon now dripped with blood and the clouds were wispy puffs of smoky grey.

The forest became quiet, too quiet, and Steph's ears began to ring. A wave of heat ran over her body as her adrenaline began to spike. She wasn't cold anymore; beads of sweat rolled down her forehead. As though a cotton ball was in her mouth, she tried to swallow it down. Fear encompassed her, tightening her chest as if her torso was being squeezed by a snake. The sky flashed with orange and red, thunder rumbled through the night as dizziness threatened to make her black out.

The door of the dilapidated house opened, and the old man in the chair wheeled out of the house and onto the porch. He met Stephanie's eyes with his and an eerie smile reached across his face. He stood, his frail body filling out into a youthful, strong man. No wrinkles, no loose skin, but a young, strong, muscular body. His face morphed as his hair lengthened, brown and shaggy. A familiar look. His formerly gray eyes sparkled blue. That eerie smile was one she recognized on his face now, clear as day.

Dan?

Dan walked towards Stephanie, following a dirt path leading him away from the porch. He met her, face to face, in the center of the yard. Stephanie couldn't move; there was no running, no escape. She was frozen to the spot where she sat, trying to force her limbs into motion to no avail. But it wasn't the fear causing her failure to move; something was happening within her body. She thought maybe this was all one giant acid trip; could she have been drugged? Was this all some weird sick fucking joke? The thoughts were irrational.

"What is happening, Dan? Where am I?" The words felt almost impossible to push out. Her chest was too heavy, suffocating.

Dan began to remove his tattered moth-ridden clothing, his face void of any emotion. He let them fall from his fingertips at Steph's feet. *Where the hell did his other clothes go?* Standing naked in front of Stephanie, he stared deep into her eyes, a darkness within his own. Suddenly, without warning, his neck cracked as his head forcefully snapped back. The door to the house flew open, ripping off the hinges, leaving a black void of nothingness in the doorway.

Dan's mouth shot open, quiet words hummed in the air, yet his mouth hadn't moved. Stephanie couldn't make out the words. One by one, the children trickled out of the dark doorway, their steps silent as they joined Dan in the unkept grass. They aligned themselves in a row to the left and right of Dan. Their pale skin almost glowed and sparkled in the bloody moonlight.

Stephanie's heart began to beat out of her chest, sweat pouring from her chin. She tried to open her mouth to scream, but nothing came out. Pain began to skewer her from within, something was wrong. Something off and it wasn't just her leg. Why couldn't she move a single muscle?

What the fuck is happening to me?

Movement squirmed inside her belly, uncomfortable bursts and sounds of explosions deep inside. Her body was slowly liquifying from the inside out. Her organs turned to ooze, the liquid making its way up her esophagus before it spouted from her mouth in violent waves. Her bones loudly cracked and splintered beneath her skin, causing limbs, fingers, and toes to go this way and that. Her body snapped and morphed into unnatural positions, still unable to release the pain with failed attempts to make sounds with her vocal cords. Her bowels released in a violent wave of feces and liquified organs, flowing onto the ground beneath her. The smell was appalling; the fact she still even had that sense unfair. Stephanie's mind was beginning to fade as her skin dripped off her muscles, an invisible inferno at its highest temperature baking her alive. Her eyes rested, motionless, on the vision of Dan and the children, and the skin of her face oozed from her cheeks as a gel. Pressure was building behind her eyes and within her head, as if her skull cap was going to blast off like a rocket at any moment.

The children's eyes faded into dark, hollow voids. Black webbed across their faces, filling their petite veins, their skin transforming into a translucent, pastier white. They smiled, displaying toothy grins with pointed teeth. A breeze whooshed through the trees, kicking up soil and leaves around them, centering them in the middle of a wind tunnel. Stephanie studied each of the children with what was left of her diminishing mind, pain overtaking her fear, filling her eyes with bloody tears. Blood pooled in her mouth before streaming past her lips and down her chin. In agony, she watched as the feet of each of the children left the ground.

Motionless, they levitated, their arms lifting and reaching out from their sides, feet dangling beneath them. In unison, their faces snapped towards Stephanie, their mouths dropping open unnaturally, jaws dislocating like a snake eating an egg.

Dan moved his head back into place and looked in Stephanie's direction, only the whites of his eyes to be seen. A web of black covered his face, reaching down his neck. With fluttering eyelids, he moved his lips to speak. "You asked me where you are, Stephanie? There's a reason your pathetic self is here."

Stephanie's eyes imploded, striking her blind. A skinned animal with glints of white bone shining through, her chest caved in as her ribcage flattened, letting out a sickeningly loud final crack. Dan's mouth hovered over what was left of her ear, his voice a distant whisper.

"This is Hell."

***

Dan sat at the bar top of The Waterhole; the musky smell of the bar reminded him of home where the children were eagerly waiting for their next meal. He twirled his long brown hair between his fingers, mimicking that of a bored yet anxious woman. Black blood pulsed through his veins. He adjusted his tight halter top; this new body would take some getting used to, let alone the anatomy of a woman. Stephanie still screamed his in mind, desperate for an escape.

A mischievous smile ran across his face. He knew it wouldn't be long until his next sacrificial lamb fell into his hands. More blood meant more power. More death meant a longer existence. It was day three of the chili festival. He looked on as the first set of patrons walked in for a hangover cure. A younger man set next to him, sunglasses on, avoiding the light of the bar. Dan looked at him through Stephanie's brown eyes, fluttering her lashes with a soft smile.

"Hey, you wanna buy a girl a drink?"

The Greatest Show on Earth

Seaton Kay-Smith

There was something about that poster, taped to a telegraph pole like a witch waiting to burn, that caught my eye. It was a poster advertising a magic show and featured a smiling magician with dark hair and an angular face, lifeless eyes and faded pupils that looked like a pair of black translucent gems with ghosts trapped inside them, and I wasn't sure as to whether he looked like me, or I like him, or if it was possible that we simply looked like each other.

Behind the man—on the poster—there was a woman. Arms tied behind her head; she dangled from an indistinct metallic structure as a fire burned beneath her. The name of the event, "The Greatest Show on Earth" was written in what I assumed was a font called 'Circus', or 'Big Top', or something cute like that. And, while the title was arrogant and I resented it, it did not stop me from writing down the web address and later indulging my curiosity by buying myself a ticket.

How quaint, I thought, how wholesome. How retrograde.

It would be something different at least from the endless torrent of TV shows and films desperately trying to capture our restless attention spans amid our increasing tolerance to intensity, each new release boasting more sex, more violence, and more violent sex, one-upping each other in their currency of blood and tits—and the very occasional flaccid dick. Something different to the perpetually compounding grit, mining reality for trauma, as they paid their tithes and made bloody offerings to the malevolent god of ratings, with an endless procession of the worst of humanity presented in 8K for our viewing pleasure. Low brow in high definition. Expensive budgets; cheap thrills.

This would be different, however. This would be an escape, a chance to step away from the world and reality. This would be quaint and wholesome. This would be retrograde.

The day passed slowly. Unable to think of anything else, I struggled to focus. I did not know why this show had such a hold on me. Was it the poster? The familiar visage of the man? The promise, which I knew could never be delivered upon, that the show would be the greatest despite the impossibility and immeasurableness of such a thing.

I tried to learn more about the show in the hopes that I might find out what to expect. There were no answers online, however, nor was there any trace of the it—or the magician—anywhere. There was the website where I had bought my ticket, but that merely consisted of a blank page in a block colour, the name of the show, the cost, and a place to enter your credit card information.

The day was torturous and long. My skin prickled. My brain throbbed. I wasn't used to being unable to sate my needs when they arose; I wasn't used to being patient.

Finally, the hour came, and I was gone, making my way downtown toward the theatre.

Cutting through the smell of sweat and excrement, which rose thickly from the gutters, I scurried past street-beggars and homeless people asking for change and crossed the road to avoid the more persistent and desperate among them. Then, stepping off the curb, I was almost hit by a car. I continued on without berating the driver. There was no time; my mind was elsewhere. Anxiety coating me in a slick sheen of sticky nerves, I darted through the gridlocked traffic, pushing up-stream, through the evening foot-traffic, leaving a choir of car horns and angry shouting in my wake.

I could not stop for the lights; I could not stop to help those who had fallen. I trampled over them and pushed through them. I had booked my ticket late and the only remaining seats had been at the front. I could not be patient or courteous or kind. There was too much at stake.

I could not bear the thought of having to make my way to the well-lit front row in awkward embarrassment once the show had already started, of shuffling obnoxiously past the knees, legs, drinks, and coats of the other patrons, in full view of that dead-eyed, fake-smiled magician; of offering myself up as a sacrifice to the bloodletting that is audience participation. The very thought of it filled me with a mortal dread so severe that to ruminate on it longer than necessary would be tantamount to torture porn, a genre of filmmaking much more enjoyable when sitting safely on the other side of a screen, eating popcorn and chocolate in the dark, watching characters get torn to pieces in front of you.

I glanced at my watch and my step faltered. The hour had arrived; the show was about to start. I had come so close. I was there, only a moment too late. I was about to turn back and abandon my plans, when an usher caught my eye.

"We were just about to lock the doors," he said, holding open the door and waving me through. "The show's about to start."

"It hasn't started yet?"

"It's about to," he said, waving his hand even faster.

I nodded, thanked him, then entered. He didn't even check my ticket.

As I stepped into the theatre I heard a loud thud behind me. The sound, I can only assume, of a heavy beam falling into place to lock the doors so that the show could start and go on, uninterrupted.

There would be no pausing, no rewinding. If I grew bored, and that was likely, I would simply have to endure it.

How quaint, I thought, as I hurried to my seat. How retrograde.

The theatre was packed and hummed with a nervous energy. The air was filled with restless mumbles and anticipatory mutterings along with the smell of whiskey, roasted nuts, and sweat.

I sat down, the lights dimmed, and the murmurs of excitement calmed, and I felt focus, like a tangible object, rise into the air and fly toward the stage, expectant and eager, as the crowd sat eerily quiet and still. It was almost as though they were not there at all.

I could hear my own heartbeat and the rush of blood coursing through my body. I could hear my organs, twisting inside of me like eels or snakes in a hessian sack, slopping about behind the thin wall of skin and tissue, squirming in anticipation and fear, for some reason. Then, I heard the drums. First slow, they increased in speed and volume, while below them, between each percussive strike, the distinct squeaking of creaky wheels.

Then, just as my eyes had begun to adjust to the darkness, the drums came to an abrupt halt and light, like a nuclear explosion, flooded the stage, washing away the shadows to reveal a large metal contraption being wheeled across the stage by a crewmember. The crewmember was dressed entirely in black, from head to toe, and even wore a charcoal scarf, which was wrapped around his head like a mask. He resembled a mummy, or some poor soul who'd recently had facial surgery and had, for some reason or other, been swaddled in black gauze instead of white.

It was all very strange. A weight began to form in my stomach, like a stone. Then, suddenly, a voice, loud and thunderous, bellowing from backstage—from everywhere at once—filled the electrified air. "Ladies and gentlemen," it said. "What you are about to experience may shock you. A once in a lifetime event, the greatest show on earth..."

I grimaced at the announcement and felt the stone in my stomach dissolve, as I was reminded of where I was. 'Once in a lifetime', they'd said. 'The Greatest Show on Earth'. I would believe it when I saw it, and even then...

I'd seen sword and sorcery epics of lust, revenge, and bloodshed; startling horrors that creep into your dreams and infect your waking life. We were awash with content. We were girt by a great sea of entertainment, her water's rose every day. We were drowning in content, as wave after wave of spectacle crashed violently upon our heads, seldom allowing us respite or a chance to breathe. I'd seen man's inhumanity toward man, toward women; jarring scenes of such affect I hadn't slept for days. Real life made fiction yet somehow more real than reality could ever be. Entertainment which held a mirror to our world and showed us at our worst, as an ouroboric society, fed on smut and filth and misery and heartbreak, and shitting out the same. I'd seen news articles detailing atrocities which had been optioned and made into films to create a new normal, raising the bar and the baseline. I'd seen agonizing, painful, horrors that left you depleted, hollow, staring at your own miserable reflection in the black glass of the TV set, post credits. I'd seen daughters murdered; slaves traded; hour long torture scenes which had left nothing to the imagination, watching, safe behind my screen, protected from the tortured existence of the characters whose heart-wrenching tales of agony were farmed for my enjoyment, watching as they routinely lived out their worst days—day after day, night after night—with increasingly ghastly horror.

I was there to watch a man pull a rabbit out of a hat.

"No matter what happens," the voice continued, "remain in your seats. Do not panic. I am a professional. There is no need for concern."

I laughed to myself at this warning. The idea that anyone might begin to panic in such a place, perhaps in relation to the threat of audience participation, but as far as the content of the show was concerned?

A knife attack in a shower might have scared people in the 50's, but now, to incite fear, we had to see each narrow incision. We had to see it in a close up, with realistic flesh, in long, lingering shots. We had to see the skin as it is sliced and opened, as it spreads beneath the finely sharpened steel of the blade, which moves slowly to ensure everything is visible and evocative and cruel. The pain needs to be visceral; the audience needs to taste the blood on their tongue from their living room.

Then, to my surprise, a woman, beautiful and completely naked, walked out onto the stage, skin glistening beneath the intensity of lights. I stared—aroused and confused—in disbelief, unable to comprehend what I was seeing.

I was at a magic show, and, as such, I had assumed it would be for families, for children. I had assumed it would be quaint, wholesome and retrograde. Yet here, now, walking gracefully across the wooden floorboards, a naked woman, wet with sweat, soaking and shiny, heading toward the contraption, seemingly unaware, or unbothered by the crowd, as though hypnotized or bored or simply absent.

She reached the contraption and lifted her arms above her head, paying no regard to the masked stagehand, as he slid her wrists into the thick leather cuffs attached to the device, and locked them in place—a clear recreation of the image from the poster.

I began to feel unwell.

Something wasn't right, though I could not say precisely what.

Prematurely, perhaps, I felt the heat from a fire they had not yet lit, but which I was certain they would. It burned through the oxygen in the room, stealing the air I'd hoped to breathe.

I glanced at the woman beside me and, before I'd even registered her unease, the musty odour of gunpowder and mothballs, and the sound of a small explosion drew my attention back to the stage, as another announcement echoed through the cavernous room.

"Behold!"

The pillar of smoke on the stage was already thinning and as it cleared further, I saw him, the same man from the poster, the man I had for some reason, beyond my own understanding, come to see.

"I am the great entertainer!" he said, waving his arms theatrically, pandering to an audience who had seen better and worse and both at once, and who offered in return only a smattering of half-hearted applause.

"A volunteer! A volunteer from the crowd!" he continued. "You!"

My body became hot, became cold, simultaneously. I began to sweat, and the sweat froze against my skin. The magician was pointing at me. His finger, all bone and malice, was aimed directly at me. He prodded me, despite the distance, practically piercing my flesh. I could feel him, wriggling his deft digits around inside me, fingering my heart, sending tremors of anxiety through my ribcage—

small hiccups of fear, making my cartilage vibrate and the sinew tremble. Fingernails, scraping the calcium off my bones.

Something wasn't right. I swallowed the accumulated saliva in the back of my throat with an audible glug. A sound he took, it seemed, as affirmation.

"Yes, you," he said, still pointing, still fingering, still scraping. "Up on the stage."

Then, with the eyes of a few hundred theatregoers turned in unison towards me, their gazes expectant, I rose from my seat, mindlessly climbed the stairs, and walked out onto the stage into the glaring lights, harsh, never completely certain I'd left my seat at all.

"Ladies and gentlemen, a round of applause for our brave volunteer."

The crowd obeyed, and eventually, in the warmth of their encouragement, I felt myself thawing, as the magician took hold of my arm, just above the elbow, and led me toward the silently waiting woman affixed to the steel contraption.

There was wood piled at her feet. It was wet, and rancid with the sharp putrid aroma of fuel. Was it gasoline? Was that why she was wet herself? Had she too been doused in gasoline?

I did my best to keep my eyes on the woman's face— her flat thin mouth, her bored vacant stare—embarrassed to be as close to her naked glistening body as I was, trying to resist the pull of her shoulders, smooth, shiny, and her breasts…

Beyond her head and eyebrows, and the thatch between her legs, she was hairless. The hair she did have was thick and matted, tangled and clumped in curling peaks. Her legs shone like wet roads under streetlights. I had seen this before, in so many different scenarios, but in person, it frightened me.

I wanted to ask if she is okay, if she needed help, as the memory of my humanity danced upon the tip of my tongue. I swallowed the urge, quashing the compulsion, as I reminded myself where I was. She was a performer. She was a part of the show and a willing participant. She was paid to be here. Her role was to entertain and to elicit emotions, excitement, etc.

The nudity, necessary or not, was an artistic choice, pandering to a crowd of onlookers who would nightly expect flesh in whatever they were watching: comedy; drama; horror; musical. To be an actor, a performer — particularly as a woman — was to accept the commodification of your body and the leering gaze of a male dominated industry indulging in gratuity as they serviced half their audience, who they knew they had at their fingertips. A million bodies to gawk at, to lust over and use as fuel for their nightly trysts.

The camera framed wide when a woman disrobed, cropping in close, above the waist, for men. This was just how it was; this was the world we lived in, and our art reflected that. She was a willing participant in it, as was I. She was vulnerable, yes, but she did not need my sympathy. Who was I to question her choices or comfort? I did not know her or share her experience… *Would she not prefer my excitement, my amazement, or my applause? My adoration, even?*

Regardless, as I looked into her eyes, downturned, pleading and unfocused, I could not shake the feeling they were begging for help—not from me, but from some unknowable uncaring God, who had banished her here to play out the violent desires of men for their own sick amusement—an unwilling extra in a sordid industry of lust and horror.

Still, when instructed, I did exactly what was asked of me.

I climbed the stepladder—which had been placed beside the woman—and fiddled with the cuffs, testing their strength and rigidity, to ensure they were tight enough so that the woman's still-wet wrists could not slide through.

"Are they secure?" the showman asked, loud enough for the crowd behind to hear him.

"They are," I replied.

"Are they real leather?"

I did not know.

"Are they real leather?" he asked again.

"There's no tag," I said, flustered, much to the amusement of the crowd, who, for their part, had seemingly settled into the show, relieved, perhaps, that the event was not as wholesome, quaint, retrograde, as they had initially feared. And, spurred on by their excited ovation, I too began to settle into my role.

There was no tag; it was a magic show, one catering to the modern audience's increasing appetite for reaching the highest highs and lowest lows of humanity in art. It was entertainment. I was there to be entertained.

I glanced down at the naked woman and saw that her head was tilted to one side, as though lilting in resignation. It was a strange choice, I thought, but the crowd seemed happy. She knew what she was doing.

"No secret compartments back there?" the magician asked.

I shook my head, no.

"Thank you. You may return to your seat."

I climbed down the stepladder and bowed to the audience, lavishing the undeserved praise heaped upon me for my insubstantial efforts.

"Another round of applause," shouted the magician.

It wasn't gasoline; of course it wasn't—it couldn't be. It was more likely some kind of jelly—a heat retardant, some kind of safety measure. My heart warmed at my epiphany, and I hurried back to my seat to enjoy the rest of the show, offering an unreciprocated smile to the woman in the seat beside me as I passed her, scuttling back to my seat, landing in it just in time to see the magician lighting a match.

A moment later, a black curtain, guided by one of the stage gremlins, slid across the stage to cover the fire and protect the illusion.

It was some kind of jelly. I smiled and exhaled my concerns in long slow breaths, letting them float away into the rafters. She was covered in some kind of jelly. I thought of her up there, behind the curtain, her flesh slathered in the stuff. Her breasts and shoulders, the wet of her hair, on her head and elsewhere, the jelly dripping over her, lubricating her as she slipped free, her soaked body sliding to safety. I could feel my body growing hot, thinking about her, as the room warmed alongside me. My palms were sweating, my neck itched. I could feel blood moving through my veins, making its way down south, and I thanked the gentle Gods I was back in my seat and not still up there on stage, filling my pants with excitement while a woman, pretending to be burned alive, screamed in agony behind me, smelling, I suddenly realised, very realistically of burning hair and flesh.

Up on the stage, the masked assistant ran across the boards with a fire extinguisher to put out the flames. Then, taking hold of the curtain, he wheeled it away.

The leather cuffs I'd inspected only a few minutes earlier dangled listlessly from the centre-beam, empty, black and charred, and still steaming from the heat.

I stared in awe and uncertainty, as all around me, as one, the crowd erupted in applause. The magician stepped forward, bowing, and thanked the audience, then, raising his hand above his eyes to shield them from the lights, he looked out into the crowd, "Another volunteer!" he said. "You!"

I twisted in my seat to see who had been chosen, and my heart turned hard and heavy—the majority of the audience were men, and worse, the magician had somehow chosen one of the few women in attendance to be his next volunteer.

My gut churned with discomfort, as a creeping nameless dread took hold of me. It was magic, I reasoned, sleight of hand, smoke and mirrors. There must have been a latch I'd missed, a secret compartment behind the contraption. Surely, she had climbed down and left the stage.

I looked up to see the volunteer he'd chosen having reached the stage. The magician was asking her who she was, where she was from, and whether she believed in magic. The answers she gave were "Therese", "Here" and "It seems so real."

The magician smiled. "Have you ever been sawn in half before?" he asked.

The audience was quiet as they awaited her answer.

Therese swallowed, and even from my seat, I could hear the thick glug of her terror, as a large device, not unlike a coffin, was slowly wheeled out.

The crowd watched, Therese trembled, and the showman gave an example of what would happen, running his saw through the middle of the empty box, then separating it into two halves.

"Well?" he asked again.

Therese said nothing, her focus fixed on the device in front of her, and on the sharpened teeth of the saw in the magician's hand.

"I'll tell you what," the Magician said, "I'll ask you again in five minutes."

The crowd laughed and Therese turned towards the audience, as though in search of someone in particular: a friend, a partner, a date? Perhaps to the audience as a whole—that throbbing, thrumming mass of hungry eyes and insatiable desires.

She made a miniscule jerk toward the stairs, as though she'd reconsidered her involvement, when another beautiful woman appeared on stage beside her. This one was clothed, though only just. She took Therese's limp hand and led her toward the device, then helped her to climb in.

Once Therese was inside, the magician closed the lid. "Comfortable?"

Therese's voice was muffled but audible. "It's a bit cramped," she said in a thin unsteady voice, which quivered like a ribbon caught in a tree.

"That's because you're too big," snorted the magician. "Maybe, when you're half the size you are now, it will start to feel a bit roomier."

This elicited another laugh from the crowd, one I did not join in on, however. I was too nervous about what was about to happen. My heart was in my throat, blocking my windpipe. I could not breathe. I leaned forward; palms sweaty. A drumroll scored the magician's actions. He raised the saw over his head, then placed it into the narrow slit at the top of the box.

Therese let out a short, surprised yelp, and I found myself tensing, squeezing the arm rests on either side of me as the magician turned to give the audience a horrifying look, the same dead-eyed smile from the poster. The one I had been so curious about and came to see.

He was there but not there. He was like a photograph of a photograph of a photograph, where each successive one lost something in the process. His smile was empty and soulless. It was the toothy grin of a hollow ghost.

I felt unwell. I thought I was desensitized, able to stomach the extremes, but now I worried that I was only capable of that when I had a remote control in my hands and when I was alone. I was used to being disturbed from the comfort of my armchair—horror-stricken out of view—enjoying a guilty-pleasured spectacle I could pause at any moment but never would. I was a carnivore, gobbling down carcasses, able to do so through cognitive dissonance alone.

Up on stage, the magician began to saw.

Immediately, Therese began to scream in agony. Her muffled cries carrying through the coffin shaped box were quickly becoming gurgles—the pathetic wet sound of bubbling death.

Once the saw had reached the bottom of the box and the screaming had stopped, the magician stood upright. He wiped the sweat from his brow. Then, seemingly content with his work, he split the box in two, separating each side from the other like a raw cracked egg, showing us what we all knew we would see.

Therese's organs, flopping to the floor, viscous and thick, landing with a wet smack, as a meaty odour, metallic and pungent, escaped alongside them.

In awe, perhaps, or terror, the audience remained quiet, staring on in disbelief. The room, silent, aside from the sound of smaller organs splashing onto the ground and tumbling out and onto the intestines already in a glimmering steaming pile of pinks, purples, reds and blues, on the floor.

Pools and rivers of blood...

...deep running scarlet streams of her insides...

I wanted to vomit. I gagged in the silence, holding it in, forcing it back. The dense silence choking me, crushing me. My eyes stung. I could not breathe.

Then, all at once, the mood shifted, and the audience began to whoop and cheer and whistle, while I sank deeper into my seat, filled with shame for what I was a part of and for what I knew I would not stop.

The next device to be introduced resembled an iron maiden, a great steal contraption, whose doors lay open like an exploded rib cage, waiting for a victim it could embrace.

"Another volunteer!" the magician shouted, wasting no time, intent to keep the energy of the show moving. His frenzy had reached fever pitch; his eyes were dark and deep with bloodlust.

Surely no one would dare to volunteer, not now, not after what they had only just witnessed. Then, turning, I realised how loosely the magician defined the word 'volunteer.' Two of the masked goons in black were dragging a young woman onto the stage, one on each arm, holding her tightly as she kicked and wriggled in their uncanny grasp. The audience, for their part, were silent. They watched hungrily, waiting, lips wet with saliva.

The showman began his next trick. He took a sword, silver and sharp, and sliced through the air around him, a red ribbon, tied to the sword's hilt, trailing behind it, dancing sublimely. Next, the magician bent the sword. He flexed its blade, then swung it again, cutting a watermelon in half, and then a pineapple. Finally, a cantaloupe. I did not know where the fruit had come from, nor did I care.

He was showing us how sharp the blade was. He wanted us to know, wanted to fuel our imaginations and prepare us for the horrors. He wanted us to know what would happen before it did.

The goons had, meanwhile, muscled the woman into the iron maiden. They slammed the heavy door on her, stifling her screams with the weight of it, while I sat, unmoving, my eyes glued to the stage, gripped by the horrible drama unfolding before me. My shirt soaked through, muscles twitching. I knew I should stand, should do something, say something, speak.

"We call this one death by one hundred swords!" The magician's voice was loud; it had to be, to carry over the guttural wails of the woman he'd chosen for the trick. "Sword one!" he said, as he plunged it into a slot in the box. "Sword two!" he shouted. "Three! Four!"

As he inserted sword after sword, blood continued to spray out each hole, fountains of blood, spurting in time to the woman's frantic staccato of screams, which became increasingly louder with each impaling until they morphed and become cries, then sobs, then finally, silence.

"There's still 96 swords to go," the magician said, smiling toward the audience in a moment of mock disappointment. "But what would be the point?"

I turned to my left, hoping to check in with the woman sitting beside me, to gage her reaction and ensure I was not alone in thinking things had gone too far, only to find that the woman I expected to see there was no longer where I expected her to be. Her seat was empty. I turned around and looked toward the back of the theatre, toward the exit, my eyes passing over a horde of theatre goers whose mouths were hanging open. The back door was still closed and presumably still locked.

I had no idea where the woman had gone to, nor did I have any idea how long ago she'd left.

Still twisted toward the back of the theatre, there was a great splash behind me. I turned quickly, returning my eyes to the stage to find the person I was looking for. There she was, the woman from the seat next to me, wearing nothing but the thick iron of a heavy chain, inside a large vat of water, struggling, writhing, sinking. Pulled down by the bulk of her restraints, she fought, twisted her limbs, wrestling with the chains which were much too heavy.

"The time to beat is 35 minutes," the magician said. He was holding a pocket watch, which he glanced at periodically for show.

I slid forward. Every fibre in my body was pulling at me like a riptide, begging me to do something to shout and scream and wail; to stand up and storm the stage and stop it; to pick up something heavy and smash through the glass, to free the woman.

I slid further forward, my head leading the way, as the veins in my neck turned into iron rods, taut with tension. The sickening gargle of her escaping air a desperate plea for help.

I remained in my seat, watching horrified as her pale muscular body spasmed and convulsed behind the glass.

Then, after a final shudder, she became still.

No longer fighting, she merely swayed eerily at the base of the vat like a single tree in a kelp forest beneath the waves. Her arms floated limply by her head as small bubbles, like Styrofoam, stuck to her pale visage and rolled upwards off her exposed white skin toward the surface.

It had barely been three minutes.

Her bag lay open by my feet. Inside, there was a phone, no doubt full of numbers she would never call again.

I had to do something.

I ran my fingers through my hair, damp with anxious sweat, and pulled at the skin beneath my eyes. I sat in stony silence, arms crossed, desperate for the show to end.

Then behind me a voice shouted from somewhere in the back. "Why are you only choosing women?" they asked.

Their voice was tremulous and uncertain. I could hear their quickened heartbeat in every word. But still, I was thankful that someone had said something.

I tried to find the speaker, but finally returned my eyes to the magician, whose face seemed genuinely confused.

"Cuck!" someone shouted.

"SJW!" shouted someone else.

The magician raised his hand to cover his eyes from the blinding glow of the stage lights and peered out into the now quiet audience. He scanned the rows of attendees in search of the man who'd asked the question.

"Who said that?" asked the magician.

The audience did not reply. They sat in silence, terrified and shaking, watching as the burned, smoldering body of the woman from the opening act began to crawl pitifully out of the charred remains of the bonfire toward the front of the stage.

Her hair was gone. Her skin was ashen, cracked and scarred. Pulling herself along the floor on her broken wrists, she was headed directly toward the magician, who was so focused on finding the person who'd challenged him that he was completely unaware of the movement behind him— the blackened mass dragging itself toward him.

I gripped my armrest. My eyes were red and desperate for moisture. Refusing to blink, I sat there paralysed, watching the wretched woman edge closer and closer to the man at the front of the stage.

"Who said that?" he asked again, as behind him, the woman pushed herself up onto her weak and tender knees, her bones cracking. She rose slowly and silently to full height behind the unsuspecting showman.

She wore that same bored expression from earlier, now masked somewhat by soot and charcoal, and the already thickening skin of scarification. Frail, she almost swayed in the non-existent breeze. Her feet were unsteady. It was as though at any moment she could collapse into a pile of ash.

Then, with a dangling wrist, she reached for one of the remaining swords, and baring her teeth in anguish, curled her crackling fingers around its hilt.

My heart was ready to explode. I could already see my terrified shadow scampering away and diving into the darkness to hide.

"Who said that?" the magician asked yet again. "You all paid for your ticket, you all came here, you all sat and watched. The theatre is full," he shouted. "It's supply and demand. Who said that?"

The magician paused, and I could see in his eyes he had heard it. The sound of scraping metal, the sound of a sword being unsheathed. He flicked his eyes to the right, then turned his back on us.

"Please," I heard him say, "I have a family. A wife and kids."

Then, a moment later, like a fresh bamboo shoot breaching the topsoil, the thin blade of the sword jutted out toward the audience, emerging slick with blood from the deep black of the magician's tuxedo.

Behind me there was no laughter nor applause, no whooping nor whistling. There were only screams as people scrambled over one another for the door and tried in vain to force it open. There was the crunching of bones and the horrible howls of people as they were buried underfoot.

Still sitting, staring forward, I watched as the woman on stage crumpled and fell, finding her final resting place on top of the man who had killed her. With her eyes still open and almost opaque, she stared into the audience, and at me, with a look that was neither angry nor sad or even disappointed, but which more closely resembled boredom.

When they found me, I was still in my seat. My eyes were still glued to the stage at the tableau of gore and horror in front of me. The volunteer, sawn in half; the iron maiden, leaking blood, still flowing; the drowned, now bloated, corpse of the woman who'd sat beside me; the contraption, burned and blackened; and its victim, long since cooled, lying in a crumpled heap atop the host of the whole horrible show.

While I sat there, soaking in the smell of death, with the bodies of the people who hadn't made it out of the theatre, lying twisted and trodden on by the door, their faces forever frozen in their cries of agony, I looked at the magician's face, distorted in a state of agony, fear and regret, and I still couldn't work it out: did he look like me? Or did I look like him? Or did we, perhaps, look like each other?

The Dark Demise of Deann Dunn

S.C. Vincent

It was a private affair. Almost as if he'd paid for the actors to perform for him and him alone. The only ones who accompanied him to the show were the cicadas muting his presence and morning mist which removed the necessity for him to blink.

He liked to watch.

As the mechanism cranked and the coffin lowered, he almost fell out of his cover, inching beyond the branches above to see her more. One last time.

"They aren't like us are they, Mister Dunn?"

During his lurid sabbatical Deann had completely lost sense of his surroundings. How unusual. The mysterious man was tall and seemingly experienced. A certain lengthy fatigue followed his deep voice, one that demanded his attention.

"How did you know her? The woman across the way?" The man looked down to Deann's left hand. "Married?"

He was caught off guard and his lack of reply only made him more nervous. Pulsating. Sweating. Thinking. Until his jaw began to click while he murmured, "we were…engaged."

"The family did not bless the union?"

"No."

The man sighed with a grimace. Pointing, just so daintily, he spoke once more. "At my age, I have lost many close to me. All gone too soon and who I wish to see again. O'Connor there, was like a brother to me."

Deann squinted as if to help see through the lavender mist. But his eyes landed upon her stone once again. Ah, to see her again…was a thought that hadn't dare cross his mind. So audacious. So immoral.

"My name is Lee," the elderly man held his hand out to Deann's, "Lee Elmond. Nice to meet you."

Deann hesitated just long enough for Lee to widen his smile. He felt as if the ground had opened and swallowed him whole as he stared into his eyes and shook his hand. It was a familiar and comforting feeling.

"Mister Dunn, I'll quit this charade. Me and my compatriots deal in the defiance of death." Deann glanced behind Lee and found who had come with him. A black Cadillac was parked yards away and a woman dressed in black stood next to it. He could only partially see her blonde hair in its bonnet because of the umbrella obstructing his view.

"I have to leave." Deann began to scuttle away but the once gentle hand of the elderly man now firmly held him in place.

"Please hear us out. Please!"

Deann could hear his jaw clicking again. To fight and flee or entertain the strange request?

"What do you know?" Deann asked.

"I know we all wish to see the ones we love. To be with them forever. No one wants death, yet it is inevitable."

Deann resigned himself to the rantings. "And what does death have to do with me?"

"Everything my dear Dunn! Look afar, what if you could see her again? See her as she was?"

"You some sort of nut?"

"I can arrange it so you can see her again." The cicadas alarm drowned out any of Deann's hesitation. Lee's voice was just so absolute. "My organization deals in death, yes, but we can't get our hands dirty. The law, you see. However, we can facilitate your access to the cemetery and guarantee you won't be bothered."

"What for? Why do this for me?"

"We believe in acts of good will. Such as allowing you to say goodbye to your special one."

Deann's jaw clicked evermore as he mulled over the proposition. Was he to look the gift horse in the mouth? No, he quickly surmised, he would not. The risk that Lee would recant was too great. "What do you want in return?"

"We want pictures," Lee replied. The charm and charisma had left the old man's voice. "Just the one, to be exact."

"Of her?!"

"Yes, the body. We will send someone along with you to take the photo. My colleague next to my car."

"I-I want one too! I'll need it to remember her by."

"This cannot be done, dear Dunn. Our photos are special and only one of them can be produced."

"Liar!" Deann leapt forward and grabbed Lee by the collar. "I'm the one getting my hands dirty – give me a copy of the picture or no deal."

Lee's once cavalier demeanor had turned to one of great introspection as he freed himself from Deann's clutches and leaned against the nearby willow tree. Deann folded his arms as Lee became lost in consideration. Deann allowed his smile to roam free.

"Agreed. Meet my compatriot here, tonight," Lee said, "One A.M. Tell no one. Bring no one."

"And the storm? Heavy one coming in."

"It's now or never."

***

Darcy felt the oncoming heat of the midmorning more than other people. As Lee returned to the car, she collapsed her umbrella and tried to open the door. It took more than she had. The second try hurt, her fingers being so weak. A breeze brushed against her legs and then upon her back as it slammed her against the car. She could see her reflection in the window as she panted. How pathetic. She was naught but a skeleton. She was only twenty-seven.

"Calm down my dear Darcy," Lee said as he held her from behind. Gently he stood her straight. "Please do not overexert yourself. You are quite precious." The two got into the car, Lee letting her in first, and he knocked on the window between the driver and themselves in the back to let him know to proceed.

Darcy removed the earpiece as she glared at Dunn spying at the funeral procession. Her eyes squinting as he grew smaller and smaller.

"You seem concerned," Lee said as he removed the microphone from beneath his tie.

"Something isn't right. He's more than just a forlorn lover. She was too pretty for him, anyway. What was her name? Alia?"

Lee smirked, "don't tell me you're jealous? Would you like your own stalker?" Lee crossed his legs as he smugly chuckled. Darcy threw him a pointed gaze. "Hmph, sorry. I see my niece has lost her sense of humor."

"Lost? You don't know what I've lost. My health, my life, my soul…every time I take those damn pictures I…"

Lee held out his palm and shook his head, "you knew the deal, Darcy. Just as your father did. The exchange for saving that precious soul of yours from your cancer. That's why you joined us, of your own free will, mind you. To save your damned soul. I know the pictures compound your illness but it's a necessity to get you well again."

Darcy peered out the window once more, the cemetery now in the distance. "I don't know how many pictures I have left in me, uncle. I don't want to die. I feel like my life hasn't even begun. And I don't want to hurt anymore of them…"

"Don't worry dear, we're confident we have perfected the spell. We simply need to test it one last time."

The car jumped as the driver hit a pothole and she fell down to the floor. Everything hurt her. She was just so fragile. "And what of Dunn?" She said as she struggled to get up. "When I deny him the photo?"

Lee bent over and put her into her seat as gently as before. "Don't worry, Darcy. Georgio will be there to help you."

***

The storm ravaged the delicate terrain as the wind shook the mighty branches of the oaks, which she could hear creaking in the comfort of the car. Like hail, the rain poured so heavily that it seemingly had no regard for the privacy of the passengers of the vehicle, herself and Georgio. She looked at him in between the flashes of lightning. Like children, they were staring each other down through the rearview mirror. Deann was taking too long.

She looked at the time on her phone and the amount of it that had passed forced her to recall the hours prior. Dunn had met them there, almost as if he had never left the cemetery this morning. Lee's associate had loosened the cemetery gate's chains just enough for Deann to unravel and slip through. He was to do the unthinkable, the freak. Dig her up and bring the body to Darcy at the entrance so she could take the picture. Poor Alia.

Up and down her fingers went across the metal briefcase. So cold... So hard. It was a catch 22. Death was an inevitability; her cancer would see to that. But her only salvation was in this camera that happened to worsen her condition. The Soul Camera – it could capture the spirit of the dead at the expense of a piece of the photographer's soul and health. Lee and his followers had been trying to perfect their spell for years – to transpose a soul once it's captured in a photograph and put it into a new body; the host's soul being banished to the ether. She was complicit in this nefarious experiment.

"Time's up, wouldn't you say?" Georgio continued his gaze via the mirror. His eyes were all the expression she could see. It was more than enough.

"You expect me to go out there? In that?! Lee is paying you a lot."

Thunder erupted and the sound of the doors unlocking followed suit. "Not that much."

She glanced at the door handle and out the window again, making up her mind. It had to be done. Lee would handle Giorgio's disobedience later. Everyone gets their just deserts. She pocketed her phone as she readied for her departure. After putting the code into the briefcase, a golden gleam shone from the inside. The fragile Soul Camera was old and mysterious. But one thing was known for sure, and it was evident in how Giorgio winced as she removed it from its metal case, was that it was radioactive. She held it securely and opened the door with all her might.

Her hat was taken by the wind and so was she as she stepped onto the gravel. It took everything she had to steady herself off the slippery car and down the path into the dark, hallowed grounds. Lee would've been angry, for he didn't want anyone in the Society implicated. But mostly he didn't want to lose the camera. She often had to remind him that she was not a member of his little group and the camera and herself were a package deal. She was the only other Mystic around who could use it other than him, after all. This dutiful reminder was what braved her way through the laughing shadows that danced upon the tombstones. However, the darkness didn't worry her because as old as the camera was it still strangely had a functioning lightbulb that had an even more powerful light than her phone. Befitting for the cursed object.

Eventually she reached the burial plot. She could hear him, Dunn, his voice so recognizable with its nasal and raspy trappings. But he spoke to no one, for he said nothing at all in the darkness alone. But he did pant and curse. Over and over. Was he still digging? No, not after all that time. The ground would've been loosened by the rain. She stepped closer, allowing the winds to deafen her footsteps. The shovel was strung across the mud so she could not fathom what was making the slapping sound from within the dark pit. As she stood above it an epiphany struck her like lightning itself.

The camera.

She was so filled with curiosity that she deemed the oddity worthy a photo. She prepared it to get a wide shot and as Dunn's panting turned to a singular climatic grunt she snapped the picture. She saw it all. His face was at the moment of the greatest pleasure and greatest sin – and the corpse, so stiff and bare.

"Hey!" He shouted from below.

Dunn continued with some expletives, but Darcy couldn't be bothered to notice. Bile, spit, mucus, all expelled from her mouth as she turned away. Never had she seen such a thing – she'd only heard of such horrors. She wanted to run.

"Give me the picture," Dunn said as he began to claim ground. "I don't care what you do with it, but I was promised one!" A strange clicking sound echoed from his mouth as he spoke – like his haw was made of fragile sticks. "I need to have her!" Darcy snapped back from her illness once she felt Dunn grab her arm and pull her towards him.

"Georgio!" She shouted, hoping that her cries for help would make it through the wind and rain. But the two continued to struggle and it was once she saw the smile on Dunn's face that she became truly desperate. She was but a plaything to him. Like a house of cards made of pitiful bone. But much like a deck of cards, she still had her ace.

With her free hand she aimed the camera solely upon him and snapped another photo – could it work? Could the camera really steal the soul of the living? His grip loosened, the rain lessened, and she removed her arm. The gravel beneath creaked as she stepped backwards. He was in a daze; eyes of which reminded her of a goldfish as they didn't gleam nor shine from the lightning above. She didn't question it. She took the camera and ran.

***

She had grown used to the smell of the chemicals used in the process and as the photographs hung above it was only a matter of time before the film developed to show the ethereal specters she captured. All that was left was her reflection, red and worn. The darkroom was hers alone; those in the Society never bothered her while she was working. As she surveyed the new lines on her face and looked at the photos above, she could only be reminded of her guilt. Her desecration of others' souls, to be used for her own reprieve, grew heavy on her conscience. But she was too far in to back out now. For if she failed, she knew she would be doomed to hell like her father before her, who had a similar disease. The photographs – the camera – were her curse.

She could hear Lee and the other talking in the chapel. "What a surprising turn of events, Master Lee," said one of the six members.

"You lot nearly got my niece killed! Your jobs are to do research and analysis – that includes psychological!" Lee's demanding voice filled the rotting halls of the church.

"But master," Darcy recognized the voice as Gloria's, "considering the time given I think we made a fair case. We all knew he was a stalker – he drove that girl to suicide. And Darcy wasn't supposed to be the one to face him in the first place."

"Quiet!" Her uncle's voice boomed so loudly that the rickety walls shook along with it. "Georgio's defiance will be dealt with in a suitable manner. One that will make you sure to never be as incompetent again lest you share his fate."

The silence that followed only made Darcy want to fill it with something beautiful to distract her from her twisted reality. Her hands wandered her pockets, looking for her phone so she could play some happy pop music. But it was to no avail. She skirted around the darkroom until her uncle's voice just barely made it through the dilapidated walls, "that woman is the only tool we have to counteract our fate. We cannot put her in positions that will cost us unnecessary photos – for every one she takes the lesser her lifespan – or in your incompetence did you forget that as well? Think of it as this – for every photo she wastes, that's one of you not getting saved. Fire and brimstone for you all because I can assure you, I will not lose my chance again!"

This was not the first time her uncle had let his true intention and feelings be known. She found her arms holding herself, wrapped around as if to ease her loneliness. She was only a tool to them. If only her father was still alive; but no, he was a tool, like her, that had all been used up. She opened the door to the chapel and saw the six members of the cult sitting in the pews while Lee sat upon an ornate chair upon the pulpit. Above him hung an upside-down crucifix. Their conspicuous visages changed as soon as she closed the door behind her. Like night and day. Cults like this knew only obfuscation. This she had come to learn far too late.

Gloria had bad kidneys. The other man, John, who spoke before, had muscular dystrophy. Another, a brain tumor too complex to operate on. The others had similar terminal diseases – except for her uncle, who quickly put his hand over the binder of spirit photos as if to hide them from her. Despite their self-pity and bitterness, they all faked their smile upon seeing her.

What were they expecting? What else could she give? "I-I," she stuttered.

"Yes, my dear?" Lee questioned.

"I lost my phone."

Much like how the cult obfuscated the truth, darkness now suffocated the light. The screams of the members proved to her that this was a surprise even to them. One of them, an accountant, would've been sure the electricity was paid.

"What's happening?!" Lee shouted.

There were no answers among them. The only sign of illumination was the strand of moonlight piercing through the stained-glass window above. Darcy cowered as the glass shattered, screaming as she hid in the pews.

Thud.

Had someone thrown a brick? No. She could tell, listening through the cult's clambering, that the rolling sound was more evident of something spherical. And the rolling grew louder, closer. Until she saw it. What had broken the window was staring straight at her. The night had returned to her in the most nightmarish of ways. The image of Dunn and Alia – the corpse – leapt across her mind. The vivid sin. What she had photographed had returned!

She recoiled further down into the floor while she muffled her screams with her hands. Crash! Crash! Crash! And two more breaking of the glass windows shook the room to its core. "An arm!" Shouted the accountant.

"A leg!" Said another.

"Whose body is this?!" Lee asked.

Darcy garnered just enough bravery to join the group in the center of the room. "I saw the head!" She answered. "It's Alia, the woman he dug up. Dunn has found us!"

"But how?"

Nobody answered but it took only a second for Darcy to realize what happened. "I lost my phone. It must've fallen out of my pocket at the grave when he was pushing me around. He must've gotten into it and got this address."

"By God!" The accountant proclaimed. "You stupid girl! You know this place is a secret."

Bam! Darcy turned to see the chapel's doors swing open and what followed was a gust of wind that pushed her fragile body to the ground. The figures above her were doubled and so were their screams as they ran. Were they leaving her? The darkness hid them – but as she looked about, she saw her uncle as he fled to his chair, grabbing the binder of spirit photos and similarly fled to the bleak shadows. As her head grew heavier and sight just as hazy, a large figure passed over her.

***

It was perhaps the smell that beckoned her to consciousness, but it was indeed the warm puddle that enveloped her which opened her eyes. As she grimaced, the pain from the back of her head reminded her of what happened. She looked around and once she saw the corpse of the accountant near her, she felt only slightly relieved. Quietly – as much as possible for she couldn't quell her shaking, she crawled over to him. Stabbed. Relentlessly. She couldn't count how many holes, and it was too repulsive to stay and do so.

Where were the others? Lee? One arm upon the pew and then another, carefully she pulled herself up as to not slip. Her chest had never felt so heavy. Her head snapped towards the belltower where a deathly curdling scream echoed from.

Dunn. She had not presumed he was capable of such atrocities, that is, until she had seen what he did to Alia's body. Others the cult tricked to do their dirty work were loons, similarly, but were patsies and almost all ended up in asylums or prison. But Dunn was different. Not his intelligence, but in his brutality. Every inch of her body told her to run – turn, and escape through the church doors. But what about the spell? If anyone died then her efforts would be for nothing. And her uncle, her only family left she could not bear to lose. Before she could search for him, if he was still alive, she was to retrieve the few things she had that could grant her any leverage over Dunn.

Just enough light guided her way to the darkroom and through it she carefully entered to not alert Dunn on his murderous rampage through the chapel. She quickly removed the camera from the briefcase and found the photos of Alia and Dunn, their souls wistfully moving about in the pictures, and pocketed them. Carefully she vacated the room and entered the halls of the church once again.

The floors creaked as she grew ever closer to where she last saw Lee; the rotten timber ached even from her lofty weight. But as she stepped behind her uncle's chair, she heard a deep 'thud' upon her footsteps. She bent down to find a hatch on the floor. She looked around to be sure Dunn was not near and lifted the door, finding a staircase descending into the dank underground.

What machinations had her uncle devised to warrant a secret passageway? As she descended, heels echoing down the damp path, she could not help but wonder if the terrors she'd encountered were a sort of divine punishment for flirting with the occult. She met the base of the steps and continued down the narrow cavern until she heard a click next to her ear.

"Don't move!" A voice demanded from within a crevice of the wall. Never had she been so panicked to be driven to paralysis. "Oh, it's just you."

"Uncle?"

"Come, Darcy. Quickly!" Lee reached from the darkness and pulled her in between the rocks. She was led along the shadows until she heard a door knob turn and a light embraced her. A panic room. But unlike most, it was filled with unholy relics of the occult. Ancient looking tomes, jars filled with taboo things suspended in time, and black candles all of which were above a symbol on the floor. A satanic star was varnished in a certain stain that she assumed to be blood beneath her. "You have your camera. Good. Behind the curtains," Lee pointed across the room, "Gloria. Take her picture."

"Dunn killed her?"

"She protected me in the skirmish." He walked towards the door and listened for a moment before speaking again. "She knew I could bring her back with my magic. So, we fled here to retrieve my gun." He removed his revolver from his suit jacket and said, "there is something strange about that bastard. He's different than before. Any blow that struck him only stopped him temporarily. We'll see how he fares against a bullet."

"I think this is my fault. Lee, I took a picture of him. And it's like the others!" She saw on a table the binder of soul photos her uncle always kept with him. "I don't know how it worked because he's not dead!"

"Yes, the camera can still capture the soul, but it can't be used in the transference spell because the soul is still tethered to the physical realm. That's why we must die before we transfer our souls to a new body. Or else we end up like him."

"So, what do we do?" Like the sound of a tidal wave smashing against a cliffside, so too did Darcy and her uncle hear the shutting of the door to the surface. "It's him!" Darcy screamed.

"Damn you girl! You left the door open?! He's followed you."

"I'm sorry – I –"

"No matter," Lee gripped his gun securely, "now is my chance. In the dark."

"No uncle, stay here. We're safe here."

As he opened the door he said, "beings without souls are resilient. This is not the first time this has happened, Darcy. His strength and will would outlast us here. Goodbye."

And with that her uncle left to face the demonic man, Deann Dunn. A monster of her own doing. It would be only moments before he became within Lee's line of fire and the sounds of gunfire would fill the room.

What was she to do? How could she help? She didn't want to die; that was the point of all this blasphemy. Yes, the greatest sin of all. She was reminded of when she saw the binder of photos on the table. One, in particular. One which was the genesis of her sorrow. A face which she had been running from but now more than ever wished to see.

Her fathers.

The sound of gunfire filled the room, and she leapt for the binder, opening it and facing her photographic sins. The pictures moved, haunted by the souls that contained them. She flipped through the pages until she found him, looking straight at her with a pleasant gaze. The gunfire continued; one shot quickly became three then five. Then silence.

She held her father's photo in her hand, her bottom lip quivering, and saw him mouth something. The door creaked open and once again turned to face Lee but only found Dunn holding his keys and gun. She knew he had one more in the chamber. Looking down to the only person she had left, she saw her father mouthing something once more and finally understood what he was saying: 'rip me.'

Once she did, it was as if time itself stopped. Dunn stood completely still with his finger on the trigger and a ghastly smoke flew from the torn photograph taking form in front of her. Her father, Christophe, looked just as he did when he was living with a gentle mustache and smile in his eyes. "Hello, my daughter," he said. "Please remain calm, I know it may be strange to be talking to your deceased father, but the forces of good can only stop time for a short while and there is much to tell you."

Darcy lowered her hands from her mouth and replied, "I'm sorry, papa, they made me take that picture of you. They said I could bring you back. You were my first photo. I didn't know -"

"That the ensnared souls were suffering within the frame. Neither did I when Lee tricked me into this wicked game of his. I didn't put it together until I saw their sorrowful faces and by then it was too late to back out."

"What do you mean by 'game'?"

"Yes, as you know we come from a family of the spiritually inclined, or as Lee puts it, Mystics. It takes one to use the camera, to take a soul. It also takes one to cast the spell." Christophe walked to Dunn and placed his hand into his, phasing through like the specter he was. Yet, it was not as if he had no impression, for Dunn's hand moved upon Christophe's will; the gun pointing downwards. "Lee began to poison me and convinced me I was terminally ill. And my only salvation would be the spell, if he could complete it in time. He didn't. Sound familiar?"

"Then that would mean… How do you know, papa?"

"He told me so himself. For years he would open that book and show me the newest photo you had taken, flaunting how close he was getting. And how sick you were becoming. I'm sorry darling; I couldn't do anything."

"Papa, what do I do now? I've hurt so many souls. Participated in the occult. Now either Dunn or Lee will kill me."

"Darcy, the souls of the oppressed can be far more forgiving than you give us credit for. But first you must forgive yourself and then…"

"And then?"

"Free us!"

Christophe stepped backwards into Dunn's body and time seemed to begin moving again as the candles flickered once more. She could tell Dunn's malevolent nature was being contained for he spasmed and seized – he could not bring his gun up to target Darcy. But it was a short snare. Slowly his will was gaining ground; her father losing control.

'Forgive yourself' and 'free them'? What did he mean? She was losing time and backed away. It wasn't until she looked at the soul photos moving in their sorrow and paint that she realized what her father meant. She was as trapped as they were. Her frame being her guilt and capture, Lee.

And so, she put herself at their mercy. She tore out each and every page, throwing them on the floor. Joining them on her knees, she took out the photos and ripped them apart. One by one ghastly figures flew from the pictures, turned to face her, and then flew into Dunn's soulless husk.

Her father was right. They were forgiving – they must've known she had been used. Tears began to fall from Darcy's eyes as the souls were freed and in this whirlwind of fate, as the occult books flew about, a shining light grew from Dunn until it blanketed the room in its entirety and forced her to look away.

It was her hair being pulled forwards that caused her alarm once more. Then the binder slipping away, tiles of the satanic floor rising, and light of the black candles being pulled into the bright void that was once Deann Dunn. She had but two pictures left. Deann and Alia. As she herself began to get pulled into the vortex, she grasped the pictures and tore them to shreds.

From the pictures came the two souls in combat, Dunn pleading for mercy, and Alia saying her parting words to Darcy. The two souls were pulled into the void, a giant light flashed once more, and the vortex and spirits disappeared. Everything was back to normal.

Her heart pounding in her head was all that was left – she couldn't breathe. All the pictures, her father, guilt; it was all gone. Gripping her chest, it all erupted as she bowled over in tears. Her sobbing was everything and with every tear she was left bereft of burden.

But as her tears dried and her breathing steadied, a forgotten sound bellowed from behind her. The sound of death. One step after another she followed the singular groan to the back of the room. Darcy pushed the curtain aside and found Gloria bleeding out from her wound. The bad kidneys were ironically not the cause of her death, and the groan was likely the last bit of breath trapped in her lungs.

"Won't you save her?"

Darcy's hair stood on end. It was Lee.

"Here is the camera." Lee brushed up against her; his demanding voice was one she would normally not question.

Darcy looked at the camera and then at Gloria's corpse and replied, "sorry uncle, I can't do this anymore. You'll have to find someone else to abuse. I'm done." She turned and walked to the exit.

"Don't you walk away from me, girl! You owe her – you owe me! Take the damn picture. Her death is on your hands!"

Darcy's hands only momentarily rested on the door frame, and she just partially turned to face him. She continued up the stairs and left behind the dark demise of Deann Dunn.

***

The sweltering heat and droning cicadas reminded her all too well of the recent tragedy. But of course, so did the granite tombstone for Gloria that stood erect in front of her. The service had just ended. A service of one.

After all the trouble and terror, she couldn't figure why she attended, for Gloria was like the others that were murdered by Dunn. They used her. But she still came.

"You look well."

Her heart skipped a beat. She turned to find Lee coming forward with a briefcase in hand. He walked to her side with a foreign smile.

"Yes," Darcy replied, "my condition's improved since the last time I saw you." Darcy turned to face the grave, not wanting to look him in the eye. She scoffed, "of course it was you."

"Me?"

"That arranged the funeral."

"Oh, yes. Well, Gloria had paid her dues. Deserved a good stone."

She shook her head, "that's an interesting choice of words, uncle. It seems everyone has paid except for you."

He exhaled but then let out a chuckle, "we left things on a sour note that night, dear Darcy."

"Don't call me 'dear' ever again," she looked at him with the most serious of intent. "Do you understand?" His brow furrowed. Gobsmacked. She was sure by his reaction that he didn't know the truth.

"Hm, fine, Darcy. You can be that way. But our work here isn't done. Look, I'm not sure what happened that night. Dean must've thought he killed me and then I awoke to find you standing next to Gloria. Whatever happened to Dunn, the photos, and the damage to my room is a mystery to me. But that doesn't change the fact that you are very, very, sick. And your sins are truly grave. Unless you want to spend eternity in hell, I advise you to reconsider working with me."

"Would you help a mosquito suck your blood? Or a tick bite you?" Darcy turned and began towards the parking lot. "Don't come to me again. I'll have a bullet in the chamber for you."

She only made it two steps before he replied, "I knew it! Once you saw her dead and refused to use the camera, I knew you wouldn't join me without the proper motivation. There is a difference between the dead and the dying." Lee reached into his suit pocket and brought out a white handkerchief. Like a magician of sorts, he held his palm out with a wry smile and gently unfolded it, revealing a rather large cicada. "Have you ever wondered why I have always sought immortality, Darcy? Unlike the others, I was not knocking on death's door."

Whatever sternness or authoritative demeaner he once had, Darcy could see no trace of it any longer. Like a snake, he had shed his skin. His eyes were alive with the fires of hell itself. "To flee hell," Darcy answered. She found herself taken aback, but only for a moment.

"No, my dear Darcy. You see, when I was a child, I had the most marvelous food. Shrimp."

"Shrimp?"

"Yes. Do not laugh at me for I had a terrible allergic reaction. I nearly died that day. But I lived in a coastal town. Shellfish was our livelihood. I was a boy! Alone. The most delicious thing I could have would bring me the most ruin."

His smile had turned to a grievous frown so once he put the cicada in his mouth she was just as surprised as she was disgusted. "Lee! What the hell?!"

"You see, cicadas contain the same deadly protein as shrimp." The smile returned to his face as the bug's guts gushed between his teeth. "I want a new body not allergic to shrimp. And I can only do that if you take my picture." He opened the briefcase and revealed the Soul Camera. "You'll take my picture, won't you? Promise me." He loosened his collar and pulled apart his tie. Darcy remained silent, but slowly she approached her uncle as he fell to his knees and grabbed the camera. "Atta girl, my little niece…" His face was swollen and glistening with sweat. "The spell… I perfected it, I'm sure. You are a Mystic like me. Just follow the instructions…Georgio-"

"Uncle," Darcy interrupted as he sat dying before her. "You said you were alone as a boy. But you were wrong. You had my father. But you betrayed him." Darcy felt a surge of joy jolt up her spine. "That's right. I know everything." Lee recoiled, falling on his behind and gasping for air. His lips were gigantic and right eye swollen. "I tore the picture of my papa and the others you enslaved to eternal torture. And you want to know what they wanted in return for saving me from Dunn? Revenge."

Darcy lifted the old camera above her head and threw it hard onto the ground, stomping on it and smashing it to pieces. She continued, "they forgave me, so I don't fear death. Will God forgive you?"

Lee began to flounder about, like a child having a fit on the floor until he seized. And finally, the fire in his eyes went out.

Three, maybe five minutes passed, and a gentle breeze struck her.

She stood strong.

Bumping Uglies

Scott Wilson writing as
S. Michael Wilson

*C*ymothoa exigua, or the tongue-eating louse, is a
parasitic crustacean of the family Cymothoidae.
This parasite enters fish through the gills and then
attaches itself at the base of the fish's tongue. The parasite
destroys the fish's tongue and then attaches itself to the stub
of what was once its tongue and becomes the fish's new
tongue.
- Marine Parasitology, Seventh Edition

The more conspicuous and more interesting part of the
genitals of both sexes, the male organ, has a symbolical
substitute in objects of like form; those which are long and
upright, such as sticks, umbrellas, poles, trees, etc. It is also
symbolized by objects that have the characteristic, in
common with it, of penetration into the body and
consequent injury, hence pointed weapons of every type:
knives, daggers, lances, swords, and in the same
manner firearms, guns, pistols and the revolver, which is so
suitable because of its shape.

-Sigmund Freud, A General Introduction to Psychoanalysis

This wasn't Richard's first STD. He'd been around. Pubic lice, party crabs, crotch crickets, clam chowder, filly fungus, French gout, ball rot, clap shack, seam squirrels, the drip, the trick, the rub, even the blush. Not the hivvies or grid lock - he wasn't queer or anything - but other than those he was pretty sure he'd had them all at one time or another.

That's what happens when you're an experienced ladies' man. You get around enough, you're going to end up dipping your wick in a polluted yeast pot, and he had the scars to prove it. So, with that kind of track record, he wasn't the type to get all paranoid over the sudden appearance of a couple of blisters or some off-color flaking in the bikini area. But this one... this was different.

He'd first noticed it as a lump at the base of his prick, just above the scrotum, small and hard, like a zit or boil. This was a couple of weeks after he and a few of his coworkers down at the futon factory decided to blow their paychecks on a weekend romp through one of the more depraved districts of Tijuana, throwing around pesos like they were millionaires and doing shit that made donkey shows look like that edited-down porn you get in hotel rooms. So, he just assumed he picked up a new bed buddy from one of the skanks at that dive with the skinned dogs hanging on the clothesline out back and decided to wait until the weekend to trot around to the free clinic and get whatever shot or ointment they threw his way.

By the weekend, scales started appearing.

Experienced as he was, this was just a tad unsettling. They were transparent with a slightly grayish tint to them, circling the entire base of his shaft like a crusty cock ring. They sort of felt like the part you threw away when you peeled shrimp. He probably should have gone to the doctor at that point, but the fear of what they'd do outweighed his concern over what it was. He wasn't going to go to the docs to save his Johnson just so they could turn around and chop it off of him. That was a fate worse than death. So instead, he spent his evenings soaking in hot baths with salts and shit from the health and beauty aisle at Wal-Mart and watched in the following weeks as the scales grew wider and slowly climbed up his pole.

Some of the guys noticed that he was a bit quiet at work the last few days, and a few made a point of busting his balls over passing on the next pussy raid, but they weren't queer for him or anything, so none of them got up in his shit and tried to find out what was wrong, which was just fine with him. Some things a man needs to sort out on his own.

The one thing that probably kept him from caving in and running to the emergency room was that it didn't hurt. It didn't itch or nothing. In some ways it felt a little numb, like it wasn't attached to his body anymore. But it still worked as far as pissing went, and he was still waking up with morning wood, man's best friend. In fact, there were a couple of times when he could have sworn he was getting bigger, and not in that scary snakebite kind of swelling way, either. He tried jerking off a couple of times, but the feeling just wasn't there. Probably just best to let whatever it was run its course. As long as it ran it pretty soon. This was the longest he'd gone without dropping a load, manually or otherwise, since he could remember. Soon as this shit shed or molted or whatever the hell it was going to do, he'd be spending the better part of the following weekend either stroking, poking, or both. Hell, he'd probably drop trow on the top of the apartment building and jerk off over the edge just to celebrate. After a while, he just got used to not thinking about it outside of bathroom duties. Wait long enough and you can eventually get used to anything.

He nearly jumped out of his socks the first time it moved. He'd just been sitting at the card table in the kitchen smoking that Sunday morning, not really thinking about anything, when he felt a tug at his crotch, as if somebody had reached under the table and given him a quick yank. He actually looked under the table, that's how weird it was. Then he felt it again. It was like his pecker was stretching or something. He watched the bulge in his underwear move the next time it did it. He tried doing it himself but couldn't figure out what to flex or where. It was like it had a mind of its own now. At least, more so than usual.

It was more and more active throughout the day, and Richard spent most of the time walking around the apartment staring at his crotch. And he could feel it again. That is, there was more feeling down there now. A lot more. And it was different. You spend most of your adult life playing with your prick; you know what it feels like when it's just dangling there biding its time. This was an entirely new sensation, and every time it flexed or stretched or - he could have sworn he felt it expand every now and then - it felt good in a way he'd never experienced in his life. Like when stretching sends a shiver through your back, but a bit more concentrated.

Something else began to return with the feeling: arousal. His sex drive had been on the low side lately, as you expect would be the case when your crotch looks like a prawn cocktail. But suddenly he was "all het up," as his mother used to put it, the urge seeming to come and go in waves, each one stronger than the last. By the time the sun had gone down, the lust had grown so strong that caution gave way to the animal urges, and he found himself sniffing around the bedroom for clean jeans and a semi-fresh shirt. He didn't care if his balls were leaking blue cheese and battery acid. This boy needed to get laid, one way or another.

Richard practically vibrated as he paced the sidewalks of the meat district. He couldn't remember ever being this horny. If he didn't sink his dick into something soon, he was going to lose his shit completely.

He wasn't even sure if he was going to be able to bust a nut. He'd tried stroking off in the shower that morning, but it was like trying to pet an armadillo. He couldn't even feel anything through the scales anymore. He hadn't even looked at it since Thursday. He couldn't. If he wasn't able to get off tonight with a professional, he'd call out sick tomorrow and hit the clinic first thing. But first... nothing else mattered except the need burning inside him. It was almost like a thirst, or a hunger. He didn't feel pressure building up as much as a gnawing emptiness.

He passed up five or six whores who looked like they knew the score. This wasn't the first time he'd looked for cash and gash with something visible rooting around down there. A pro would turn him away before he'd gotten a chance to cop a feel. He needed some fresh meat, someone too green to know to inspect the goods beforehand.

He finally found her next to the truck docks on the corner of South and Forty-Second. Young but not jailbait, too homely to be attractive, no real curves, just a stick in spandex with a dead stare. She looked used, but not enough to be streetwise. And you could tell she was behind on her quota by the way she kept glancing around. She'd be perfect.

He wooed her by not trying to talk her price down, which was way more than her street value, probably trying to make up for a slow night. She took the bait like a good little suckerfish, and he followed her down a block to one of those by-the-hour inner city motels designed specifically for shooting up or getting off. The retired strip-club bouncer behind the front desk cage didn't even glance up from his smart phone as the girl grabbed a key and took him up the stairs; probably pays a flat-rate for repeat visits through her pimp's cut. Cost of doing business, as they say.

He could feel the bulge in his pants growing as they made the journey from the corner to the room. It wasn't just the stiffening he was used to with a gradual erection. There was the sensation that his member - it barely seemed like it was his anymore - was uncurling from his scrotum like a pill bug. He could feel grinding little shifts and clicks, as if the scales surrounding him now were rearranging to allow the expansion of his length and girth. His need swelled with it. It was a miracle he didn't tackle her in the stairwell and take her right there.

The minute the door closed behind them he was on her. There was no pretense, no masquerade of intimacy or foreplay, even more so than usual. He backed her into to the barely made bed, where she fell and unceremoniously hiked up her skirt. She might have been new, but she'd already been through enough that she understood this was a no-nonsense call. No panties, of course. She was unshaven but well-kept which relieved Richard somewhat. Nothing put a dent in the mood more than a hooker who let herself go down below. It wasn't just unappealing; it was downright unprofessional.

Richard didn't waste any time. He undid his belt and let his jeans drop but left his underwear on until he was crouched down in front and over her and blocking her view. He couldn't even bear to look at himself. It felt like it was going to explode, and he was afraid glancing down would confirm the feeling. He just hooked a thumb under the elastic waist and pulled it out and around his hard-on. He had to pull it pretty far to get around. He was definitely larger, and harder than ever, even more than he'd been as a kid when he had copped a feel off his babysitter while she was napping on the couch. It was like gripping a club when he grabbed it and pointed it at the girl's fuck hole.

He should have been worried about how it felt; those scales practically locked into place, smooth and rigid, lined up like the studded grip on a bike handle, and cool in a way his warm, rigid flesh down there had never been. But the moment his fingers curled around the base of his shaft, a bolt of pure pleasure shot from his asshole, up his spine, and through his shoulders like flaming wings. It was more amazing than any orgasm he'd ever had, and he wasn't even on the road to shooting a load yet. Somewhere, beneath this sudden flood of pleasure, it registered that this was just a promise, a glimpse of the climax to come, and the sudden fear that something, anything, could prevent what this new thrill was merely hinting at threw him into action, and he shoved himself fully into the girl in one forceful motion.

It wasn't the first time he'd skipped the introductions and got to the point with a rent girl, so the look of shock on her face when he drove in up to the hilt in one thrust wasn't alarming, and even if it had been, he was too overwhelmed by the rush that flooded through him as he filled her. There had been times when he'd wondered about what it must feel like for women when they were fucked, suspicious that they probably enjoyed it more than the man did. Whatever he had tried to dimly imagine, at its most fanciful it couldn't have been more than a fraction of what was flooding through him now. Time froze. His body expanded, a raw itch crawling over every inch of him as if his skin were stretching like a balloon. His heart purred in an erratic staccato, threatening to splay his chest like the neck of a cobra. He could feel sparks everywhere as this moment hung in the air for eternity.

The look of shock on the girl's face morphed throughout this euphoric moment into a look of fear and anguish, and a scream barely touched her lips as it ripped from her throat. Richard panicked. Not out of concern for the girl, but because she was threatening this, whatever this was, and this was something that couldn't be allowed to stop. He hooked his arms up under her legs, threw the weight of his body onto hers, and clamped both hands over her mouth. She bucked and surged beneath him as he rode her struggling body like a mechanical bull.

She clawed and scratched at his arms and shoulders; her feet clamped tight against his ears by his arms as he did his best to muffle her. Her nails drew bloody tracks down his biceps, but they barely registered over what he was feeling. He was dimly aware that he wasn't thrusting in and out of her as much as he was sunk in and hanging on, but the sensation was as if he was pile driving her relentlessly, drilling through as if it was possible. There was no buildup, no increasing pressure and release. It was as if he was coming nonstop, in steady pulses that just rolled over one another.

Comprehension dimmed in this unyielding wake. His hands gripped the girl's mouth tighter as sounds vibrating beneath them became more frantic, and he was vaguely aware of wetness washing over his groin, down his thighs and knees. He didn't even notice when she stopped making noise, only that her eyes stopped rolling around and stared blankly over his left shoulder. He had no idea how long he was lost in the void of that relentless pleasure. It was only in the aftermath of the throbbing echoes chasing through him that he noticed the girl wasn't struggling anymore.

He collapsed on her as he breathed heavily, willing his body to retain the physical memory of what had just happened, and realized that his hands were on the girl's shoulders instead of her mouth. He lifted his head up and looked at her face. The eyes were still looking up at nothing, her mouth hanging silently open from her last attempt to vocalize whatever it was that had last gone through her mind. He could still see the imprint of his fingers on her cheeks.

He stared at her in disbelief. She couldn't be. She had been trying to scream, but that doesn't mean anything. He shook her a bit, got no reaction, then realized that he was still inside her. When he pulled out and looked down to discover why his legs were all wet, he almost screamed himself.

***

Rust-colored carpet/Box springs silenced, soaked in blood/Last trick was no treat.

Detective Abston surveyed the squalid hotel room while the lab boys took their photographs and samples. Everything needed to be documented, from pictures and belongings to blood and fiber samples. It was like harvesting a Death Garden off season: you never knew what would produce, or when. The lab rats had the corpse and its surroundings covered, so Abston spent most of his time concentrating on the young girl's small dresser. Ramshackle hotel property, probably picked up at a flea market or snagged off a street corner on garbage night. She had more clothing than she probably needed, some of it too nice for the surroundings. A drawer for makeup and toiletries, common when you're sharing a bathroom with the other three rooms on the floor.

Shoved in the far corner of the top drawer was a plastic snow globe with a unicorn in it. It was on its side, the white and silver specks gathered in the concave glass just above where the unicorn's head was. The beast's magical horn was buried in the pool of fake snowflakes, penetrating it is if caught in the act of diving through into a different, better reality. He had the overwhelming urge to take the decoration out and shake it, place it on the dresser and watch the snow cascade around the mythical creature, like the dead girl laying spread-eagled in a pool of her own blood behind him had no doubt done countless times herself. Instead, he left it where it was and closed the drawer.

There really wasn't a reason to be here. Any real evidence worth noting would come from the lab boys or Doc, and the flunkies at street level were interviewing whatever neighbors or potential witnesses they could gather up. If everybody could have been trusted to do what needed doing without him acting as ringleader, he could have handled the whole case from his desk back at the station. He wasn't playing detective out here as much as he was playing manager. Not that he wouldn't have shown up at the crime scene anyway. It seemed wrong not to. To deal with a crime like this from a distance of pictures and lab tests would be the final act of dehumanization for what was once the less cynical among him would refer to as a person. He wasn't just there in his official capacity as an officer of the law. In many ways, he was here to bear witness. Otherwise, there was no point to any of this.

He looked over the room again. The faded wallpaper separating at the seams, an outdated floral design caked with a decade or two of nicotine and inner-city exhaust, almost complicated the dingy warped furniture. Below it all was a slab of shag carpet so old and unaccustomed to any real attempts at housekeeping that you could probably drag a comb through it and come up with a decade worth of biological residue. Getting any useful DNA evidence from a crime scene like this was impossible. Lab crews would just go through the motions, then later run betting pools on how many different DNA matches came up. It was a cynical and demoralizing tradition. Abston had won twice.

It was a small room, typical style and size for these tenement-style hotels, slivers of building you could usually find wedged between factories and warehouses in industrial districts that were never properly zoned. They were the kind of hotels tourists and travelers didn't seek out, and wouldn't find even if they did, since the owners never bothered to advertise. Word of mouth was the only reason you'd step foot into one of these dives, and if a mouth offered you words that delivered you to a place like this, you were probably too far gone to care. He didn't give the order to knock on doors for statements; the building undoubtedly emptied out the minute whoever had found the girl opened the door and saw the blood.

There was a lot of blood, and no real confusion as to where it had all come from. The dead girl was spread-eagled on the bed, knees hooked over the side, and a cone of dark-red fluid was soaking into the sheets and carpet, the congealing mess originating from the epicenter of where her legs met in the middle, as if she'd given birth to a tidal wave of gore. He didn't need to go sticking his nose in any closer to guess that somebody had gone at her down there with a knife or something. The only other way you could have gotten that much blood out of her would have been to grab her head and roll her down like a tube of toothpaste. It happened more often than anyone was willing to admit. The knife thing, not the toothpaste tube thing. Obviously.

A commotion in the stairwell broke the silence of the crime scene, but nobody in the room acted like they heard it. They were all familiar with the sound of a med team hauling a gurney up a flight of stairs. The sample guys started packing up their kits. Everyone had run out of things to do, Abston included, so he made his way to the landing and waited for the stairwell to free up.

***

Richard still couldn't believe he'd managed to walk home.

He had obviously panicked. One minute he was getting his rocks off, the next minute he was kneeling in a pool of blood from a whore who'd been dead for at least part of the time he'd been fucking her. He was also still high from whatever it was that had come over him when he came - hell, from the moment he'd first entered her - and so the whole thing seemed distant, as if he was watching it on a TV with bad reception. He'd simply stood up, pulled up his pants, and walked casually out of the building. He'd gotten two blocks before realizing that he was leaving a blood trail and had to duck into an alley and rummage through dumpsters for something to change into. He managed to stiff-leg it the rest of the way home before dawn in his bare feet with his bloody clothing and sneakers in one garbage bag he had emptied out and his naked ass wrapped up in another. They were all stuffed in the oven now until he figured out what to do with them.

What to do was the big question. What the fuck was he going to do? Not just about the dead hooker, which he was sure the cops would be kicking in the door any second to ask him about. What was going on with his penis? He'd done all he could to pretend the problem wasn't there and hope it would just go away on its own, but the dead whore whose blood he had recently waded in was a little hard to ignore.

After he showered, he dragged the kitchen chair into the bathroom and stood on it naked in front of the medicine cabinet mirror. That was not his prick. The grey scales covering it had spread down past the base and over his crotch, becoming less uniform as they faded away like pubic hair. In place of pubic hair, really. He tried to peel back one of the scales along the edge but stopped when it hurt. It was like trying to peel off his own skin.

His dork wasn't dangling like it used to. Instead, it was curled up underneath, wrapped up like a coil and tucked into his scrotum like an elephant's trunk. Or like it was sleeping. He couldn't get the proper angle to take a close look at his balls, but he slid his fingers under and felt the bulge he expected but covered in scales. He could feel them up until about halfway across his taint, where they faded out like in front. What in the fuck was going on?

He was almost afraid to touch it. How sad was that;a man afraid to touch his own dick. He took it between two fingers and slowly uncurled it, as if he was afraid it would leap up and bite him. The scales pinched his skin now and then as they shifted with the movement, but he didn't stop until it was stretched out to its full length. It was definitely longer by at least two inches, and he had to suppress a smile. The head of his cock was pointing right at him in the mirror. It looked more alien than the rest of it, a little less like the head of a penis and a little more like a conch shell, a little wider and a little less pointy. His piss-hole looked larger too, maybe twice as wide, and he fingered the tip curiously to spread it open.

That's when it snapped at him.

***

"So, what have you got for me, Doc?"

'Doc' was actually Doctor Eugene MacDonagh, chief medical examiner for the county and the twenty-third precinct. Abston called him Doc because it pissed him off, and he let Abston get away with it because Abston knew about the mutilated cadaver photos that Doc sold to some of the more deviant one-percenters on the Upper East Side. It was a tenuous but long-standing relationship.

The examination room was a small offshoot of the morgue, and in a city this big and ugly, it was never in disuse long enough to be properly cleaned. The important parts were always scrubbed down; Doc wasn't a slouch when it came to the job. But the floors and walls always had that grungy greasy spoon kitchen look, good enough to pass a cursory health inspection, but not a close one. Abston had thrown a smock on, more for Doc's benefit than anything else, and was standing on the opposite side of the autopsy table as they looked over the newly carved up corpse spread out between them. She had been undressed and cleaned up, and the lack of blood and clothing left nothing to the imagination. Due to the nature of the wounds, Doc had elected to prop the girl's legs open over some stirrups like a post-mortem OB/GYN. Seemed a shame that she was being forced to assume this position in death.

A perp you can't nab/and a corpse spread like steamed crab/makes a drab lab slab.

"What we have here," Doc said, "Is just your average, everyday prostitute, minus the lower third of her innards."

"You mean whoever did this removed some internal organs?"

"'Some' is a gross understatement. This poor girl has been hollowed out like a Tauntaun."

"A what?"

"Star Wars reference, not important."

"So, the killer sliced her open and removed what, exactly?"

"Everything." Doc wiped his brow on the sleeve of his scrubs not speckled with gore.

"Uterus, fallopian tubes, lower intestine, colon... when I say hollowed out, I'm not just generalizing. The walls of her abdominal cavity were practically scraped clean."

Doc took hold of two clamps at the base of the large incision bisecting the girl's abdomen and pulled them back like he was opening a picnic basket. This wasn't Abston's first medical examiner visit, so he didn't flinch or wince. But he was still surprised. The Doc hadn't been exaggerating. Somebody had hollowed out this poor girl like a canoe.

"She wasn't sliced open, either. You were at the crime scene?"

Abston nodded.

"You probably couldn't see it clearly with all of the blood, but there were no exterior wounds. Whatever was done to the girl's innards, it was done without so much as a vaginal tear."

"No signs of excessive trauma from stretching? I mean, from pulling stuff out. I'd imagine the guy would have had to get his hands in there to do the kind of damage you're describing if he was actually dressing her like a Thanksgiving turkey."

"Nope. There's nothing here to indicate that anything larger than she was prepared to take was forced inside of her. Or pulled out, for that matter."

"Jesus. It's like one of those kitchen tools that lets you puncture an egg and scramble it without cracking the shell."

Doc just stared at him.

"Sorry. Been a long day."

"Tell me about it. I spend one more evening hunched over a dead body instead of my wife, I'm going to end up on a slab myself."

"I lucked out. Mine left me. When can you get me the full report?"

"I'll have one of my flunkies run it by your desk tomorrow morning. I would drop it off myself, but I've got to take off early tomorrow. Wife's dragging me to the fucking Ice Capades."

This time, Abston flinched. "Man, how much is that going to suck?"

"Probably not as much as your next alimony payment."

"Fair enough. What about signs of her being bound or secured somehow?"

"No ligature marks on her hands or feet, but somebody definitely had a hand clamped over her mouth pretty tightly. Don't even bother asking about prints, though."

"What am I, a newbie here?"

"Just saying. But the hand marks do raise the question of whether this was a one-man job, because whatever was done to her, she was alive when it happened."

***

"Don't worry hon, this is my alley, we rent it in shifts. Ain't nobody going to disturb us."

He had tried to put it off, tried to resist. The cops had never showed up at his door with guns drawn, but that didn't mean he was in the clear. He'd seen enough of those crime shows on TV to know that they eventually found some kind of stain or residue that led back to the killer. He'd also burned the bloody clothes in the incinerator at work, and that made him feel better, but it kept nagging him that he might get caught. Then that fear gave way to the urge.

It was even worse than before. Horny is one thing, but there was something boiling up in him that needed release, and it was more painful than the worst case of blue balls had ever been. Lust didn't even begin to describe it. On top of that was the memory of the climax of that night, and that was almost more maddening than the lust. His head swam just thinking of that rush, that shotgun blast of euphoria that had emptied him when he came that night. But it was like smelling an ashtray when you were trying to quit smoking. All thinking about it did was make the need grow stronger.

Whatever it was between his legs was feeling it too. It started writhing around on its own again a couple of days after the dead hooker incident but had started moving around the same time that the hunger came back. By the end of the week, he wasn't sleeping. He would just lie in bed all night clenching his fists, trying to think about anything other than sex as his plated member flailed around down there like it was having a seizure.

Then, one evening, it started nipping at him. The first time he wasn't sure what it was. But after the second and third sharp pain he climbed up on the chair in the bathroom and saw the three tiny bite marks in his upper thigh near his groin. Something told him that they were just warning shots. They were just the excuse he needed to stop resisting. He couldn't be sure of anything anymore. The desire was so strong at this point that any thoughts in his head not about getting laid were moving in slow motion and in the wrong direction.

So here he was, several hours later, with some redheaded skank positioning him between two dumpsters in a blind corner of her own private alley. She dropped to her knees once she had them positioned them in the sweet spot and started fumbling with his belt. He'd brought a change of clothing this time, stuffed in a backpack he bought at the chink store on the way, now resting on top of the dumpster to his right. He'd told the dumb bitch he was going camping later when she asked him about it. She laughed as if she thought he was trying to be funny. Didn't matter if she believed him or not. He still wasn't sure how or where he'd change, but he still felt smarter for having brought them. He didn't look down. He pretended that he was watching the alley, but he really just didn't want to look down. He felt the belt go and the zipper of his jeans slide down. He knew she would see it. She was eye level with it, after all. So, he waited. He felt it snap to attention the second she pulled his underwear down, as if it was spring-loaded, a switchblade shooting out of his balls, and the moment he heard the beginning of the word 'What' coming out of her mouth, he grabbed her head and pulled it toward him, towards it.

He missed her mouth. He'd face-fucked enough sluts to know that the angle of her head was all wrong. But that thought exited his head as quickly as it had come, because he was suddenly inside her, and as the white light travelled up his spine and engulfed everything he was, it didn't matter where or how, as long as it continued for as long as possible.

He didn't know when she stopped struggling, only that it was way before he finished, and that he was way beyond caring.

***

"Three fucking pages on a snow globe? Do you purposely pad your reports with this shit to piss me off?"

Abston was in the captain's office. Doc was on the way up. Captain Fallion was a career man in every sense of the term, a never-ending supply of machismo, stress, and misplaced rage, all distilled through thirty years of active duty into the hottest mug of stereotypical upper management you've ever tasted. Abston loved provoking him.

"No, that's just a happy side effect."

"Well cut the shit before I bring you up on administrative charges, I don't care how fucking good you are at your job. And enough with the goddamned Haikus. What the fuck is this? *'Bricks and cobblestones/catacombs of stained mortar/industrial tombs.'*"

"The new victim was found in an alley."

"Then why don't you just fucking say that?"

"I thought I did."

Doc burst in nearly as angry as the captain was and threw a thick folder on his desk so hard that it slid across it and landed in his superior's lap.

"Ocular penetration followed by traumatic excavation of the entire cranial cavity. There, I just saved you twenty minutes of reading and twelve visits to a dictionary and could have done the same without being dragged up to your office."

"Well then, save me another ten minutes and tell me what that means in non-geek English."

Doc paused to shut the door to the office behind him. "Somebody skull fucked the woman then sucked her brains out through her ravaged eye socket."

Fallion waited until Doc had taken the other seat in front of the desk to respond.

"Is that your final assessment?"

"No. That's what I'd like to be able to sign off on. Unfortunately, half of what I've found contradicts that hypothesis, and even then, the other alternatives don't make much more sense."

"So, she wasn't skull fucked, as you say," Abston asked.

"No, that much is definite. There's no traces of semen to confirm that the penetration was sexual in nature, but I did find a pubic hair caught in one of her earrings, and signs of trauma are consistent with repeated ocular penetration by a blunt, phallus-shaped object."

"And the brain sucking?"

"It's just like the girl we found last week. This one's skull has been completely emptied, right to the bone."

"So," the captain interjected, "Somebody went to town on her with a shop-vac and emptied her head with the extension nozzle?"

"No Home Depot receipts to track down for this one. Any kind of suction tool would have left residue behind in chunks. Besides, I found the interior of the skull pockmarked with what appear to be - and I have no definitive evidence that this is one hundred percent accurate - teeth marks."

That earned a moment of silence while everyone attempted to wrap their head around it. Abston was the first to jump in.

"You aren't talking about human teeth, are you."

"No. These are small, almost rodent-like, but the marks aren't consistent with rat bites. I've already sent samples out for zoological identification. Also, the one remaining eye has definite bite marks on the optic cord, and it was only partially distended so the bites most definitely took place from within."

"Alright, so it wasn't a rat. But some sick bastard out there is shoving some kind of animals into these girls and letting them eat their way out."

"Except that there's no evidence to support that. No claw marks, no traces of urine or feces left behind, no hair or fur whatsoever, and absolutely no damage to the face - or anywhere else for that matter - consistent with a rodent attack."

"So, you don't know what kind of rodent the guy is using on the women. We don't need to name the fucking species."

"Maybe it's a new species," Abston offered. "We could name it after you. Skullfuckus Fallionious."

"It isn't rodents," Doc fumed.

"You just said it was some kind of rodent."

"Is he hearing a word I'm saying?" Doc asked Abston.

"I don't think he's hearing you."

"So, what are you telling me, that I should release a statement that this psycho is feeding these girls to rats, only they aren't rats?"

"I don't care what you tell anybody, but I have better things to do than sit around your offices making shit up to feed the press."

"Like what, the Ice Capades?"

"Fuck the both of you."

Doc left the office even angrier than he had entered. The captain tossed the ME report in Abston's lap and pointed at him menacingly.

"I find a Haiku about skull fucking in your next report, I swear to God and Christ on the Cross I am going to fire your ass."

"That should free up your budget for a rat catcher."

***

It was starting to get easier.

Richard hadn't been nearly as scared after leaving the last one behind. Everything cleaned up easy enough, and the closest the whole thing got to him was when he saw the headlines at the newsstand he passed on his way to work. Less worry, less guilt; even the aftershocks of the orgasm's high seemed to last longer. He could get used to this. More likely than not he would have to. Might as well get into a rhythm. He'd forgotten to bring a change of sneakers with the clothing though, and ended up walking home barefoot again. He should probably start making a list now, so he didn't forget again in the heat of the moment. He couldn't afford too many more mistakes. Not at this rate, anyway.

His new target was a name he'd heard a couple of the guys around the shop whisper about in more drunken moments, a solo streetwalker named Kitty that had started making house calls. You didn't find many outside of the expensive escort services that would take the risk to hit you at your home, especially not without a pimp to check up on them. This sounded like a quick opportunity, and easier than running around town with bags full of bloody clothing. Then again, he wasn't sure what he'd do about a dead whore in his apartment.

Getting rid of a body seemed complicated. Maybe he'd just leave it and move on. That was probably the best idea.

Those crime scene scientists were going to find a fiber or molecule or something eventually, so why stick around waiting for them to show up? There were probably only so many women you could leave behind dead before it was time to move on. Maybe he'd travel. He'd never really done any foreign chicks before besides the occasional wetback, and that didn't really count as a foreigner if you were sharing a border with her. He wondered if French trim would land him a different high.

Setting up the meeting took a bit of time, but eventually he found somebody who knew somebody who could arrange a visit, and money changed hands with the promise of more to come. He gave his address; they gave him a time the following evening. Yep, it was just that simple. Maybe next time he would ask them to bring their own garbage bags.

He spent an hour or so cleaning the place up before she was supposed to show up. Why the fuck not. No reason to make the girl grab her last lay in a pigsty. What little he owned was packed and ready to go as well, no reason to stick around for pillow talk and cuddling after. He could feel his pecker jerking around in anticipation as he picked up and moved stuff around. It was like it knew what was coming. Eager little shit. Vacuuming seemed like a lost cause, especially since he didn't own a vacuum, so he compromised and left the lights off. He was actually lighting a candle as a goof when he heard the knock on the door.

Kitty wasn't disappointing. She wasn't escort service fuckable, mind you. Even the prettiest whore starts looking a bit haggard after a year or two. But as far as street whores went, she was pretty hot. Heels were too high for reason, of course, but the legs were nice and the shape of the red skirt they disappeared under was full of promises. Nice rack, too. The eyes were dead inside, of course, but that was to be expected. He actually liked that now, come to think of it. Made it all just a little bit easier.

He let her in, and she took her high heels off at the door, which he thought was odd. Must be part Jap or something. Once again there were no words spoken; they both knew what they were here to do. He led her over to the couch and they made out for a bit. Richard didn't usually go for the foreplay bullshit, but she was hot enough that he didn't mind sucking face for a bit beforehand. Not like he was in a rush or anything. Besides, this was kind of special, in a way. She wasn't his first, not in the sense of what now passed for sex in his life, but she was the first one he would take where he felt like he was in complete control of the moment. She was his. She just didn't know it yet.

Eventually the making out started feeling too high school, and he moved his hand down to slip up under her skirt. He'd wanted to get a feel for what she had going on down there before he wrecked it, but she pulled his hand away before he got a chance. Before he could protest, she had rolled him back on the couch and straddled his lap, her red skirt riding up high enough to show him a flash of red panties. She grabbed his other wrist and moved them both behind his head.

He crossed his fingers and laid back. Why the fuck not? Things were going this smoothly, why not let her do all the work. He'd have to grab her once things got started and she tried to climb off, so might as well enjoy being serviced while he could. He looked at her, and she maintained eye contact with him as she undid his pants and freed his member. He hadn't worn underwear, didn't see the need to waste another pair, and he could feel it shoot straight up from his crotch once the fly was open, like a baby bird straining for food. If she noticed that it felt different, she didn't let on. She didn't look down, either. She just looked him in the eye as she reached down to hike up her skirt and pull her panties to one side. She raised up and over him, and he couldn't help but smile at her as she lowered herself onto him.

***

Abston was the first on the scene, along with a couple boys in blue for support. Doc had risked the wrath of Mrs. Doc with extra hours spent poring over the Rat Catcher corpses (Abston leaked the name to the press just to piss off Fallion) and lucked out with a partial thumbprint on the alley corpse's remaining eyeball. The perp came up almost immediately, a perpetual loser by the name of Richard Johnson that had wound up in the sex crimes database for two counts of domestic abuse and an instant parole verdict on an underage prostitute. They tracked him at work first, but he had been a no-call/no-show the past three days, so they hit his apartment as fast as they could scramble a raid team. They got directions to the room from a slightly inebriated super, and the uniforms went through the motions before barging in with Abston close behind.

The smell hit him before he crossed the threshold, and he thought "Yep, that's a three-day smell all right" before they found the source. The greener of the two uniforms made a dash for the bathroom, the other one merely gagged and covered his nose and mouth.

The body was sprawled out on the couch in the center of a large pool of blood. Still fully clothed like the last one, and the blood definitely originated from the genitals like the first. But that was where the similarities ended. Even in the dim light streaming in from a distant window, Abston could see without getting any closer that a complete mess had been made of the entire crotch. You could see the chunks of frayed flesh lining the edges of the massive wound.

The uniform in the bathroom came out wiping vomit from his mouth.

"Is that our guy?"

Abston nodded. He recognized Johnson from the mugshots.

"What the fuck happened to him? Looks like he was castrated."

The other uniform moved in closer.

"With what, a weed whacker? Is it laying around anywhere?"

Abston suppressed a smile as he watched the uniforms check under their feet.

"I wouldn't waste your time. I don't think we'll be finding any spare parts under the couch. And I've got twenty that says they find teeth marks where they used to be."

He sent them around to knock on doors and used his cell to report in and get a crime scene unit out there. As he waited for them, he dragged a kitchen chair out of the bathroom and slouched back in it, so he had a full view of the crime scene. The look of horror on Johnson's face spoke volumes.

Abston pulled the pencil from behind his ear, where he used to keep a spare cigarette in his younger days. Vices change over time. He scribbled in his pad while waiting for the crew to arrive.

Passions devour/both the predator and prey./We are all hunted.

It would have to do. For now.

An Idea With Merit

Carson Demmans

He was thinking of rotten vegetables.

Not just spoiled vegetables, mind you, but actually rotten ones. Vegetables in the process of decaying, which were too soft to touch without your finger going right through them, releasing a stench that would sicken the strongest of stomachs. Perhaps some mould would be nice too? It would add to the bouquet of aromas as well as the visual display; mould that was not only encrusted but that would release a cloud of spores with the slightest of touches, spreading itself and possibly disease.

How delightful.

But what kind of vegetables? Tomatoes? Cucumber? Squash? Oh God, yes, squash! Filthy, unwashed, disgusting, mouldy squash! But squash were too small. Maybe a related vegetable. Zucchini? Pumpkin?

Oh yes! Definitely pumpkins! Huge, rotting, prize winning pumpkins! He found himself getting aroused at the thought of the wave of stench hitting his nostrils until an unwelcome voice brought him back to the present moment.

"Detective?" the young police officer asked him. "What did you say about squash?"

"Crush," he replied. "I said crush," he lied.

"Well, yes," the young female officer said. "The victim was crushed. At least, parts of him were. The killer used that hydraulic vice over there."

She tried to be casual as she gestured to where the corpse was found, but it would have been the equivalent to a survivor in Hiroshima explaining what happened the day before as simply saying, "The bomb fell over there somewhere, I think." and then nodding towards a giant radioactive crater. No matter how casual the survivor tried to act, it didn't make the scene of the carnage any more normal itself.

To describe the machine shop as a slaughterhouse would have been an insult to slaughterhouses and the people who operate them. Slaughterhouses are businesses, forced to operate under strict government regulations as well as collective agreements with unions; both the government and the unions try to regulate the carnage to not only protect the health of the public and those who work there, but to try to protect the collective consciousness of society as a whole. By making slaughterhouses as clean and hygienic as possible, the collective guilt of those eating the products that come from there is eased a little bit, and they only have to worry about becoming nauseous from gastrointestinal effects from the bizarre combination of porridge made from porcine internal organs and shoved into sausage casings that they enjoyed eating and not form the knowledge of how the disgusting things were made.

Some would have called the scene a torture chamber, but those people made the detective chuckle like the ten-year-old schoolgirl his father had forced him to dress like as a punishment for licking toilet seats. Torture chambers, at least form the point of view of the torturer, were a place of business, and as such had to be organized in some way as to be functional. Even in the days of old when the Knights Templar were executed on the stretch rack by having their arms pulled off after being stretched past their limits, the detached limbs were stored in barrels as the knights bled to death so the torturers wouldn't trip over them.

What the current scene was, in the eyes of the detective, was chaos. Parts of the victim had in fact been crushed in a hydraulic vice and had been crushed beyond the point where the vice operator was doing anything other than seeing how much the vice could crush a human body. The blood spatter indicated that some of the damage was done while the victim had still been alive, but most of the injuries had been postmortem. There was little point to most of the injuries.

The injuries at least could be categorized after the fact. There were no bullet wounds, signs of strangulation or electrocution. What there were a lot of were various types of wounds. Other than the body parts that had been crushed, some had cuts to them of various lengths and depths and judging by the different textures to the edge of the wounds, had been inflicted with a variety of instruments with different degrees of sharpness.

In the abdomen there were some very amateurish attempts at surgery. An incision had been made and the skin pulled apart to expose the organs below, but that was it. It looked like something out of a textbook.

"Online shoppers?" the detective questioned himself silently in thought. "Testing purchases of different types before deciding to return them or not? I've done that, but only on myself."

There were also punctures of different diameters and depths. One set was clearly done using various bits from a cordless power drill set, a pattern he was familiar with, but few other people were unless he had accidentally allowed them to see his scars on his feet. The other punctures on the corpse were all made with various items he couldn't identify, but forensics would be able to after a quick examination of the business. Judging by the fresh blood stains on various tools left in plain sight, the culprits had used whatever was handy in the machine shop.

Lastly, there were ligature marks on what was left of the limbs, and lots of them. Someone had not only tied up the victim but had over-tied the victim using lot of unnecessary rope and knots. A quick search by the detective discovered the ropes that had been cut off the corpse to expose more skin area to disfigurement. There were examples of at least ten different knots, but who knew that many different knots? Even the highest priced dominatrices the detective knew, and he knew many who charged extra for each variety of knot, knew at most eight different types of knots.

He stopped himself in mid thought. He kept using plural, not singular nouns, in describing whatever lucky bastard had created this carnage. Why was that? What in his mind was telling him that there was more than one perpetrator?

"Is this machine shop always unlocked?" the detective asked, trying to draw attention away from his growing erection by pretending to care about what the young woman was saying.

"No sir," she replied, quickly looking at her notes. "The people who found him had a key. One of them is the son of the owner. But they aren't suspects. They're real boy scouts."

"Oh?" the detective asked suspiciously. "How long did you speak to them?"

"A few seconds, less than a minute, sir," the policewoman replied, unsure of where this line of questioning was going.

"And you could tell that they were of high moral character in that short period of time?" he asked. "That they were real boy scouts, as you put it?"

"I said they were boy scouts because of their uniforms," she said with a smile. "They're sitting over there," the young cop said, pointing to three nervous twelve-year-olds sitting in a nearby office, nervously shaking in their Boy Scout uniforms and fingering their badges.

"I'll be the judge of that!" the detective snapped as he walked off. The three boys were the ones who had found the mutilated body of the victim. Judging by the condition of the corpse, the killer had wanted both the victim and whomever found the victim to suffer by deforming the victim as much as possible. The detective had seen seasoned police officers reduced to quivering bowls of Jell-O after finding a body in that condition. Three young children, one of them obviously the sheltered son of a successful businessman, couldn't prevent this situation turning into anything less than a traumatic experience that would leave them scarred for life in the long run and nearly comatose with post-traumatic stress disorder in the short term.

At least, that's what the detective hoped for so he could quickly return to his fantasy world of rotten pumpkins.

"What's six times eight?" the detective asked abruptly as he reached the three Boy Scouts.

"Forty-eight!" they all answered in unison and without a moment of hesitation. The detective frowned. At best they should have only looked at him blankly for asking them such an inappropriate question which had nothing to do with the situation at hand. Instead, they acted like three straight A students who were taking an oral test at school. But even A+ students couldn't react that quickly to an exam they weren't expecting. These kids had been expecting to answer questions of all kinds and were deliberately alert as a result.

"Strange place for a Scout meeting, boys," the detective said. He deliberately put this to them in the form of a statement without any question attached. The three boys acted as if he had asked a question anyway.

"We were collecting empty pop bottles from the lunchroom here," one of them said quickly. "My dad owns this business, and he lets us take the bottles and sell them and give the money to our troop. We wear our uniforms so people will know we aren't stealing."

The young man had given him a perfectly reasonable answer and that made the detective suspicious. Twelve-year-old children in this situation should not act perfectly reasonable. Unless, of course, they had memorized the correct answers to the questions ahead of time.

"So, people don't suspect Boy Scouts of bad things," the detective said. He stated it as a fact, but one of the boys answered him anyway.

"We're here on official Boy Scout business," the second boy said, "so we wear our uniforms."

"In my day," the detective said, "pop bottles were actual bottles. Thick, heavy glass bottles. How many bottles do the workers here go through in a week?"

That time he had asked a question, but none of them answered. They had not thought to think of an answer to that question ahead of time.

"Two dozen," the owner's son said. "Last week there was at least two dozen empty bottles."

"Two dozen pop bottles," the detective repeated. "See, when I was a kid, that would take three guys to carry. But today, pop bottles are made of light plastic. One of you could easily carry that many without any help at all."

The three boys looked at each other, each desperately urging the other two with silent glances to say something.

"Sometimes there are homeless people hanging around here," one of them finally said. The other two quickly chimed in on this theme.

"That's right!" another one said excitedly. "There's always homeless people wandering around, but if there are three of us together, they leave us alone."

"So, in other words, you all knew you could find a homeless man nearby? Maybe an unconscious one?" the detective asked. There were no answers. He changed the subject. He glanced at a nearby piece of flat bar with desire. It would make a perfect tool to spank himself with, but how could he smuggle it out of the crime scene? No, he had to remain aware of his surroundings and at least appear that he cared about questioning these boys.

"Nice merit badges," he said as he pointed at their uniforms. They only had one badge in common among all three of them, and he pointed at it on one of them as he asked, "What's this one for?"

"First aid," one of them said as the other two nodded in agreement.

The detective nodded. That one subject was at least one thing they all shared an interest in. He paused. Parts of the corpse had looked like textbook examples of various wounds, including surgical incisions. But what else might have such illustrations? An instruction manual of some kind? Maybe the type used to learn first aid? There were a lot of manuals like that.

There were also ones that taught you how to tie different types of knots. Lots of different kinds, and easily more than ten.

"So, you have all studied about accident victims?" he asked. They all nodded with broad smiles. That was clearly a topic they were all fascinated by. "Have you ever seen one?" he continued. They all looked at each other.

"You mean before today?" a different boy answered. They were taking turns answering questions so no one of them would remain in the spotlight for long.

"This was no accident," the detective said dryly. "It was done deliberately and slowly on a victim who was probably already in an alcoholic stupor. If I remember my first aid training, you boys would have learned that there are three types of wounds: lacerations, punctures and crush. Now, book learning is one thing but even a photo doesn't teach you what the real thing looks like. And yet, the three of you suddenly had the opportunity to see perfect examples of all three in one convenient location."

The three boys exchanged silent glances again, but this time they each raced to be the first to talk.

"It was his idea!" one of them exclaimed while pointing in the direction of the other two, both of whom assumed they were the one being accused.

"I just said it would be neat," one of the accused boys replied. "You're the one who said we should do it!"

"But he's the one who said he could find us a victim!" the third boy exclaimed to the detective without bothering to identify who he was accusing. "He comes here every week to get bottles, and this time he told us to come along! It wasn't my idea!"

"But he's the one who tied the victim up!" yelled the business owner's son.

"I had to!" one of the accomplices replied. "Neither of you two idiots ever learned how to tie knots!"

"Did you have to try every knot you know?"

"Did you have to puncture both of his eyeballs to watch the fluid squirt out? Wasn't one enough? The second one was going to be exactly the same as the first one!"

The detective walked away from the boys as the policewoman who had directed him to them stared in disbelief. One of her co-workers calmly walked up to her, as she was clearly in a state of shock.

"But how…" she said as her voice trailed off. Her question remained unfinished, but her co-worker had known the detective for many years and had seen many others display the same disbelief.

"Nobody knows how he does it," the veteran cop said. "But he always does it. And the gorier the case, the quicker he does it. While everyone else is recoiling in horror, he simply analyzes the problem and finds a solution. He really knows how monsters think."

The policewoman looked at the Boy Scouts and saw them for the monsters they really were. She looked around for the detective so she could look deeply into his eyes and perhaps catch some glimpse of how his brain worked, but he was already gone. She then glanced around the room as something else seemed to be missing too. She had thought there had been a long thin piece of scrap metal on a nearby worktable, but it had disappeared as well.

Duty Calls

Diana Parrilla

"Aha! Gotcha!" I shouted, capturing my prey. Everyone in the room turned to glare at me.

"What? There was a damn mosquito buzzing around. Had to kill it," I defended, shaking the magazine where the bug's carcass was now smeared.

"As I was saying," Eulena continued, "We've detected suspicious activity in our community recently. It appears humans have managed to open a portal somewhere in purgatory, using condemned souls and temporarily transferring them into cloned bodies of politicians. They're exploiting their terrifying power to sway voters through... unconventional methods."

I interrupted. "Count me in. Who do we need to kill?"

Stuart, beside me, fixed his piercing blue eyes on mine. "Rena, if you're participating in this mission, I could accompany you."

I looked him straight in the face and smiled. "Sure thing. I'll let you know when it's time to dispose of the body. Or bodies. You never know. But remember, next time wait for me to ask, got it?" I gave him a resounding slap on the cheek that left him clutching his face.

"The mission is to return the souls to purgatory where they belong, not on Earth," Eulena said. "I'll assign two of you. Let's see... Stuart and Passiflora."

"Seriously?!" I complained, slamming my fist on the table. Self-control wasn't my strong suit. "With all due respect, boss, don't you realize there's no one better than me for this job?"

Passiflora's shimmering wings fluttered as she spoke. "But Rena, you're only on leave. Your place is in prison. You haven't finished serving your sentence. Your case is even worse than the souls in purgatory."

"Exactly, darling. That's precisely why. You know what they say—it takes a thief to catch a thief, eh? It's not that I want to do it, but duty calls."

Eulena brushed aside strands of her blonde hair, pondering. "Perhaps you're right. No one knows more about these schemes than you. After all, you used to pull them yourself," she admitted. "Very well, you'll go with Stuart. It's settled. I'll send you the details."

I looked at Stuart, still nursing his cheek. I crouched down to meet his gaze, which he was now avoiding.

"If we're going to work together, I just ask that you don't be a wimp and don't let your trigger finger tremble. To return those tortured souls, we'll need more than pretty eyes and a nice speech. You follow?"

"I understand," he said timidly, but I saw him heading to speak with Eulena. Either he wanted to back out or request a partner change. Tough luck.

Meanwhile, I made my way to the armory. Oh, what a pleasure. I'd need as many guns as possible. I chose a laser sight, a silencer, a shotgun, an automatic, a semi-automatic, a sniper rifle, a revolver, some grenades, a few mines, and why not? A handful of knives in case I ran out of ammo. Armor-piercing, of course.

Stuart appeared behind me. "Aren't you taking too many weapons? That backpack's going to weigh a ton."

"Nah, it's nothing, dear friend," I said, handing it to him to feel the weight. His face fell. I laughed. "Well, I think I'll just take the stun gun and tranquilizer darts. We don't want to hurt them. After all, humans took them; it's not like they wanted to escape," he said, looking like a lost puppy to me.

"That's where you're wrong. Once they're with our enemies, there's no mercy. Pity and mercy are weaknesses. It's like when someone points a gun at you," I said, aiming my sleek black pistol at him. "If I start saying, 'Don't move or I'll shoot,' what happens, huh?"

"I get scared and raise my hands?" he said, lifting them.

"Exactly. And by raising them, they're closer to my weapon, until you snatch it from me. That's the flaw. So no speeches, no warnings. If you see a bad guy, shoot. Understood?"

"But that's not my style," he mumbled. "We have to follow the rules. That's why you're in jail, even if you're on leave to help with these missions."

"Don't worry. If something goes wrong, they'll blame us both, and you'll come to the slammer with me. I can give you a tour of the place," I said with a wink.

I headed to purgatory to check how many were missing. What a view. The place was like the deepest depths of the sea, with as much light as when you open a refrigerator at midnight. The rocks and other decorations only served for the creatures to take out their frustrations on something other than the guards, who also got their fair share.

I approached a guard's booth where a man was calmly eating a three-story cheeseburger. "Hello, I need the list of the missing for a mission," I said.

The man looked me up and down. "You're going on the mission?"

My childlike appearance had always earned me disapproving looks. I was used to it, but that didn't make it less annoying.

"No, your brother from the fifth floor is going," I said. "Look, I don't have all day, you know. So give me the list, and I'm out."

The man's face transformed. But no, he wasn't looking at me anymore, but behind me. I hadn't sealed the booth door when I entered, and one of the creatures was slipping its tentacles inside.

The man immediately grabbed the communicator. "Alert all units! I have one trying to break into booth number 58!"

I pulled out one of my knives and started cutting the creature's tentacles, which began oozing a viscous liquid. "When you're done chatting on the phone, let me know," I said. "What a useless idiot."

I drew another knife and, with both hands, began dodging the undulating tentacles of that skeletal octopus. But one of them hit me, and I fell to the ground. That's when the creature entered the cabin completely.

I reached under my black jumpsuit and grabbed the gun with armor-piercing bullets. Meanwhile, the guard had drawn his laser pistol and started shooting it in the face. That destabilized and annoyed the creature so much that its tentacles went berserk, grabbing the guard and lifting him into the air.

I had a clear shot at the monster's head, but I waited. "You doing alright up there, big guy?"

"Help me!" he cried, sobbing.

"Now you want my help? I thought I wasn't good enough for this kind of work."

"I'm sorry! I didn't mean that before, but please!"

The monster squeezed tighter. "I can't hear you," I laughed.

OK, enough. I gritted my teeth as I aimed. It wasn't just about blowing their brains out; you had to shatter that grotesque metal protrusion. That's where the cameras were nestled, because that rotting meat-sack wasn't truly theirs. Inside writhed a soul, twisted and perverted, and those cameras were the eyes of its vile disguise, the way the abomination perceived the world. Obliterate that, and it's like dropping it into an endless void. I knew because I'd festered there, trapped in that lightless hell for what felt like eons. I'd been one of those corrupted souls. Or maybe, deep down in the putrid core of my being, I still was.

I squeezed the trigger, and a spray of gore erupted as the bullet tore through circuitry and rotted flesh. The tentacles, now spasming wildly without guidance, released the guard. He plummeted to the ground with a sickening crunch, bones shattering on impact. Blood and viscera oozed from his limp form as he lost what little consciousness that meat-puppet ever truly possessed.

The stench of ruptured organs clouded the air around us. Not knowing where it was, the creature moved erratically, though its juices, acidic and disgusting, kept flowing. I climbed onto the cabin chair and grabbed the fallen guard's weapon. With the laser, I tore open the creature's head. I wanted the soul to come out.

"Come out! You're surrounded!" shouted the guards arriving from other units.

The soul emerged—a man, or what was once a man, came out from inside. His features were darkened, skin torn in strips, veins larger than his body hair. One of the guards approached him with handcuffs. They would take this one to prison; that's what they did with the uncontrollable monsters from purgatory.

Maybe it was because it's what my twisted mind would have done, but I eyed that man suspiciously, even as he choked on his own blood and bile. Strings of crimson drool hung from his mangled lips, mingling with chunks of God-knows-what as he wheezed and gurgled. Without hesitation, my hand snaked to the grenade launcher strapped to my back. The satisfying 'thunk' of the launch was quickly drowned out by the wet explosion of flesh and bone.

A red mist filled the air as the man's torso erupted, showering the area with a slurry of liquefied organs and shattered ribs. As his mangled corpse slumped to the ground, twitching in its death throes, a hidden revolver clattered from his spasming fingers. The stench of cordite mixed with the foul odor of his bowels, creating a growing pool of bodily fluids that seeped into the cracked concrete.

Call it instinct, or maybe just the depraved intuition of a mind as warped as mine. I'd saved them, and they barely thanked me. Perhaps they thought it was my fault for not sealing the door behind me—a consequence of my impulsivity. What did I care? I didn't need their recognition. The sound of my weapons reloading was satisfaction enough. You might wonder why I'm so rebellious. What has life done to make me this way? What bad experience have I had, or whose love did I lack as a child? I'll tell you: Nothing! Nothing has happened to me. I'm like this because it's my character, and I don't need to have experienced anything traumatic to always feel like killing someone, capisce? So, the next person who asks me that can consider themselves dead.

In the tunnel passageway to Earth, Stuart joined me. "Here's the plan: the portal will give us access to Mr. Osvald Posth's office, the hotel magnate financing the election campaign of the party we suspect is stealing condemned souls. He must know where they're keeping them since they're the ones using them. So, I'll hack his computers to find out where they are, okay?"

"Sounds good. You know how to hack, I don't. Too boring. I need more action. I'll go look for this Posth guy."

"Oh no, it's best if we take them quietly, without them knowing we were there."

I wasn't keen on the idea, but I wasn't about to kick-start a brawl that'd likely leave one of us pushing up daisies. And let's just say, I was packing enough heat to turn any would-be adversary into Swiss cheese.

The portal took us to an enormous office with large windows and a gold desk. "Posth will be in a meeting next door. I'll go to the computer room," Stuart said, with his perfect human avatar and business suit to blend in.

I hadn't bothered to change. My human body and high bun matched my black jumpsuit and flat, high black boots. If it didn't match, I couldn't care less. It was comfortable, period. Fashion had always mattered to me as much as the shape of clouds after a summer storm.

I was left alone in the office. "How's it going, Stuart?" I asked through the earpiece.

"Good, I've started the hack. 5% scanned."

Pfft, this was going to take forever, and the guns were burning in my pocket. I pressed my ear to the adjacent door, listening to the meeting:

"And so, we'll not only increase votes but also ensure the 'security over privacy' law passes without incident. Any video leaked on the internet will no longer be considered illegal, as the entire population will be recorded at all times."

"But I have a young daughter, a minor. Does that mean authorized personnel could see, for example, when she changes her clothes and such?"

"Dear McKlein, don't worry. There are no pedophiles among those authorized to review the recordings. In fact, machines will do it. You have nothing to worry about."

The sound of his demure laugh, intended to be reassuring, carried a tone that didn't convince anyone, not even that fool McKlein. I'd had enough. I broke the fire alarm glass, and everyone rushed out of the room to see what was happening. Only the boss, Posth, remained, his bloated form quivering like rancid jelly.

"What the fuck's going on?" he wheezed into his phone, sweat beading on his greasy forehead.

I burst from my hiding place. Grabbing a fistful of his lank, greasy hair, I yanked his head back, exposing the wobbling flesh of his throat. "This is what's happening," I snarled, jamming my gun against his kneecap and pulling the trigger. The satisfying crunch of bone giving way to hot lead filled the air as Posth's leg exploded in a fountain of gore and shattered cartilage.

As he collapsed, shrieking like a stuck pig, I snatched his phone from the floor, now slick with blood and other less identifiable fluids.

"Where are the souls from purgatory?" I growled, shoving the still-smoking barrel against his temple. The coppery reek of fresh blood filled my nostrils.

"I don't know what you're talking about, you psycho!" he blubbered, fat tears cutting tracks through the grime on his face.

Without hesitation, I blew out his other kneecap, relishing the wet pop as the bullet tore through flesh and bone. "Are you sure, you bloated cockroach?" I hissed, twisting the gun in the pulpy mess that used to be his leg.

"Jesus fucking Christ!" he howled, his voice cracking as he writhed in agony. "What the hell's wrong with you? Are you out of your fucking mind?"

A twisted grin split my face as I leaned in close, my lips nearly brushing his ear. "Oh, you have no idea how batshit crazy I am," I whispered. "Now, tell me where they are before I start peeling you like a rotten orange."

The pounding of boots echoed down the hallway, and I felt a grin spread across my face. My hand found the grenade, fingers caressing its deadly contours like a lover. With a cackle that would make a demon proud, I lobbed that beautiful little ball of destruction through the doorway.

The explosion ripped through the space, scattering shredded flesh and shattered bone. The walls trembled, splattered with a fresh coat of red as chunks of what used to be human beings painted abstract horrors across every surface. So much for subtlety—I'd always been a sucker for carnage anyway.

Those charred, twitching heaps of meat? Just a fancy new carpet for Mr. Posth's office. Exclusive, one-of-a-kind, and still smoking. Burnt hair and seared flesh created a bouquet that made my nostrils flare with perverse pleasure.

"Jesus fuck!" Posth shrieked, his eyes bulging as he took in the grisly scene. "They're in the basement, you psychotic cunt! The security code is 25E486!" His words came out in a strangled sob as he realized his reinforcements were now nothing more than a steaming pile of hamburger meat decorating his previously tasteful decor.

I licked my lips, savoring the terror in his eyes.

"Did you hear that, Stuart?" I tapped at my earpiece.

"Received. I was already 55% through the hack, but anyway, okay. I'm heading there to open the portal for them," Stuart said over the communicator.

Then a black miasma surrounded me. It was... impossible. Mr. Posth was possessed by a soul from purgatory. Of course, why hadn't we thought of that? That explained his actions. An obscured aura took shape—with two eyes like knives protruding—and it lunged at me.

"Rena, I've found them. Hurry to the basement. The portal will close in 3 minutes, and we won't be able to open another one for a long time!" Stuart's voice came, desperate.

Damn. Yeah, that was another one of my quirks—a bit of a potty mouth. Always had trouble keeping it in check, no matter how hard I tried. "Listen, Posth was actually possessed by one from purgatory who escaped on his own. That's why he was bringing his own to Earth using this plan. Posth's nefarious political intentions must have attracted the attention of the purgatory beings."

"That's extremely serious. I'll alert Eulena right away, but for now, you need to move. The portal is closing!"

The creature sank something into my neck that wasn't teeth but razors, or at least that's how it felt. Instinctively, I should have moved away, but I remained frozen for a moment, pulling the grenade from my pocket. Summoning strength from the frozen depths of Cocytus, I managed to shove it into its mouth. This distracted it, and I broke free, leaving the meeting room and firing at the ceiling with the grenade launcher.

The ceiling groaned, chunks of concrete raining down like diseased hailstones. The creature, a writhing mass of tentacles and pulsating flesh, launched its grotesque form towards the glass wall. Its slimy appendages left trails of mucus across the floor as it fled the impending concrete avalanche.

Mid-leap, the grenade detonated. The air filled with a cacophony of wet pops and sizzling meat as the abomination's bloated body ruptured. Gore sprayed in all directions, painting the shattered glass with a Jackson Pollock nightmare of viscera and ichor. Chunks of still-twitching flesh rained down, sizzling where they landed.

The resulting explosion created a perverse fireworks display—a gothic spectacle of burning offal and the last bits of the creature's remains pattering down like a grisly rainfall.

"Rena, the portal has closed!" Stuart shouted tearfully.

I smiled. "Better. I think I'll enjoy staying on Earth. There's a lot of trash to clean up here. You know how it is— duty calls."

The Stone Man

Michael Errol Swaim

Billy Reese sat quietly at a table in a filthy and dimly lit kitchen, slowly slicing the meat off a human femur with an old, worn filet knife. At the other end of the table, a much older man sat with his right hand inside his coveralls, rubbing his cock while he watched the younger man work.

"What happens if ya cut too thin?" the older man asked. His voice was gravelly, with a deep southern drawl.

"If I cut the meat too thin, it will absorb the marinade more quickly, the meat will dry quicker, and we will have crispy jerky, Mister Jeb," Billy replied.

Jeb nodded as he ran a hand over his greasy, balding head, grunting as he stopped masturbating long enough to steady himself while standing up. The wooden chair creaked under his bulk. With labored breathing, he stopped briefly to rest, then quickly jammed the hand back inside the overalls. Slowly he began pacing from one end of the table to the other, right hand still furiously jerking his cock.

"What if ya cut the meat too thick?" he asked as he switched hands.

"Thicker cuts will take longer to dry but will make a chewier jerky, which will cause it to retain more of the meat's flavor."

"Good, that's why we need to be precise in our cuts, to get the flavor just right," he said as he began to masturbate faster, "and what happens when you don't do your job right?"

"Then the business suffers, and I get punished, mister Jeb," Billy said with a slight look of fear.

"That's right, and we don't want that, do we?" he asked as he leaned forward, inches from his face.

He could smell the foul stench of alcohol in the older man's breath and could see his rotten teeth. His breath was so horrifying. Jeb walked up to the table, undid the straps on his overalls, and let them drop. A powerful smell assailed Billy's nostrils, and he nearly hurled; it smelled worse than a rotting corpse. Jeb shot him an angry look, and Billy stifled the urge to vomit. He knew that would just piss him off.

"Now, push the marinade over here so I can put the secret ingredient in," Jeb said, inching closer to the table.

Billy slid the translucent plastic tub full of a dark liquid substance across the table as Jeb lifted his gut so he could see where he was aiming. It sloshed and a little bit of it spilled on the table. Luckily, Jeb didn't notice. He was too busy trying to jerk off into the marinade. Jeb grunted as his cum shot into the tub. He gave it a few final strokes and put his cock away and snapped his overall straps back on. Billy wondered how he could be so calm about whacking off in public.

"Stir that up nice and good. When you are done cutting, the meat will be ready to go in the dehydrator tomorrow." He instructed Billy and stepped away from the table.

"Yes, mister Jeb."

Billy grabbed the handle and stirred the marinade mixed with the fresh strips of flesh around until the older man's jizz disappeared into the mixture. Three cockroach corpses floated to the top as the contents were disturbed. He looked at Jeb with a concerned look on his face. He tried to keep the roaches out, but they breed so fast it's hard to do anything about them.

"Don't worry about it. The roaches give it flavor," said Jeb as he patted Billy's shoulder. "Finish your work and clean up. Tomorrow, I will try to bring you a fresh corpse."

Billy sighed in relief and looked up at Jeb to see him grinning, his rotten teeth on display. The smile was nauseating, and the smell lingered. He imagined punching out those nasty teeth, and the thought comforted him. He smiled. Just that one simple thought gave him a tiny amount of comfort. Perhaps someday he would just go for it. Or even better, Jeb would just keel over and die. Then he wouldn't have to put up with all of his bullshit.

Billy returned to work, carefully slicing the meat to the correct size, and putting the slices in the marinade. He worked in silence, and the monotony soon began to calm his tortured mind. He hated the work but was resigned to his fate, and he was good at it. He had been slicing meat off people for several years now. Jeb still didn't trust him to do it right. He quizzed him every day. Today, he was working on the meat from the legs and buttocks. He would be glad to get the fresh corpse tomorrow. This one was starting to stink.

Billy stood and stretched when finished, then walked to the sink to wash off the knife, rinse his hands, and began to clean up the mess. The tub went into the fridge, and the blood on the table started to dry, so he scrubbed it with an old rag and rinsed it in the sink. Jeb was not big on cleanliness, so he did the bare minimum.

He never really enjoyed his work, although he was good at making jerky. It was the only life he had ever known, and he often wondered if it was wrong. He had lived with Jeb for as long as he could remember. All he did know was that he got fed well and had a house over his head, and if he did a decent job, Jeb would leave him in peace. When he made mistakes, however, Jeb would become angry and violent.

Shuddering at the thought, he began to wipe the blood and gore off the table. The cuts and nicks that covered the surface made the cleaning difficult, but he took his time so he would do a decent job. When the table was clean, he took the basket of bones and leftover meat and fat outside to the incinerator, fired it up, and tossed everything in. He returned and checked on the jerky, smiling in satisfaction at how it looked.

Billy retreated to his room when the cleaning was complete. It was his only sanctuary, where he could find peace away from Jeb. As he shut the door behind him, a wave of relief washed over him, and he began to relax. Jeb very rarely bothered him there.

It was a small and sparse room, but to him, it was paradise. There was no window, but at least he could lock the door. He had a small bed, and beside that was a bookshelf that was his pride and joy. It was crooked, but he made it himself and was proud. All the books he owned had been given to him by Jeb, and most were Westerns, but his favorite was a book about Cherokee mythology. Reading kept his mind off his miserable life.

He sat on his stained mattress and ran his hands over the books. They were his only friends. He smiled, picked up his favorite book, leaned back against the bedframe, and began to read, but his eyelids soon became heavy, and he put the book back and lay down, quickly falling asleep.

***

He awoke suddenly sometime later, hearing someone wildly pounding on his door. He opened his eyes and sat up in alarm.

"Billy!" Jeb hollered, "Billy, open up!"

He sounded scared, which was highly unusual; Jeb wasn't afraid of anything. He got out of bed and began to open the door, and Jeb frantically barged in before he could open it all the way.

"Billy, I screwed up. I screwed the damn pooch!" he exclaimed.

"What happened, mister Jeb?" Billy asked.

The older man sat down on the bed and threw his hands to his face. He had never seen him like this. Something was wrong.

"I was in the woods, walking toward town, and I found a native couple naked in their tent, so I snuck up on 'em and was about to watch 'em fuck, so I had my cock out, ready to jerk it. I ain't never seen any natives naked before, and my dick was hard as a rock. That bitch screamed when she saw me holding my dong, though, and my boner went south real quick. The guy got out of the tent and started yelling, so I punched him right in his stupid face. He fell to the ground, and I picked up a rock and bashed him over the head before he could get up. Bitch was screaming the whole time! I could swear he was dead. I had to chase her down cuz she slipped by me, but I finally caught up to her. I dragged her all the way here and threw her bitch ass on the table!" Jeb spoke frantically.

"Is she dead?" Billy asked.

"Damn right, she is! I slit her throat!"

"So, what's the big deal?"

"I brought that slut to the kitchen, dropped her off, and went back to get the guy, but he wasn't there! I looked around for a while and couldn't figure out where the fucker went. I had popped him a good one, and he had a gash on his forehead, so I knew he was hurt. We gotta go get him!" Jeb exclaimed.

"How far away was this?" Billy asked.

"Not far. Let's go," Jeb replied, "I'll get my gun, and you get some knives."

Jeb went toward his room, and Billy ran toward the kitchen and stopped as he entered to examine the dead woman lying on the table. Blood was still dripping from her neck wound and had pooled onto the table below, which in turn began to drip onto the floor like a bloody waterfall. It was beautiful, and he became mesmerized by the sight and the sound it made as it hit the floor. *Tap, tap, tap.*

"Billy?" Jeb queried as he walked into the room.

The noise broke his reverie, and he shook his head and looked around, noticing a set of bloody footprints leading from the door to the table and back to the door. He pointed and looked at his uncle.

"Fuck, he musta been in here," he stated firmly. "All right, let's find this bastard. I brought my shotgun."

"Let's go then," Billy said as he reached into a drawer to grab two long knives.

They quickly left the kitchen and went outside, and Jeb led the way since he had already been to the camp and knew where it was.

"Maybe that guy wasn't dead and followed you here to get her back, mister Jeb?" Billy asked as they made their way deeper into the forest.

"That's what I'm thinking," Jeb replied as he stopped to look around. "We're almost there."

He kept walking, and the campsite abruptly came into view.

"Shit!" a shocked Jeb asked.

It looked like a tornado had hit the campsite. The tent had been smashed and strewn about. Clothes and garbage were scattered everywhere. Something had snapped the tree limbs and left them dangling, and a man was sitting against a tree. Billy stifled his rebelling guts when he noticed the man's skin wasn't where it was supposed to be. Blood dripped down the length of the body, and there was a bloody pile of skin and clothing on the ground under the corpse. They both looked at the sight in shock and disgust.

"Sweet Jesus!" Jeb said and genuflected.

"I don't think Jesus wants any part of this," Billy replied.

Suddenly, the man's head moved, and he reached out a hand.

"Nun'yuni'wi," he said quietly.

Billy was horrified.

"No fucking way!" He exclaimed, stepping backward in shock.

"Nun'yuni'wi!" the flayed man said again with more force.

"What the fuck does that mean?" Jeb asked, looking over at Billy.

"It means dressed in stone or stone coat," Billy said, visibly shaking. "I read about it in one of my books."

"Stone coat?" Jeb asked.

He was getting anxious and looked around wildly as he spoke.

"It's a human-like creature with skin so tough that allegedly no weapon can pierce it. It is said to be a powerful sorcerer, devours humans, and can control their minds." Billy explained.

"It eats people?" Jeb asked in a hushed voice.

"We need to leave right now, Jeb," Billy replied.

Jeb turned back to where they had come from and took several steps before a giant cane suddenly came crashing down on his head. It exploded like a watermelon, and bits of brain and blood mixed with pieces of the skull splashed all over Billy. Jeb's body crumpled and fell to the ground, and Billy screamed when he saw the creature. He closed his eyes, too frightened to run, and fell to his knees and prostrated himself before the towering figure that had appeared.

It walked by him, unconcerned with his presence, toward the flayed man next to the tree. Billy opened his eyes briefly to see a nine-foot-tall creature with white skin made of inch-wide stones. The beast was swallowing the body. He closed his eyes in fear and heard bones breaking and noisy chewing. It made a satisfied grunt, and it walked by him again, the cane thumping on the ground with each alternate step.

He opened his eyes as it picked up Jeb with one hand and tore his clothes away with sharp arrowhead-shaped fingers with the other. Once finished, it touched the body with the cane, and the skin began to bubble and slide off the corpse. The creature's mouth opened, the jaw unhinged and then opened even further and began to shove Jeb's body into its stony maw.

When it finished eating Jeb, it turned its attention to Billy, still crouching on the ground. It lumbered over to him and looked down. Billy raised his hand in defense as if he could ward off a supernatural creature. He was trying to make peace with death and was surprised to hear it speak to him in a deep, monotone voice.

"Billy. Punish." It said.

Billy looked up at the creature and instantly regretted it as the beast pointed the cane at his forehead and touched him right between the eyes. The eyes caught fire as soon as he said the words; the flame was so hot it burned his eyes out while simultaneously cauterizing the sockets. In pain and agony, he fell to the ground.

"Do better." It said and began to walk away.

Billy could hear it stomping away through the forest. He was alive, his uncle was dead, and he was free. The thought gave him hope for the future, and he was thankful to be alive and have a chance at a better life. He accepted the punishment the stone man had given him and was happy to be alive. Blind and in pain, he knew he had to find his way out of the woods if he wanted to survive.

He began to crawl.

BooDoo

John Schlimm

<u>One Year Ago Today</u>
<u>*Calico, South Dakota*</u>

The deal was quick and easy.

Devil: "I will make all your dreams of fame and fortune finally come true, and I'll show you exactly how to do it. All you have to do in return is promise to create pain and suffering."

Maynard Kritzpatrick: "I promise."

***

<u>Nine Months Ago Today</u>
<u>*Birdsmuir, California*</u>

The body odor—a combined swill of ripe pine needles, curdled milk, swamp ass, and maggot-writhing roadkill—hung in a constant bubble around Curt Martin, who was nose blind to his own stink, as he peddled along the old country road. The amateur survivalist was midway through a two-week, solo cycling trip, which included only the clothes he was wearing, camping at night, foraging for food, and zero showers.

The five-mile stretch of backroad that Curt was currently biking was lined on both sides by tall, thick wild rose bushes in full fuchsia-and-ivory bloom with a sunny, cloudless blue sky overhead.

Curt crested a hill that dipped deeply in front of him. He howled and pumped hard going down full-speed in the righthand lane, accelerating to twenty-seven-miles-per-hour, then twenty-eight, twenty-nine . . . thirty-four, thirty-five . . .

This must be what the path to Heaven looks and feels like, he thought with a smile, raising his fist victoriously as fresh, rosy-scented air broke wind around him and tussled his helmetless head of thick, wavy hair. *Pure freedom!*

Turning his head to the left to hock a loogie, Curt never saw the large chunk of rock that his front tire hit, exploding and catapulting bike and rider separately high above the road towards the voluminous briar patch.

FUUUCK!!! Somersaulting midair, from the corner of his eye, Curt saw his bike swallowed whole into the rose bushes behind him.

Seeing a soft, romantic blur of hot pink and ivory, Curt's outstretched arms struck first, the thorns embedding beneath his fingernails like sewing needles, lifting them up and off with a crackling, the branches yanking his arms backwards into submission; his finger, wrist, and elbow bones snapping, his shoulders dislocating, the ball-and-socket joints shattering. He felt the two-inch-long, razor-sharp spikes penetrate his forehead and slice down—exposing his skull, then gouging out one eye and tearing another in half, then butterflying both ears, then grating his nostrils into flaps ejecting globs of snot, then ripping away his lips attached to sticky strings of stale spit while plucking chunks of diseased gums and discolored tastebuds from his screaming mouth. His entire body bulleted through the web of petals, branches, and thorns, sounding like a load of softwood logs being savaged by a crackling campfire—the thorns stabbing his neck, fileting his phlegmy throat, popping open jugular veins, then stripping off shirt, shorts, and skid-marked underpants, then peeling away flesh and muscle fibers along his back, chest, and sides as nipples tore off and ribs cracked, then shredding his tender groin and fraying his butt cheeks, piss, shit, and cruddy bits of smegma splatting out as pelvis bones crunched, and then drag racing the length of his legs like hundreds of Exacto knives, finally yanking off his sneakers, offering his rank bare feet to the vicious blender of nature, gashing his heels and arches in long, wide trenches and then the bottom of toes on one side while on the other scratching along his thick and ridged, mucous-green, fungal-infected toenails, and in between them scooping out gunky toe jam.

Eight feet into the tight, claustrophobic bushes, Curt's mutilated body full-stopped, his one-hundred-and-eighty-six-pound, skinned and slimy frame sinking onto thousands of thorns like an over-pinned, poorly dissected specimen in a first-year Biology class. A beefy, putrid soup of bodily fluids and fleshy chunks the consistency of runny cottage cheese streaked the branches, thorns, and beautiful, fragrant petals behind him. None of it visible from the road.

A car passed and was gone.

Blood and syrupy goop oozed from Curt's suspended body, like from a slowly squeezed musty sponge, running over branches and trunks, then swallowed into the fresh soil.

Another car passed and was gone.

Curt moaned once before all air escaped from his collapsed lungs and splayed throat, his brain registering terror and hope for help that he knew would never come in time.

***

Today
1:00 p.m.
Nickel Museum of Contemporary Art, Ficksdale, Illinois

Like the Museum itself, which covered one whole downtown block in the gentrified small rural town, the gallery space resembled a large white box—four twenty-foot walls, no windows, two sets of double-doors along the back and front, and a clear polycarbonate ceiling that offered an open-air, ethereal vibe.

An audience of two-hundred spectators from across the country, and even international, sat in ten rows of straight-back chairs. Each had received their ticket via a lottery system weeks ago. A dozen Arts-related media jostled on a raised dais in the back.

At the front were two, 15' x 15' x 15' white wooden cubes with paper fronts marked "1" and "2."

The Nickel's Chief Curator, Evelyn Worth—a dead ringer for Anna Wintour, sunglasses included—emerged from behind the cubes.

"*WELCOME*, ladies and gentlemen!" she exclaimed into the handheld microphone, with an overly lilting, elitist accent of unidentified, possibly made-up, origins. "Welcome to *THE ART EVENT OF THE YEAR*, right here at The Nickel!"

The crowd clapped and cheered wildly, their phones already raised to arm's length, recording every second. Their invitations specifically instructed them to photograph, film, and, if possible, broadcast live across all their social media platforms.

"Today, we have *THE GREAT HONOR* of unveiling Maynard Kritzpatrick's *GROUNDBREAKING* new work, *Reckonings*."

More applause.

"In the *SPECTACULAR* tradition of *ICONIC* works such as Chris Burden's *Shoot*, Marina Abramović's *Rhythm 0*, and Yoko Ono's *Cut Piece 1964*, this *UNPRECEDENTED* debut work of immersive, participatory and interactive Performance Art by Maynard will introduce the world to a creative genius who is hidden no more. An artist whose work is *SO RAW* and *SO SIGNIFICANT* to the times in which we live. And you, the chosen few, will get to see it and partake live in *Reckonings'* two-part installation today—right now and again at three o'clock. Like our Nickel staff and the media, we ask that you please also take photos, record footage, and go live across all your platforms, so as many people as possible around the globe can be included in this *ICONIC, AWE-INSPIRING ART MOMENT!*

"Now, ladies and gentlemen, please give a *WARM WELCOME* to my new, dear friend and your soon-to-be new favorite creative phenom, *MAYNARD KRITZPATRICK!*"

The audience jumped to their feet, phones soaring, their thunderous applause earsplitting as the room shook. The Arts media in back telegraphed every bit of it across planet Earth.

After a moment, the fifty-two-year-old artist emerged from behind the two giant cubes. Gaunt, gangly, 6'7", with a John Waters' pencil mustache, he resembled a living, breathing iteration of Giacometti's four *Walking Man* sculptures.

The artist smiled sheepishly with a slight wave. This was new, mysterious, and wonderful to him.

"Thank you, thank you," Maynard said awkwardly in a low monotone into his own handheld mike. The one thing the Devil couldn't give him was a more spirited personality—as is, his charisma meter leaned more toward Norman Bates than P.T. Barnum, despite the quirky-cool stache. "Thank you for coming, thank you for coming."

The audience applauded a moment more, then sat, quieted and tense with anticipation.

Once the room stilled, Maynard continued, "Today, I'm honored to present my new work, *Reckonings*, which has been a year in the making."

The artist walked over to the cube marked "1" and tore away the paper front.

The audience and media *gasped*.

Inside the otherwise bare white cube were two visuals for their consideration. The first was what appeared to be a mannequin, but remarkably lifelike in every way. Reminiscent of Duane Hanson's hyper-realistic sculptures—*Supermarket Shopper*, *Jogger*, *Tourists II*, *Woman Eating*, *Surfer*.

"This is *Number One*," Maynard said in his colorless pitch, motioning towards the figure—a handsome male, with a wide, open-mouth smile, clad only in navy swim trunks covered in kelly-green sea monkeys.

"And this is a table," Maynard said, matter-of-factly.

The audience laughed.

"On this table," he continued, "is a butcher knife, cashmere sweater, sand paper, a garbage bag, twenty-feet of rusty barbed wire, cotton balls, hot wax, a cheese grater, a clear bucket of dog shit, a basket with peanut butter, jelly, and bread, a stuffed teddy bear, a curled hose connected to a large pump on the other side of the back wall, and a red tin heart."

The artist paused a moment to allow the audience time to let the scene before them settle in.

"I will choose one of you in the audience to come up here," Maynard said with a dull tone. "The only rule for that person is: there are no rules. You are free to do whatever you would like to *Number One*."

The audience clapped and yelled in excitement. "PICK ME! PICK ME!" several started to scream, cresting into a full, collective mob chant.

The artist studied the crowd, which purposely spanned the spectrum of age, gender, sex, race, faith, socio-economic status, and geography—urban, suburban, rural, domestic, foreign. The Nickel's staff had purposely curated this melting pot of twenty-first century humanity when choosing the guests from the supposed lottery-style submissions.

Scanning side-to-side, front-to-back, Maynard zeroed in on row seven.

"You," he said softly, pointing, "the woman in the short-sleeved, red-checked shirt."

The woman motioned to herself to make sure.

"Yes, you," Maynard confirmed, smiling.

The woman screamed excitedly, jumped up and queefed loudly, laughed at herself, screamed again, and plodded in front of the others in her row, stomping on several feet, until she was free to run down the side of the gallery like a contestant on *The Price is Right*.

She threw her arms around Maynard, who froze, then squirmed free of her. Up close, he realized that her face and bare arms were inflamed with untreated adult acne and rosacea. Engorged, scarlet-purple lumps, clusters of white-tipped zits begging to be popped, crusty scabs, open sores seeping. And moist scratch marks—self-inflicted according to her dirty, crimson-tipped fingernails. Her lips were dried and cracked, several teeth missing behind them. He could practically feel the pain and burn of her sick flesh and inside her mangled mouth.

Fighting back a shot of bile slithering up his throat, Maynard saw Evelyn, off to the side, also shiver at the site of this rancid human pizza with all the clotted, flaking, leaky-pus free toppings you could ever hope for.

"Are you ready to become a part of Art History?" Maynard asked with a deadpan timbre, swallowing back more bile. He never bothered to ask her name. It wasn't necessary.

The woman rushed over to *Number One*.

She stood eye-to-eye with the figure, her back to the hushed audience.

After a minute, the woman slapped the left cheek of *Number One*.

The audience and media *gasped*, their phones raised and recording.

She then slapped the right cheek, clawing this time, drawing blood.

The audience and media *gasped*, their phones capturing it all.

Maynard stood to the side, expressionless. Next to him, Evelyn was wide-eyed and thrilled. "This is revolutionary and so iconic," she whispered to him, then burped a grody puff of her expensive lunch, sending the icky gust of sushi, liver pâté, Limburger cheese, and Merlot vapors into his mouth and up his nose. "Oh, excuse me!" she apologized, covering her mouth.

"You like that, you sick fuck?" the woman said. "I know you do!"

She then wrapped her right leg around the crotch and ass of *Number One*, pumping her hips back and forth. The woman humped the figure several times.

"Feel good, you sick fuck?" she yelled, slapping *Number One's* face again and pinching the nose.

The audience and media *gasped*, their phones devouring the performance.

"Let's see how *you* like it this time, you sick fuck," she scowled. "Now I'm the one in charge!"

The woman turned and approached the table.

The audience and media leaned forward.

She picked up the butcher knife and waved it in *Number One's* direction. Next, the barbed wire. Then the tin heart. "*Ahhhhh*," she said. "FUCK YOU!" She hurled the heart at the figure.

The audience and media *gasped*, their camera phones working overtime.

Maynard remained straight-faced, while Evelyn was enthralled. "Simply ICONIC!" she said, looking up at the artist who was about a foot taller than her, even in her five-inch Jimmy Choo heels.

The woman now picked up the coiled hose. She examined the wide nozzle end. When she squeezed the handle, a thick substance shot from the end like uncased sausage.

The audience and media *gasped*, then instantly fell silent, straining to watch every detail.

To those in the first few rows, the mixture appeared to be mayonnaise, ketchup, and raw, ground hamburger meat.

The woman unfurled the hose and approached *Number One*.

"You like to give it, so let's see how you like to take it, you sick fuck!" she growled, placing the nozzle end inside *Number One's* open, smiling mouth and pulling the handle.

The sound of the substance squirting into the figure's mouth was that of muffled, wet farts, one after another after another after another.

As the full-blast odor of raw meat mixed with warm mayonnaise and ketchup reached the first few rows, hands went to throats to restrain gagging in addition to hands growing numb from holding phones in the air for almost fifteen minutes now.

Maynard stared at the performance, satisfied. Evelyn covered her nose, continuing to smile ear-to-ear at the glorious spectacle that was sure to launch The Nickel's growing reputation into the Art World stratosphere.

After five minutes with hose to mouth, *Number One's* belly began to swell.

"Take that, you sick fuck!" the woman said. She then turned towards the audience with a wicked, toothless smile. The audience cheered her on.

After ten more minutes, *Number One's* torso was swollen to twice its size.

More gasps rippled through the audience and media.

At twenty minutes, glops of the runny, meaty blend began seeping from *Number One's* mouth. Undeterred, the woman kept force-feeding the figure. "You've had enough when I say you've had enough!" she screeched.

At twenty-three minutes, forty-seven seconds, *Number One's* torso burst, spewing blood and chunks all over the woman.

The audience screamed, then jumped to their feet, applauding.

"HELLZZZZ YEAH!" the woman screamed, turning to the crowd and pumping her fist.

Maynard smiled for the first time, while Evelyn was overjoyed by the audience's reaction. "MARVELOUS!" she exclaimed. "SO ICONIC!"

The woman raised her hand towards the room, silencing the crowd. She wasn't finished yet.

While *Number One's* dismembered upper body and head lay on the floor, leaving only his legs standing, the woman turned to the audience. She lifted her red-checked shirt, flashing her bare breasts, shaking and bouncing them up and down while letting rip a primal growl.

The woman then returned to the table and examined the items once more, finally selecting the clear-plastic bucket of dog shit.

She walked back to center stage, the remains of *Number One* behind her.

She smiled at the audience, reached into the bucket and retrieved a handful of dog shit.

The audience and media *gasped*, still recording everything while plugging their noses.

The woman opened her mouth wide and shoved the turds in, chewing and swallowing with a grin.

Some audience members vomited on the floor and on the backs of people in front of them. Others ran out, mouths covered, before they spewed.

The woman devoured another handful of dog shit, sticking out her tongue as if to show-off a gooey whip of chocolate frosting. More audience members gagged and puked.

Maynard continued to smile. Evelyn was giddy with this brilliant masterpiece she had curated.

The woman reached into the bucket for a third handful. This time, she hurled it at the audience.

Audience members ducked, many ran, as fistfuls of dog shit were rapid fired at them.

Rake County Fair, Beekertown, New Jersey

"Ladies and gents, boys and girls, welcome to the Forty-Second Annual Rake County Fair's Rot Dog Eating Contest!" local radio host DJ Bubba Cheeks announced into the mike. "Along with nine new contestants, here in the middle we have *TWENTY-FIVE-TIME*, returning Rot Dog Champ Roddy Boil back to defend his crown! *Dude, twenty-five!*"

Roddy—5'9", thinning hair, soul patch, skinny frame with a potbelly—raised his arms in the air to the thunderous applause and cheers from the hundreds of gathered fans and spectators at the fairground, the colorful, flashing midway attractions spreading behind them for as far as the eye could see.

"Unlike those lightweights at that *other* hotdog contest up on Coney Island," DJ Bubba Cheeks teased, "our guys and gals here in Rake County are tough mother-truckers. This ain't no dainty tea party, folks; our competitors eat nasty, rotten, stinkin' hotdogs. Can ya'll smell 'em in the buckets up here? *Peeeee-YOOOOOOSA!*"

The crowd roared.

"Which reminds me, folks," he added, "don't forget the Yucky Yogurt Eating Contest tomorrow right here on the Rake County Fair's Main Stage! You won't want to miss Muggy Slims returning to defend her crown! And, by the way, I saw, *and smelled*, the buckets of spoiled yogurt this morning. *Peeeee-YOOOOOOSA!* They all had these *grayish-greenish-pinkish-pukey* layers of fuzzy mold and smelled like a corpse with diarrhea in an outhouse. I'll tell you what, no one gussies up yogurt or hotdogs like we do here in Rake County. We don't mess around. I'm telling ya'll; our county motto should be 'Poop or Get Off the Pot'!"

The crowd roared again.

"Okay, Roddy—our King Rot Dog—remind us what your record was last year," DJ Bubba Cheeks said, shoving the mike in the reigning champ's face.

"Fifty-six rot dogs in ten minutes, DJ Bubba Cheeks," Roddy said proudly. "This year I'm aiming for more, a lot more!"

The crowd hooped, hollered, and began chanting, "RODDY ROT DOG! RODDY ROT DOG!"

"Alrighty, let's do this, *bitches*!" DJ Bubba Cheeks yelled, then sneezed a thick spray of spittle reeking of stale beer and chew all over the contestants' backs to his right. "Wow, sorry about that!" he said, wiping his drippy nose and mouth with the back of his forearm. DJ Bubba Cheeks then sneezed again, and again, this time misting the contestants to his left in the gooey, brown drool. "*Damn*, I must be allergic to these here rot dogs," he joked, this time wiping the snot and slobber with his other forearm and laughing and ignoring how the contestants were frantically wiping the backs of their heads, necks, arms, and legs.

"Okay then, ya'll ready?" he asked the ten contestants.

Each hoisted a thumb's up. They were behind a long row of school cafeteria tables onstage. In front of each contestant were three things: a clear bucket—marked "BIOHAZARD" next to the cartoon image of a laughing pig—full of one-hundred, uncooked, fungal-green hotdogs that reeked of sunbaked animal guts, a monster cup of cool water, and another empty bucket for vomit—the use of which was grounds for immediate expulsion from the contest.

"On your mark, get set," DJ Bubba Cheeks said, flashing the crowd a big, gold-toothed grin, "GOOOOOO!"

The large digital clock behind the contestants started ticking down from ten minutes.

Barely a dozen rot dogs in, three of the contestants puked, and were disqualified.

By twenty rot dogs swallowed, two more exited the race, continuing to projectile vomit as they ran off stage, even spewing gooey globs on audience members.

At thirty-three rot dogs downed at six minutes, fourteen seconds, three more competitors were out, one laying nearby on the ground groaning for dear life.

The crowd was going crazy.

That left only Roddy and a woman named Snookie to duke it out, New Jersey-style.

Around forty rot dogs consumed at seven minutes, forty-five seconds, Roddy began to feel pain in his lower gut—like a corkscrew twisting, penetrating. But he knew he could do fifty rot dogs in his sleep, so he labored on, biting each rot dog in half and swallowing the moldy, decaying, three-inch pieces whole.

Forty-eight rot dogs in, the pain spread, feeling like termites were munching their way up through his stomach and chest. He glanced over at Snookie, who was smoothly choking down one rot dog after another, no problem.

The crowd now broke into raucous teams, some screaming "RODDY ROT DOG!" while others countered with "SNOOKIE ROT DOG! SNOOKIE ROT DOG!"

Fifty-three rot dogs down at eight minutes, twenty-five seconds, Roddy could feel the actual clog form in his upper stomach. Like a backed-up toilet. But he was so close to a new record!

Fifty-four, fifty-five, fifty-six, FIFTY-SEVEN—record broken! But Snookie was also still going strong. He heard DJ Bubba Cheeks announce that she was on rot dog number fifty-eight.

Roddy was shoving, plunging, and swallowing, shoving, plunging, and swallowing the rot dogs. At nine minutes, two seconds, he felt his gut expand like a balloon. Still, he shoved, plunged, and swallowed, deep-throating like a champ. Sixty, sixty-one, sixty-two . . .

The pressure inside grew, inflating him. He could feel the skin around his stomach stretch, stretch, stretch. His lungs labored and burned against his ribcage.

Sixty-six, sixty-seven . . . .. Nine minutes, thirty-one seconds. He looked over. Snookie was still chomping away.

Roddy stopped, looked up at the crowd, the midway behind them—everything was blurred, spinning, warping in and out of nauseating focus.

He reached into his pocket and pulled out his truck key.

"Don't stop now, Roddy!" DJ Bubba Cheeks said. "Only twenty seconds to go!"

The crowd yelled, "RODDY ROT DOG! RODDY ROT DOG!"

A slimy, pinkish-green foam with tiny wads the consistency of tapioca bubbled and dripped from Roddy's mouth. He lifted his shirt and plunged the key through the belly-button of his bloated gut, sawing one way, then the other, crudely ripping skin open and unleashing mashes of fatty deposits that looked like warm potato salad, desperate for relief.

The audience screamed in terror now, while Snookie kept eating rot dogs, completely in the zone. Ten seconds left on the clock.

"DUDE!" DJ Bubba Cheeks yelled. "WHAT THE FUCKITY FUCK?"

But it wasn't deep enough. Roddy had only torn the skin and top layers of potbelly fat.

He grabbed the handheld microphone from DJ Bubba Cheeks and stabbed the bottom end into the red-and-white, marbleized slab of his exposed stomach muscles.

Three seconds left on the large digital clock.

But the stomach had already burst around the seven-minute mark, flooding his torso with gastric juice—acids, salts, and enzymes—and undigested halves of rot dogs. The rot dogs had initially been stopped, then backed up, by a rare, undiagnosed, golf ball-sized tumor known as a teratoma—that looked like a giant cluster of warts with actual hair and several baby teeth protruding from it (*Seriously*, Google it—GROSS AF!)—blocking ninety-percent of Roddy's pyloric sphincter, which is the valve that allows food to exit the stomach. Adrenaline and competitive edge had masked the pain at first, enabling the reigning champ to push on initially.

Roddy now swung one more time with every last ounce of strength left, the microphone finally penetrating his abdominal cavity, igniting a fatal, high-pressured gut burst that splattered the front rows of the crowd with bloody gunk—the bulk of his slimy intestines slamming down on the Rake County Fair Queen in a grisly, real-life *Carrie* moment—and fired the teratoma like a bullet at point-blank range, its serrated baby teeth crudely carving a bystander's sunburned cheek with the messy scrawl of a dull ninja star.

Nearby, at ten minutes, Snookie ingested rot dog number eighty-one to become the new Rake County Fair Rot Dog Eating Contest champion!

3:00 p.m.
Nickel Museum of Contemporary Art, Ficksdale, Illinois

Maynard stood behind the large wooden cube marked "2," waiting for Chief Curator Evelyn Worth to once more introduce him for part two of his *Reckonings* installation.

Part one had been a smash hit, just like he knew it would be per his deal with the Devil, who had laid out the full plan in graphic detail for him to simply follow, then reap the rewards of critical acclaim, money, and popularity. Central to the hellish plan was BooDoo—the ancient art of creating life-sized effigies, resembling human bodies crafted with haunting precision, that were used to curse, punish, torture, and defeat enemies in the most painful and gruesome ways possible.

One year ago, Maynard Kritzpatrick was by all societal, cultural, and professional standards a total loser with no prospects in sight. His creative work was constantly rejected for years, leaving him desperate to take whatever jobs he could find to survive—bagging groceries, pumping gas, sorting garbage at the local recycling center in his hometown of Calico, South Dakota. Then the deal was made, followed by a $250,000 grant check in the mail the very next day, and a week later came the call with an invitation to debut his work at the hottest, new Art World mecca—The Nickel in Ficksdale, a town that was quickly becoming known as "The New Marfa."

Nine months ago was his test run for *Reckonings*. A lifelike figure constructed from an adult-size, med-school skeleton that Maynard covered in a thin, plastic-bag layer of pig-and-chicken blood from a nearby farm and then skin he constructed from an original concoction that resulted in a startlingly realistic epidermis that he planned to patent. He especially enjoyed adding the details—brown eyes, wavy hair, big smile, and whimsical swim trunks. His muse was a bastard of a bully whom he had known through all twelve years of school named Curt Martin. Daily, for nearly all that time, Curt relentlessly taunted the young Maynard, picking on him for his height and quiet, mumbling, awkward nature, and beating him up multiple times, including forcing him to regularly lick urinals in the boys locker room and swallow a newborn bird once—all of it left unaddressed by his parents and the schools, who relegated the abuse to the "boys will be boys" shit pile.

He titled the creation *Test Dummy*.

Clad only in one of Maynard's old swimming suits, *Test Dummy* was suspended midair in his garage as if flying. With a wide board filled with the pointed ends of nails in one hand and a leather whip in the other, the artist slashed and eviscerated the figure.

A week later on Facebook, Maynard was pleased to see that Curt's body was found in Birdsmuir, California. That's the moment he realized the deal he had made three months earlier was consummated.

Number One from part one of the *Reckonings* performance at one o'clock was inspired by Roddy Boil, a scrawny prick whom Maynard had known in college. He was a nasty perv who couldn't keep his slimy paws off girls or guys, purposely sneezed on the salad bar in the dining hall, picked his nose and ate, even slurped, boogers—the bigger, runnier, yellower, bloodier, the better—and claimed credit for a final, senior-year project the two of them had completed together, which resulted in Roddy getting an A and Maynard being expelled for plagiarism just days before graduation. Maynard looked forward to eventually, hopefully—if all went according to plan—also reading his obituary soon.

Evelyn re-introduced Maynard, calling him "one of THE MOST TRANSFORMATIVE and ICONIC artists of our time!" He walked around cube "2" to the applause from two-hundred adoring fans and the media. The grisly debris in cube "1" was still on full display. Despite the graphic, gut-wrenching, barf-worthy part one of *Reckonings*, the audience was hooked. Everyone in the audience and media had returned for the sequel.

Maynard reminded the audience of the logistics—he'd choose one person to approach the front, and nothing was off limits when it came to the figure titled *Number Two*.

The artist tore away the paper front of the second cube.

The audience and media *gasped*; their camera phones raised.

Number Two was identical in appearance to *Number One*, which was identical to *Test Dummy*. Only the real-life human target had changed, and this figure donned purple swim trunks with pink flamingos on them.

The contents of the nearby table were different from the first one. The audience was captivated when they saw the selection—a two-gallon watering can, a six-inch shard of glass, a stack of hundred-dollar bills, a cupcake, a clear bucket of colored thumbtacks, an adorable yelping puppy in a cage, a pitchfork, a jigsaw puzzle, a pillow inside a silky floral case, a cup of toenail clippings, a bottle of Scotch, and an aquarium that housed a five-foot-long, black timber rattlesnake with its tongue flicking towards the audience.

"Who to pick? Who to pick?" Maynard said in his droning voice while scanning the crowd.

All the audience members strained their hands into the air, volunteering. "ME! ME! ME!" they yelled, even demanded. The puppy barked; the rattlesnake banged its head against the aquarium's glass wall.

"You, sir, the man in the business suit in the third row," the artist finally said. "Yes, you. Please come on down to the front."

The man was at the very end of the row, and hurried to the front, flashing a victorious smile towards the audience.

When the man arrived up front, Maynard shook his damp hand and saw that his face was oily, textured like scrotum skin, and scattered with blackheads, and accented by several untrimmed ear and nose hairs—wax the hue and texture of crusty butter behind the former and a tiny nugget of dried booger hanging from one of the latter. The artist also noted that his business suit was cheap polyester, puckering at all the seams, with a brown stain on the lapel. And strangely, the man smelled of Chanel No. 5, which competed with his wretched breath—unbrushed whiffs of day-old, microwaved fish, onions, and an abscessed molar.

Maynard motioned for the man to commence with *Number Two*, then he took his place beside Evelyn off to the side. She reached up and patted him on the back. "Iconic," she whispered.

The man wasted no time. He immediately grabbed the bucket of thumbtacks. As if on a time clock, the man stuck tack after tack into the figure at a feverish pace. He'd work in one area—face, chest, thighs—then move around *Number Two*, focusing on the posterior—neck, back, ass— and then return to the front—crotch, knees, feet.

The puppy yelped at the man from its cage on the table. From the aquarium, the rattler's beady eyes were now focused on him, in devotion and admiration.

After twenty minutes, the figure was dotted with the red, blue, green, and yellow ends of tacks, each one drawing thin streams of pig-and-chicken blood, turning *Number Two* into a ghoulish Yayoi Kusama-meets-Jackson Pollock sculpture.

The man set the bucket down, turned to the audience, and bowed.

The crowd replied with a standing ovation.

He motioned for them to sit.

Once the room was again still, the man turned towards *Number Two*. He screamed at the top of his lungs, not even realizing that he had ruptured an eardrum.

He raised his hands claw-like, then began to dig his nails into the figure, tearing away chunks of the faux skin.

The audience clapped and cheered him on, their phones raised. The media were mesmerized. The puppy's barks escalated in volume like a warning siren. The rattler's flicking forked tongue and bared fangs begged to get in on the action.

Clump after clump of skin and bloody-red plastic matter was ripped from *Number Two*.

Unlike during part one, the audience didn't even flinch when the metallic stench of animal blood engulfed them.

Then came the nose, the eyes, the smiling lips, clawed from *Number Two* and thrown to the ground in a series of *splats*. The hair, the fingers, the toes were ripped off next.

The figure fell to the ground where the man continued to dismember it—arms, legs, and head broken off, the fake ribcage cracked apart, and the pieces tossed across the gallery floor—the man himself becoming drenched in a vinegary-marinade of adrenaline-and-rage-infused sweat mixed with the foul pig-and-chicken blood.

The puppy now whimpered, appearing defeated. The rattlesnake settled into a satisfied and comfortable coil.

Evelyn leaned into Maynard, and exclaimed, "ICONIC!"

He glanced over at her with a grin, noticing for the first time that the Chief Curator's power bob was lightly salted with dandruff flakes.

Cooks, Louisiana

Trent Bixby stood naked waist-deep in his backyard swimming pool and pissed, the water in front of his crotch turning yellow before fading. It was his pool, and his wife and teenage kids were away for the day, so he'd do what he wanted. He farted—long and hard, then turned to watch the noxious bubbles rise and pop at the surface. He scooped the polluted air towards his nose, recognizing the odor as a gassy mix of the bratwurst, cabbage, and broccoli he'd had earlier for lunch.

Mali, the family's Irish Setter, barked from the side of the pool.

Trent smiled and threw the rubber ball into the yard, close to where the manicured lawn was separated from farmland by a broad border of tall grass waving in the wind. He then farted again—sharting this time, sending a scum of juicy stool and mucous into the clear water. He laughed, thinking how he better lay off cabbage for a while.

A moment later, Mali returned to the edge of the pool with the ball. Trent once more threw it, and Mali again fetched and returned.

"Good girl," Trent said, throwing the ball extra hard this time, sending it into the tall grass.

Mali ran to the grass but stopped short of going into it.

"Go on, get the ball!" Trent encouraged her, splashing water in her direction.

Mali stood still and barked at the grass.

"Mali, get the ball!" Trent yelled, scratching his crotch and farting again.

Mali barked but stood her ground.

"Come on, Mali, get the goddamn ball!" Trent said, growing annoyed.

After several minutes, Trent hopped out of the pool, trying not to notice how shriveled his buck-naked dick was, and headed over to Mali.

"You are so spoiled, Mali," Trent teased her, running his hand gently over her soft head before stepping into the knee-high grass to look for the ball.

Mali barked.

"Where the fuck is it?" Trent said, bending over and beginning to swipe his way through the high grass.

"There you are, fucker!" Trent said victoriously, reaching into the sticky, warm blades and grabbing the ball.

Mali barked.

Tickling itches spread up Trent's lower legs—over his feet, shins, and calves.

Trent looked down. "What the . . ." he said, seeing brown, sesame seed-sized specks covering his legs from the knees down.

He plucked one off for a closer look, then realized what they were.

"OH FUCK, TICKS!" he screamed.

Mali barked in the distance.

Trent turned to get out of the high grass, but stepped into an old groundhog hole, his ankle cracking sideways and causing him to lose balance and fall into the undulating blades. The ball flew into the air and disappeared.

"FUCK!" he screamed, realizing that he was now cradled in a nest of voracious parasites.

Glancing down to his broken ankle, Trent saw that his full legs were now covered in longhorned ticks—a particularly invasive species that can number in the millions and is notorious for infesting farmland like the property next to his backyard. He reached down, scratching. The ticks were already burrowed into his skin, sucking and drinking his blood like a frenzy of miniature vampires.

The harder Trent scratched, the more his flesh turned into a relentless itch that couldn't be reached or abated. He tried to sit up, stand up, but couldn't get his balance on the lumpy surface, the two-and-three-foot-tall blades blowing in the breeze around him. It felt like flailing in the churning stomach of a stringy green monster, its gastric acid quickly making him disappear.

The ticks now covered Trent's bare crotch and ass, the invaders marching up his stomach and chest. Trent scratched harder, all over, even picking away chunks of his anus.

Mali barked.

As the ticks swarmed his arms, neck, and head, his body looked like a loaf of rye bread. They soon began to swell with Trent's delicious plasma. He scratched vigorously, deeply, his fingernails scraping and digging away skin, drawing his own blood. Which only encouraged the ticks more as they raced into the red trenches and devoured the fresh juice until they were pea-sized.

Trent screamed for help, but his voice was lost into the wind of the surrounding farmland. Only Mali responded with a bark several feet away.

Insatiable, the engorged ticks blanketing Trent's body began popping, each with a squirt of blood.

Trent panicked now, ripping into his skin with even more crazed determination, desperate for relief. Full chunks of arms, legs, and belly skin, fat, and muscle were removed and flung, landing nearby on matted grass. This only encouraged the ticks more as they now had entry into the gutted craters.

Screaming, Trent worked furiously, clawing away more handfuls of his flesh. The full-body itch and fear superseded the pain. His broken ankle no longer even registered.

The ticks scurried into Trent's eyes and ears, up his pitted, bulbous nose, and filled his mouth, working their way down his throat. He yanked at his ears until they were severed from his head. He gagged, ripping out his tongue. He grunted, picking out his eyeballs.

Mali barked.

Trent ripped off his dick and slit open his ball sack. He dug through his abdominal cavity, pulling out handfuls of runny veins that looked like marinara-soaked spaghetti and unpacking his stomach, intestines, liver, and kidneys onto the grass. The ticks filled in the empty spaces, feasting until ballooned, then bursting like bang pops on the Fourth of July.

Having skinned and gutted himself alive, which only encouraged the ticks to indulge all the more in this all-you-can-eat buffet, Trent forced his hand and arm up under his exposed ribcage, grasping his beating heart. With one, final yank, the insufferable itch ended.

Mali barked, then barked again, then returned to the shimmering blue swimming pool where she lounged and fell asleep under a sunny, cloudless sky.

Somewhere, the Devil smiled.

One Week Later
Calico, South Dakota

Maynard sat smiling in front of his computer with two open documents—the obituaries for former Rot Dog Champion Roddy Boil and scum-ball lawyer Trent Bixby.

He had crossed paths with Trent years ago when the asshole passed through Calico. They met at the dive bar where Maynard was a dishwasher at the time. When police raided the place, Trent hid the coke and heroin he had in Maynard's backpack. This resulted in Maynard being fired and serving eight months in the local prison and an additional two years on probation, while Trent coasted back out of town scot-free. Back then, Maynard believed his lifelong run of bad luck would never end. But then it did, one year ago.

The phone rang.

"Maynard, I have GREAT NEWS for you!" The Nickel's Chief Curator Evelyn Worth said.

"What is it?" Maynard asked dryly.

"Since your ICONIC debut last week with *Reckonings* went VIRAL, I've received over two-dozen requests from the biggest, most iconic museums around the world for YOU to install YOUR WORK," she replied. "And this is ONLY SEVEN DAYS LATER. Just IMAGINE what is STILL TO COME!"

"I've already started working on *Number 3* and *Number 4*," the artist said matter-of-factly.

"FABULOUS! Plus," she continued, "multiple media outlets want interviews, and a gaming company is offering an OBSCENE amount of money for you to collaborate with them to create a video game edition of *Reckonings*!"

"Wow," Maynard said. He was grateful that Evelyn and The Nickel represented him, which was part of the plan from the start.

"AND a young horror author named Rod Sterling—no relation to *The Twilight Zone* guy—called and wondered if you'd be interested in CO-AUTHORING a SPLATTERPUNK novel with him! Have you EVER in your life heard that WORD before? I didn't and had to look it up. IT'S . . ."

"Oh, got to go; someone is at my door," Maynard said flatly, ending the call.

Maynard opened the front door to see a thirty-something woman standing there.

"Hi, are your Maynard Kritzpatrick?" she asked.

"Yes," Maynard answered in his monotone cadence, towering over her.

"I'm FBI Agent Millie Strong," the woman said, flashing her shiny badge.

"You look like Clarice Starling in *Silence of the Lambs*," Maynard told her.

"You mean Jodie Foster?" Agent Strong asked.

"Like Clarice Sterling in *Silence of the Lamb*s," Maynard repeated tunelessly.

"Okay," Agent Strong said, smiling politely. "I have some questions for you about Curt Martin, Roddy Boil, and Trent Bixby. Are those names familiar to you?"

Maynard pretended to contemplate whether or not he had ever heard of those men, knowing full well that he was the only thing connecting all three of them together and that Agent Strong knew that as well. He stared into the agent's green eyes for a moment, then finally said, "Why don't you come inside where we can talk."

"Sure," Agent Strong said, stepping into the house.

"But before we talk, I want to show you some figures I'm working on for my next art exhibition," Maynard said, thinking how Agent Millie Strong would be the perfect model for the female BooDoo figure—*Number 3*—at his next *Reckonings* installation.

The gifts just kept coming, fast and furious, literally landing right on his doorstep.

Eyes of the Beast

P.J. Verfall

He sat in the twilight created by the small overhang cave's opening and looked out, surveying the world beyond. His eyes did not see as those of a man all the time, nor did they see like a beast at all times, but they watched the world intently at all times. How depended on what was deemed necessary and when. No matter the sight he used at this moment; he did not like the view it presented him.

The men wearing blue had turned the fall dirt red on this day. Crimson stained the earth turning quickly to brown, causing the mother of all pain at all this pointlessness and premature return of her creation. His vision told him that these men had wasted their kills, letting them lie on the ground to be had by buzzing insects and by the creatures of the ground. But not by him; they had created no meal for him this day. Even if the men rode away on their panicky horses now, he would never be able to lope down there in time to save the precious meat before the rot had begun to take it in this heat. Anyway, he was no scavenger; when the heart stopped pumping and soon after the blood began to congeal it was time to move on and leave it to lesser beasts.

But it was his food the men had killed, and they should pay for that.

Something else troubled him, but not in the animal way that his loss of future meals did. There were children of the people being shackled by the men in blue. They were being dragged to a wooden contrivance and forced inside of it. This caused a pain in some forgotten part of him; he felt that small part of himself release cries of outrage deep inside as the young ones were taken. The children of the people should not be in chains, they should not be dragged from their wikiups by these men in blue clothes. What the wechuge did was hunt for his food, and like any good hunter, he respects the meal his prey provides him. He was outraged by the waste. The long-forgotten human part continued to scream to be heard. It said loudly, "This is a sin! It must be avenged! The children of the people must be allowed to return to the people!"

Body low to the ground, the wechuge slunk from his cave to get closer to the men in blue clothing.

What the wechuge was now was hard to say for sure. To the casual observer, if there was such a thing, it would appear as the largest wolf they'd ever seen. But if the observer continued watching they would see things that betrayed the reality that there was more there than any dire wolf from the land of faerie. It moved with intelligence, it hunted by setting traps, it thought like a man, and it did it alone with no pack around it. Because of this melding, there were no casual observers. Wechuges brought death. If you saw it, it smelled you long before and it was planning your demise already.

The reason for its behavior was simply explained; it had been a man once. A man who had been cursed or possessed, who had his will artificially overcome by one of the great spirit animals, so that now the animal had sway even over the poor unfortunate's body. Over time the body changed, and less and less man remained, and more and more the spirit became the flesh, while the man lurked beneath, only able to watch as less of himself remained except for the submerged mind that had to bow to the will of the animal instincts. There was no comfort for a man such afflicted. Almost immediately he would be driven out of his tribe, if not outright killed, because the tribe knew that one day soon the wechuge would need to feed, and what he would feed upon would be them.

At the moment, that afflicted soul was trying not to growl out curses under its breath as it approached the former village. All of this waste! Not even a bite had been taken, all would turn to rot! Someone would need to pay for that alone. But the man buried deep inside reminded the beast that there was more wrong here, someone had taken the children of the people away, something even the wechuge would not do. The young ones needed to be freed from the men in blue clothing. The wechuge was what haunted all of the people's nightmares, and if he would not touch the children, then no other was allowed to commit such a crime.

The men and their wagon were long gone by the time he reached the village. It didn't matter. The smell of the horses hung heavy over the air, blotting out everything but the wasted blood. Men and horses needed to rest, the wechuge did not; he would find them. He would see them again soon enough.

Colonel Bartholomew Winslow rode back to the wagon and past it. He wheeled his steed around and let it skip forward to pace the slow-moving army issue vehicle. The skittish stallion tried to indicate its annoyance with the slow pace with a snort and a toss of his head. Winslow looked over at the private and the sergeant that were sitting on the spring seat. They acknowledged his presence with a nod. When he had turned the horse, he couldn't help but notice the private had been waving a piece of jerky behind him. The piece had since found its way into the mouth of the boy's own guilty-looking face.

"I wouldn't waste your time or your rations young man," Winslow said with a fatherly smile on his face as his horse finally settled into an easy gait alongside the wagon.

"I told him so," grunted the grizzled-looking sergeant who held the reins.

"Sergeant Pennyworth is absolutely right young man. They aren't hungry enough to be desperate enough to trust you. They'll have to be good and famished before they'll be willing to risk being poisoned by us," Winslow confirmed.

"Why'd we even take them then?" the younger man asked, his face twisted in puzzlement.

Both the sergeant and the colonel laughed out loud at that. Finally, Winslow got a hold of himself and said with a smile, "Oh to be so young in the ways of the world again. Son, there's a nice lil' Californian home, just got free of the yoke of the Mexicans that'd love to have each and every one of them papooses.Get to own 'em young when they're easier to break. By the time any of them are old enough to sprout a hair on their balls or snatch, have 'em trained up just like you want 'em. Someone in Sacramento valley is just pining away for a farm laborer or a house servant right now and they don't know we already have them under lock and key."

The sergeant leaned over with a grin to the younger man. "Ain' donchu' worry yeself none, Colonel har' is an honorable man. He'll cut us in on what he gets from the slavers fer' 'em, and no mistake!"

Winslow smiled almost a saintly benevolent grin at that. "Thank you, of course, for your vote of confidence,

Sergeant Pennyworth. We'll need to stop for the night before we call on the slavers tomorrow on the other side of these mountains. If you gentlemen will excuse me, I should check to see how Aimes and Fitzgerald are coming along scouting us out a campsite."

As the officer rode ahead, the sergeant leaned over to the younger man, his breath carrying an assault of rot in the young man's face, "I tols ye Private Timmons, ye stick with ol' Pennyworth; I'll see y'all come out ahead of the game in this man's army!"

They made camp that night in the open desert. The nearby hills weren't useful at night to camp against; they were too small, too easily climbed. If anything, someone wanting to ambush the small unit of men would use the hills to get above them, and sleeping on top of them was out of the question, none of them had enough flat space to make camp. Better to stay out in the desert for the night and hope they made good enough time to meet the slavers in Tehachapi tomorrow. Their unit had gotten what they wanted out of the raid on a small village of Chemehuevi, and one night in their bedrolls on the ground wouldn't hurt them any. It was nothing a hot bath while being looked over by a loose woman couldn't cure.

Today had been a resounding success from planning to execution. Winslow had poured good liquor down the throat of a free Indian trader until the man had slurred a rough location of the native camp, and once Winslow had it, they'd made good their raiding party. Of course, when it was written up for the books, it would say, "Reports of hostile natives, possibly Apache." The word Apache always got the suits in Washington to piss themselves just enough that they'd just agree with the reasoning and file it. Truth was there wasn't a single Apache within a few hundred miles of here, but none of those pencil pushers knew better.

He might even get a commendation for diligence in the war to bring the west to heel.

The Chemehuevi had never seen the raid for what it was, not until the soldiers were already firing on them. The men of the village had died quick, and with young Timmons left to guard the children at the cart, the women had died slower. The young soldier had really thought it was a sortie against a hostile group, but it was hard to believe anyone could be that naive. Not that it mattered; with the extra money in his hands when they sold the children, and with Pennyworth guiding him through the realities of this world and a posting in California, the boy would learn soon enough how to get along. It was why Winslow had brought him along on this. Best to start his education now. And if the boy wouldn't learn, well, they had been dealing with hostiles, after all, and one casualty wouldn't raise an eyebrow. Winslow was pleased with how he'd reacted to the news. Instead of outrage, the boy had responded by going right back under Momma Pennyworth's skirts. The boy would learn.

The men were laying out blankets on the dusty ground while others were finishing up the last of the stew they'd prepared. Winslow wasn't particularly worried about the fire. With the previous raids they'd made into the desert, Indians were scarce in this area, and those that were there knew not to bother with anyone bold enough to light a fire. Winslow noted to himself that Indians were getting scarce enough they'd soon have to try their luck in the mountains if he wanted to continue with his enterprise. Not something he relished. Horses ceased to be an advantage when hunting for men in the mountains, as they put you up high as a target for would-be ambushes. Any advantage the speed of a horse gave you vanished in the steep, rock-strewn terrain. It was one of the reasons he needed to get young Timmons up to snuff. He'd need every man he could clear from the post if he wanted to hunt for slaves up there.

Corporal Aimes got to his feet and handed his whiskey bottle to Fitzgerald before making a beeline for the wagon.

"Hey Aimes! Be careful back there, don't want no rattlesnake biting yer dick off!" Fitzgerald called after him.

Aimes grinned back. "When ah'm pissin', ain't but one snake in the vicinity!"

That got a loud round of laughter from the men.

Aimes stumbled a little as he went to a spot where the other men were far out of sight. His loose legs were no surprise; between him and Fitzgerald he'd need a new bottle for his pack when they got into town tomorrow. His desire to be well out of sight wasn't caused by any shame of being exposed or in his wobbly legs. Frankly, he just didn't want to smell his own piss all night. There was one more part to it that he'd never admit to. Not only was it more hygienic to put some distance between himself and camp, but he also just liked these little moments away. Just himself under the cool desert sky. Stars glittered above with no moon to drown them out tonight. Little diamonds pinned to the sheet of the sky, twinkling joyously like the gems of your imagination do. Up there as far as he could see and further again maybe it was right in front of him as he stared upwards, and he just didn't have the eyes to appreciate the halls of God when he saw it. Whatever it was, it was quiet, it was peaceful, and it sure was pretty.

He also considered today's killing in this quiet moment. It had been easier than it should have been. It felt like he hadn't earned it when it was that easy. The men of that village had barely had a working rifle between them, and when they realized what the soldiers had come for it was far too late. They'd slaughtered the Indians like dogs. There was no good story to tell the next time he was in a saloon;

he'd have to elaborate a bit. He had plenty of good stories, so maybe he'd just forget this one altogether.

After enough fumbling, he finally got his britches open enough to get his dick out. One hand on his thigh and the other waggling his member about, he finally released a hot stream of urine into the cooling night. Aimes let out a sigh of relief. He'd needed to piss for a while now, but he wanted to make sure he'd gotten enough of the whiskey down so he'd feel it before he trusted it to that dirty pig Fitzgerald. He knew as sure as he was standing here, there'd be significantly less of the amber liquid sloshing in that bottle by the time he got back to reclaim it. If he listened carefully, he could almost hear the bottle glugging its way to empty from where he stood.

Aimes opened his eyes after closing them in relief and blinked in shock as right in front of him a part of the night detached itself. Before he could think to shove his dick back into his pants and react it no longer mattered. He no longer had hands for one thing, or a dick to hold. It took a further moment for him to register that all of the liquid falling and splattering on the ground was no longer piss. It was too dark, it was too thick, it had to be his.... blood. He fell to his knees. Aimes opened his mouth to scream out the pain his brain had just begun to register. As Aimes' mouth opened, another mouth clamped over it, one with fangs that dug deep into the flesh of his face.

Whatever sound he had wanted to make became a muffled one. A few ticks of a clock later he no longer had the strength to make a whisper. It was almost with detached bemusement that he felt whatever had clamped down on his face use those fangs to pull the flesh away.

So many stars out there.

"What in the hell is taking Aimes so damned long," Winslow snapped.

Fitzgerald laughed; his lank blond hair flopped into his face as he did. "He can take all the time he wants; it'll give me more time to finish this here bottle."

Winslow stood up. "Have too much of that corporal, and you'll be in no shape to do a turn on watch. I know we think we're in safe territory here, but all it takes is one foul up and one group of bandits thinking we're easy pickings and we're all dead. I want us at least halfway competent until we're in the valley tomorrow. And that includes having a piss and deciding while you're there to have a shit or a wank without telling someone!"

They watched the Colonel stalk off into the night to look for Aimes.

"I love when it's Aimes on the shit list," Fitzgerald grinned.

Pennyworth grinned back, "Only because it means yer off in it fer a moment."

Whatever the other man's retort was going to be was cut off by the sound of the Colonel's boot steps rapidly approaching. The sergeant was already on his feet before they could see his face in the firelight. The Colonel looked like he'd seen a ghost.

"What seems to be all the stir, sir?" Pennyworth asked.

The colonel took a few gasping breaths before he replied firmly, "Put out the damned fire, Sergeant! Do it now!"

Pennyworth moved at once; he'd been with Winslow for more than a few years now. He knew that the man did not make demands like that without reason. He was already pouring the tin pot that would have been tomorrow morning's coffee onto the fire.

Timmons stared at his superior officer, dumbfounded by the command. "But why sir?"

Winslow glared at the private as he began to kick dirt over the embers the water hadn't quenched. "Because right now, Corporal Aimes is a shredded, mangled pile of flesh back there. Whatever did that to him can damned well see us pretty well, but we can't see it! At least not until we have a moment to get our night vision up to snuff. It sounds to me like you and Fitzgerald just volunteered to keep an eye peeled while Pennyworth and I get the damned fire out!"

Fitzgerald grumbled as he got to his feet. Timmons on the other hand gulped in real fear, the first he'd had since his first skirmish as a soldier. Thanks to competent commands above him, after that first terror, he had never felt that he was in a battle that his unit wasn't destined to win after that day. He was not reckless by nature; it was just that the expectation of victory lessened the fear to something manageable. Not tonight. Here was an unknown threat, hiding in the darkened, unfamiliar desert. As he reached for his rifle with shaking hands, he knew fear had returned.

The big powerful Mississippi rifle could drop most things, but that was only if the man aiming it hit his target. Staring into the starlit night, he had his doubts about his accuracy, or if he would have time to reload, for that matter. He could only hope that he'd have time to pull the Colt Paterson on his belt that his father had gifted him when he joined the army, and maybe have better luck with that. At least he'd have more chances to shoot.

As they stood on their feet and squinted out into the darkness around them, nothing happened. No further noises came to them speaking of approaching bandits or other monsters of the night. Just the scuffs and kicks of the sergeant's boots as he covered over the last of their fire. Eventually, even that <u>stopped,</u> and they sat there in the dark The only light not coming from the stars was from the lantern hanging from the wagon that had been dimmed earlier. Timmons could finally feel the tension leaving his body. He almost felt he could collapse.

At last, the Colonel broke the silence. "Who, or whatever it is doesn't seem ready to attack right now. Maybe it was just an animal, but for the life of me I don't know what animal would do that. I don't know what man would, either. We need to be able to ride at first light regardless; you'll be fucking useless to me exhausted. Timmons, you're a young lad, you still need your sleep, so why don't you get some? Fitzgerald, you're halfway to passed out anyway; join him. We'll wake you a few hours before sunrise to take a shift on watch."

"Are you sure you'll be alright, just the two of you?" the private asked timidly.

Pennyworth chuckled, "Don'chu worry yer pretty little head bout that, boy. Me and the colonel been in a few scrapes over the years. Somethin' come, we'll hold it off long enough fer y'all to get yer hands off yer cocks and onto yer guns."

The colonel smiled indulgently. "I wouldn't have put it quite like that, but it does cover the gist of it, private. Enjoy your nap. It will pass all too quickly, I'm sure."

The air was dead tonight, and that was good. The men would not be able to smell the wechuge on the wind, and he did not need a breeze to smell them. They glowed like fire to him in the night, and yet to them he was only one of the shadows. He had worried that the men would stay on alert after he had taken the first of them, but he could see that was not the case. Good, this was a blessing for the hunt. What he had been able to tear from the one barely sated the eternal hunger for man meat that he had been cursed with. He would have them all tonight... He would save the children of the people in the process, and maybe the spirits would consider a good deed, and for a day his stomach would not groan and growl at him. Life had not gifted him with such a satisfying confluence of circumstance in so very long now; maybe not since the downfall caused by his pride.

He waited until the two who slept near the wagon settled further. He listened carefully as their breathing deepened into true sleep. The wuchege's tail twitched involuntarily with impatience as he waited for the younger of the two's breath to even out. His first goal was the one that reeked of the poison that men drank in such vast quantities. He had logic there; not only would the besotted one make less noise, but since he had to kill all the men in the blue coats he might as well get this one over with and wash the taste out of his mouth with the blood of the others.

His claws carried him carefully closer to the two under the wagon where the deep shadows lay to hide him. He timed every movement to the speech of the two men who sat by where the fire had been, staring out with half-blinded eyes into the night. His teeth were almost touching the stubble-covered throat of his target. The stench of him assailed the wechuge's perfect snout. He hovered, waiting for the moment to strike.

Brother rabbit decided to come to his aid at just that moment. Something spooked the little creature a short distance from the camp causing it to explode out of the bushes. "What they hell wuz that?!" the fat old blue coat yelped. Even as the words exited the man thing's mouth, the wechuge let his powerful jaws clamp down on the throat of the smelly one. In one quick yank, most of it came away in his mouth, leaving the man with no throat at all to yell for help. If only the man hadn't managed to slam his hand to the ground and let out a wheeze of shock before the blood had rushed away from his brain.

The wechuge vanished into the night leaving a trail of gore behind it.

Winslow had quickly identified the rabbit for what it was. What had worried him more was the thump that had come from where the men were sleeping. Maybe it was one of them having a fretful dream; it certainly seemed a night for it. Although he had been the only one to see Aimes' corpse, the thought of what had occurred would be sufficient to fuel all his nightmares. The thing was, he wasn't sure that's what it had been, and with Aimes already dead, he felt he needed to check.

"Wait here," he breathed to Pennyworth as he started towards the still forms of his men.

"Sir?"

Winslow turned and put a finger towards his lips, his eyes blazing in the dim light to indicate that what he had just heard had best be the last thing he heard from his sergeant. He moved cautiously towards the sleeping men, sweat beaded on his brow despite the dropping temperatures of the desert night. He was roughly four feet away when he saw that he needn't worry about waking Fitzgerald. The white of his spine gleamed in the gloom that surrounded the two forms, right through the gaping black hole where this throat had been.

Shaking himself out of his reverie of horror, he moved quickly to Timmons and kicked lightly at his covers. There was an edge to his voice that betrayed his fear. He barked, "Come on boy, up on your feet!"

Timmons groused drowsily, "Already? Seems like I just fell asleep." His eyes were half closed as he got out from under the covers and stumbled to his feet. His eyes drifted down to the lump that had been Fitzgerald, causing sleep to fall away from his eyes immediately. A small squeal escaped him involuntarily.

B "Get your roll together boy. We're gathering the horses and leaving; I'm not sitting out here all night just to get picked off one by one. We aren't getting any damned sleep anyway; we might as well try to save our own lives with that time."

Timmons was wide awake now and moved to comply without so much as a word. First, he rolled up his blankets and walked them over to one of the horses. Pennyworth was already ahead of him and was checking the harness on the cart horses and putting the collar back on them with practiced efficiency. The colonel had joined the sergeant in going over the tack to make sure it was in place. None of them moved to deal with Fitzgerald or Aimes, or their gear. Timmons wondered for a moment if he should volunteer, but decided against it. It was wasted time and he wanted to be out of here as badly as the colonel. He'd been able to see Fitzgerald's bones through the wound!

Coming back to the cart, he held the two horses they had for the wagon in place while the colonel and the sergeant moved with practiced efficiency running the leather through the pole and hooking it onto the horse's tack. Timmons started to feel anxious to leave, and the horses' eyes were wide as well. Maybe it had more to do with being woken in the middle of the night than anything they had sensed off the young private, or maybe they could smell what was killing the men hiding out there in the night.

Finally, the colonel clapped his hands lightly. "All right, I'm going to tie the spare horse to the back of the wagon and let it trail. Pennyworth, you and I will ride, and the boy can direct the cart. We've enough experience riding at night that we won't fall from our saddles."

"Sooner done, sooner we's movin' sah," Pennyworth nodded.

The colonel grabbed Aimes' horse out of the picket and took it back behind the wagon. Pennyworth grinned over at Timmons, "Ain't no need to be worryin' more, we'll be out of har' soon enough. If anyone ken direct us out of har in the dark, it's the colonel."

Timmons was about to reply when a cry from Winslow split the night.

Pennyworth growled, "Summbitch!"

In an instant, he was gone leaving Timmons standing there feeling foolish. Foolish and afraid. Prodding himself into action, the young private made his way to the rear of the wagon, his rifle pointed out before him like a totem to ward off evil. He was greeted by the sight of the colonel on his back, and Pennyworth was bent over him doing something hurriedly down by Winslow's legs.

Timmons kept moving in a semi-circle to get a better view. A moment later he wished he hadn't. The colonel's right boot was missing, taking the stocking with it, and the white foot had splatters of dark on it that could only be blood. Blood that came from the mangled bloody mess that was the man's ankle.

Pennyworth was desperately tying a tourniquet further up the calf to stem the bleeding. Finally satisfied with the knot, he reached up and removed the officer's own revolver from its holster.

"My gun," the wounded man gasped.

"Sorry sir, I be needin' somethin' to wind up the rag so y'all don't bleed yerself dry. And I ain't seein' a tree to give me a branch for miles. Tell ye what? Ye live, I'll make sure ye get it back from the sawbones who works on ye. Cain't ask for better'n that, least not where we are right now." The sergeant had a rictus of a smile as he said it.

"Can't ask for fairer," the officer gasped as his head sunk back down to the earth.

Timmons took a few steps away from the scene and turned away to look into the night. If anyone asked, he could say he was keeping watch, even if that wasn't true. Seeing the colonel injured like that brought a new and more fatal feeling of fear up to settle on his heart. This was the man he trusted, who he expected to save them from whatever had killed Aimes and Fitzgerald, and if that man lived it would only be because the smelly old sergeant thought faster than the blood could flow. Something out there was killing them and doing it easily. A thief in the night coming to take their life away.

The wechuge saw the boy turn away from the other blue coats; it was too much to hope for! So easily the men in blue coats could be made to look one way when he lurked in the other. It was almost nonchalantly that he sprang from the shadows and tore a huge mass out of the side of the old fat one. It was so satisfying! A weaker animal wouldn't have been able to snap the rib cage to get at what he wanted. Luckily, he was beyond any animal alive, the man's ribs snapped and cracked easily, allowing his front teeth to seize the delicious liver behind them and pull the whole gory mass free.Working the bones loose to drop on the dirt, he quickly bolted down his gory prize into his gullet.

The man thing he had wounded earlier finally processed what he had just seen and started to yell, making the boy turn and face him. The wechuge almost laughed upon seeing the boy clutching his fire stick in trembling hands. The boy tried to point it at what he thought had to be the largest wolf that had ever lived. The barrel twirled and twisted, more likely to kill the wounded man thing than even come close to the wechuge.

He let out a growl as he stood over his meals; a low sound full of menace and intent. A stain could be seen even in the dim light on the front of the boy's britches. Even without it, the smell would have been enough for a man to detect, let alone the wechuge's nose.

The wechuge let out a lunging bark. The boy responded by letting out a yelp and dropping his gun, letting it clatter on the ground. The wechuge's teeth showed brightly in the dim light. The boy couldn't know that he was laughing at the young one's terror. Composing himself quickly, the beast lunged at the boy again.

The boy let out a whimper before bolting into the night.

The wechuge turned his attention to the man thing that was still alive. He could tell by the scent of him that this would be the best meal he could hope for. Nothing but fine meals building this one's muscles. He would be tender and not pumping with poisons.

The man's hand fumbled at his leg where the knot was tied. The wechuge recognized from his memories that he was trying to get another fire stick from somewhere in his coverings. He dealt with it the easiest way possible. He bit the man's hand, eliciting a groan of pain. Not hard enough to remove it; just hard enough to crush the fine bones that it needed to grasp and fire the weapon.

The man moaned and struggled to strike the wolf with his good hand while the wechuge removed his boots, the tourniquet, and then his pants, opening the snaps and tugging them down with his teeth. The man thing struggled futilely, trying to beat the monster away, but already the blood loss made him too weak to offer more than token resistance.

The wechuge was full of the ecstasy of anticipation, living flesh, right off the bone, and from someone who tasted as fine as this man promised to be. How long had it been? It was a foolish hunter indeed who wandered out into the beast's territory alone and unaware at night. Normally he found his meals after they'd been lost for some time in the wilds, catching them half-starved, not healthy and hale as this man.

He grabbed ahold of the man's thigh, sinking his teeth in before pulling back a huge gobbet of bloody flesh. The man thing screamed, but the wechuge barely registered it, so full was his pleasure at the meat he held in his mouth to savor. He sat down on his haunches, as it would take quite a while to eat so much fresh man-flesh; he might as well be comfortable.

The screams pierced the night for some time before they became rasping, throat shredded wheezes that lasted not nearly as long as the screams had. Soon enough, the night had returned to something approaching peace except for the sounds of a pair of jaws masticating.

The wechuge lay on its side, belly distended and painful. For the first time since it had become what it was, the spirit of the wolf and the body it resided in actually felt full. There was more man meat about, meat that was still fresh enough to eat, that he himself had killed, but yet at this moment he did not crave it. Curious.

Deciding that he would need to get moving to take the children to a small village of people he knew to the north, the wechuge dragged himself painfully up on his paws. He considered for a moment if he should track down the last of the men in blue coats, but dismissed it. That one was young; maybe he would learn the error of his ways and find better company to keep after this night. Also, more importantly, the wechuge was still full, it would be wasteful to kill the young one now.

He briefly reared up and put his paws on the back of the wagon. Listening closely, he could hear the steady breathing of the children inside. There was the occasional whimper of a nightmare, but the screams had stopped long ago, and they were children who had been through much. Without an immediate threat, their tired bodies had taken the only refuge available. He hoped they stayed asleep so they could wake up to a world that was much better than the one they'd finally succumbed to sleep in. A world with no men in blue coats.

The wechuge was thankful to the men, and not only for the meal. They had hooked the wagon up to the horses, which made the rest of his night easier for him. He could see the whites of the animals' eyes as he slid up to them. They knew the wechuge was dangerous. Worse, the scent was confusing; his smell was all wrong for his shape. It mattered not, as he was possessed by a spirit animal, something beyond just flesh and bones. He could make them do what he wished, as he knew the way of the beasts. For the first time in many years, he remembered clearly being a man, and remembering that time, he knew that the great wolf spirit dwelt inside him. It was punishment for his own sins. It taking him over had made him what he was now. Maybe this good act would sate the wolf spirit, and he could finally move on to being just a man again. But who knew such things?

What he wished for right now was for the horse to move this contraption. He let out a low growl and in response, the wagon began forward, creaking and clattering in the empty night.

The wechuge once more considered the meal he had left somewhere hiding in the darkness. He could track the young one easily and return before the wagon had gone very far at all. Again, he dismissed it; for he knew that a good hunter never kills what he does not plan to eat, and a good man does not hunt children.

Piece by Piece

Karly Foland

The droopy skin beneath her bloodshot eyes fluttered like a spider's web alerting the predator to prey. With every twitch, she scraped her fingernails along the porcelain sink, pressing harder until *snap,* one flipped backward and tore low, exposing the sensitive skin under the nail. "Ow, shit," she shook out the pain and dug through a messy drawer for clippers. She trimmed it as best she could and bandaged it to protect it from ripping it further.

The harsh light above her flickered and she caught her haggard reflection in the smudge-covered mirror. "God I look like a zombie," she sighed. Pregnancy and old age conspired to manifest a myriad of strange ailments, and she could never tell which to blame, figuring she'd know by which stuck around after the birth. *Geriatric....advanced age...*whatever terminology was now in vogue and written in cloying pastel fonts in the waiting room pamphlets all meant the same thing. She was too old to become a mom. Life had siphoned away what little beauty and verve she had in her youth by the end of her 30s, and now, mid-40s, here she was asking her deteriorating body to grow another one.

On a whim after a couple of weeks of stomach cramps, she gasped at the improbable plus sign on the pregnancy test. Panicked conversations with her husband followed. Worst-case scenarios from Reddit posts convinced them their old bodies could only produce a grotesque creature worthy of a nuclear-era sci-fi story. Throughout the entire first trimester they half-joked, *We don't want a monster baby,* and researched abortion laws in their state. But as test after test come back normal, and their doctor declared 45 the new 35, which was of course the new 25, they settled into the idea of becoming parents while some of their friends welcomed grandchildren. Uneasiness remained, though, and she grimaced at every grainy ultrasound displaying the contorted body and giant head of the alienesque fetus inside her. Mistaking her disquietude for awe, the doctor warmly intoned, "Meet your future daughter." All she could think was, *parasite.*

Medical reassurances didn't stop the nightmares. In one, she stood in front of a massive glass wall, behind which endless rows of newborns dozed and cooed in a cavernous, decaying factory. As she scanned the infinite space for her own, a gaunt, hunch-backed nurse in a 1950s-era uniform handed her a child she didn't remember giving birth to. The "baby" weighed 30 pounds and had long, light brown hair tied up in two spiky pigtails.

"Wow, you look just like me... exactly like me," she marveled.

The little girl responded with vacant, black eyes, and a flat voice, "I'm made from you."

She cleared her throat and glanced back toward the glass, where thousands of new mothers now held their tiny babies. She compared them and pled, "Isn't she kind of big for a newborn?" But no one responded. Instead, synchronized heads turned towards her. The moms inched closer and glowered at her with an implied insistence that she accept this baby-toddler. So, although she felt no connection to the child, she hoisted her up to her hip and carried her out into the darkness beyond the hospital. She awoke to a racing heart and shallow, tortured breaths.

Another night, she dreamt she gave birth to an animal-human hybrid. Gray and brown fur flowed from the baby's head and poked out of random spots of its scaly, molting skin. Its brown-streaked teeth alternated between sharp and dull, and its pale eyes glowed with reflected light. Nurses and patients gaped and pointed at this creature with horror. She stammered out simultaneous defenses and rejections of her child, but as their hostility grew, she grabbed the creature by the scruff of its neck and spirited it away. It twisted from her grasp, climbed up her arm and clung to her back with sharp claws that dug into her soft flesh, tearing out yellow, subcutaneous tissue like stuffing from a plush toy. She woke writhing in agony, as if someone had stabbed her in the kidneys. After pleading suggestions from her husband to see a therapist, she stopped sharing her dreams and fought to temper her physiological reactions to them. This led to bedsheets drenched in sweat and teeth clenched so tight her molars sprouted tiny cracks.

Still at the mirror, she ignored the memories of these haunting dreams and picked some flaky skin off her forehead and winced as she popped the zits rimming her nostrils. Though she took a sick pleasure in expelling the thick pus from her body, she was irritated that she hadn't experienced any of the famed pregnancy glow and bemoaned these other weird changes to her body. She wished the whole thing were over.

Her husband sidled up and wrapped his arms around her, resting his palms over her now protruding belly button.

"I hope she gets your eyes." He kissed the back of her neck and she recoiled. Six months of this pregnancy made her protective of her body. She already felt invaded from the inside out, as her parasite leeched away her energy and nutrients and sanity. Any outside stimuli set her skin ablaze with horripilation and overwhelmed her. She took care to hide it from her husband, though. He cared. His outreach was sweet in any normal context. But she didn't feel normal anymore.

A sharp pain pierced her stomach. She spasmed and doubled over the sink in a coughing fit. Her husband patted her back as if practicing burping their baby, which revolted her, and she swatted his hand away. A string of slimy red mucus dangled from her mouth, and she gripped the sink with shaking white knuckles. She retched and spewed out a glistening piece of tissue about an inch wide. It landed with a *thwack* and splattered the cream-colored sink with red droplets like thick pasta sauce. Her husband gagged and she shooed him out, sweat trickling down her neck.

"It's just phlegm, I'll clean it up," she slammed the bathroom door shut in his worried face and slid to the floor, holding her stomach in that way pregnant women do that she swore she'd never do. She had gotten used to placing her hand further from her core as her body swelled, but felt, just for a moment, that it had shrunk down a bit. She shook this off as dizziness-induced spatial confusion, tore some toilet paper from the roll next to her head, and wiped off her blood-stained mouth.

She heaved her heavy body up to the sink and peered into the basin. The bloody starfish-like mass she spat up sat stuck to the side, and she could have sworn it pulsated. She stared, disgusted but intrigued, and had no idea what to do. A soft knock on the door and offer to help sprung her into action. She couldn't bear to throw it away, so she emptied out a glass jar of cotton swabs, used two of them to pick up the mass, delicately placed it in the jar and secured the lid. She hid it in a box of now superfluous tampons and let her husband enter as the rest of the blood, now pink and frothy, washed down the sink.

By month seven, several more fleshy masses had gurgled up from deep within her. They alerted her of their emergence through a tearing pain in her stomach, as if someone was scraping parts of her away like the guts of a pumpkin at Halloween. The masses then slithered up her esophagus, catching in her throat and choking her until she loosened them and hawked them out, leaving a coppery taste and viscous film coating her tongue. The latest, another, though bigger, starfish, landed with a *plop* on her dinner plate. It sat there, leaking bile and staining her already slimy bok choy a putrid shade of its former self.

Her husband gawked and covered his mouth. "Another one? This can't be normal; what did the doctor say?"

She dismissed him with a wave. "Pregnancy hormones often cause an increase in mucus and congestion," and rolled her eyes at his concern.

"But it looks like a piece of raw meat, and you don't even eat meat!"

She cut him off with a quick, "It's fine, pregnancy is gross, ok?" And dashed into the kitchen with her plate, where she put on the theater of loudly scraping the entire thing into the trash. In reality, she pocketed the new mass in a crumpled-up napkin and slipped it up her sleeve. She then hurried to the bathroom, ostensibly to rinse out her mouth. She slid out the now blood-soaked napkin, smearing a sticky crimson trail along her forearm and carefully unwrapped it. Stray pieces of rice stuck to it like maggots, so she plucked each out and, satisfied with its appearance, secured it with her growing collection.

Though the early masses were flaccid and soft, they had taken on a rigidity lately, like an internal scaffolding underpinned their fleshiness. They flopped less when dangling from the end of the tweezers she used to transfer them to the container. And they'd grown large enough that she'd graduated to using tongs. But she never touched them and never rinsed them off (she couldn't bear the thought of any part of them being wasted, though she wasn't sure why, other than they came from *her* and that was sacred) so she had little investigative facts with which to explain their composition. She noticed that the pieces had gotten stuck together in the jar and, though this strange coagulation wasn't growing, because that would be impossible, tiny fissures had nonetheless splintered the glass. *I must have stuffed too much in, that all,* she reasoned, and resolved to find a larger container.

She waited until her husband went to work, taking a justifiable sick day for herself. The second the door clicked shut, she threw off the covers and bolted out of bed. She stood shivering before the container and felt her armpits moisten. *Why are you nervous?* She chided herself and unsealed the lid. Tangy, earthy odors crawled up her nostrils and induced her gag reflex. She let it pass, breathed in deeper, and marveled at how the smell, like old, wet flesh, reminded her of a rawer, gamier version of herself. She wondered if airing it out would help it or make whatever it was becoming spoil. It had stayed moist and bright in the jar, like tumors made of overlapping maraschino cherries, and despite still being unsure of what it was, she knew she didn't want to ruin it.

To conduct the transfer, she reached for the purple latex gloves she had used when cleaning out the litter box while her husband was away but reconsidered. She rolled up her pajama sleeves and sank her bare, trembling hands into the pulpy meat and pulled it out. Warm to the touch, it throbbed almost imperceptibly. As she turned it over and examined it, one of the starfish latched on to her finger. Stars flooded her vision and she swayed. *Is...is that a hand?* She peeled it off, leaving a sticky residue behind, and dropped the thing back in its old container, where it slid down, *squelching* as it settled back into its own juices. She collapsed with a thud onto the gray tile floor, panting and willing herself not to faint. *Your mind is making patterns where none exist. It's nothing, it's just phlegm. Your old, disgusting phlegm.* After a few minutes, she inched back up to the counter. She rubbed her bruised tailbone, smearing the light blue material with bits of this thing. She let out a frustrated "shit" at the mess, but relaxed when she observed that nothing had changed. Though her mind had conjured the potential horrors awaiting her, no creature had escaped the container. Nothing had scurried away to tear tendons out of the necks of her two cats. Nothing jumped out to stick itself to her head like an octopus and engorge itself by sucking her brain matter out through her ears. She blamed her wild imagination on pregnancy hormones and decided to throw this abomination away.

First, in case it *did* grow legs (or, maybe it already had legs, but she refused to examine it again) she unceremoniously dumped it from the small container to the larger one and snapped on the lid. Then she hurried to the kitchen and rummaged under the kitchen sink for a trash bag. As she grasped one, waves of guilt rushed over her and she froze. *It'd be a shame to get rid of it now.* Then, as if in a trance and without understanding what she meant, whispered, "It just needs a little more time." She dropped the bag, straightened, and waddled back toward the bathroom.

She passed the full-length mirror in the hallway and stopped to gaze at this stranger in front of her. She slipped out of her pajamas, unclasped the beige utilitarian bra meant to aid with nursing in a month, and wiggled out of the soft underwear hidden under her belly. She stood naked in front of this heavy, gorgeous mirror, framed by pristine holly wood with intricate carvings of plants. She had blown her emergency budget on it in her 20s but always loved how looking at herself in it built her confidence. Until now. "Wow, I look so…deformed." Shiny stretch marks criss-crossed her protruding belly, iridescent streaks shimmering like abalone shells; beautiful, perhaps, in another context. Her breasts sagged with new weight and the skin, though always pale, was now stretched so thin that rivers of blue veins were visible. As she stared, she once again wondered if her belly wasn't as big as it should be. She never voiced this concern to anyone and, weary of pre-natal check-ups, vowed to skip the final ultrasound appointment. *Would it be so bad if something was wrong and you ignored the warning signs?*

She stepped over her clothes, ignoring the ruddy stain that had seeped from the material onto the wood floor, and returned to her charge in the bathroom. She held the jar up to the light and the backlit contents glowed as if she were deep in chummed waters gazing toward the surface. Now too large to squeeze in the tampon box, she stuffed the jar in the back of her closet, under a pile of jewel-toned sheath dresses that no longer fit. She paused for a moment, whispered, "soon," and imagined commanding meetings again in those dresses. The cats, usually eager to dart into any open cupboard or closet, approached, then hissed and backed away. Orange and gray fur stood on end to intimidate the unseen threat within. She shoved them away with her foot and, from then on, the once cuddly tabbies avoided her.

By the end of month eight, carpal tunnel contorted her hands into claw-like appendages. Her feet had ballooned up like microwaved marshmallows. As her body grew foreign to her, her discomfort reached a fever pitch and she screamed at her belly, "It's been long enough, get out!" Spittle darkened her drab, gray maternity t-shirt and she flinched. Though still large, her belly was not the same size as all the women in the pictures online. When she thought about it, she realized it seemed like it had stopped growing awhile ago. *Old moms often have underweight babies*, she reminded herself, and chalked it up to that. She hid it from her husband, who was eager to check in on the progress of their growing baby.

"How are my girls?" He cooed.

She shoved him away and lectured him on body autonomy, "I'm not a zoo animal!"

He shrunk back, fumed, and reminded her pregnancy wasn't an excuse to be rude. Feeling unloved and misunderstood, she burst into ugly sobs. He released a sigh she chose to ignore as she buried her face in her hands, rivers of tears and snot oozing through the spaces between her fingers. He snatched some tissues from the box on the kitchen counter and patted her face and hands clean while silently counting down the days until her due date.

The next day, she checked on the contents in the jar. "Oh, fuck!" The lid was loose. She lashed out at herself. "Didn't you screw it on all the way?!" What looked like bloody entrails had surged to the top and seeped out, thick, gooey tentacles now clotted on the outside. Fresh blood from the main mass somehow trickled up and over the lid and dripped from each like melting icicles. Her favorite dress, amethyst-hued with an angular collar, once sexy and modern, now lie caked in rust-colored stains. It crackled as she grabbed it and stuffed it deeper under the pile. She scrambled into the bathroom with the jar and scraped the mess off the glass with her bare hands, leaving tiny pieces of warm flesh under her nails. She piled this escaped viscera on top of the mass in the jar but realized it had outgrown its confines again. Her head swiveled around as she marched through the apartment on the hunt for something larger. She spied her husband's terrarium in the living room. A big glass cylinder, it had plenty of room for things to grow. She grasped it with both hands and offered a limp, "sorry, plants," and ripped out the ferns and moss by their roots and dumped the layers of moist soil and slick rocks into the trash. The erstwhile terrarium became the latest home for her abomination.

Exhausted now, she sprawled like a melting blob on the loveseat. The cats curled up together in the far corner of the bigger couch, too tired to move to another room, but taking turns keeping one eye on her. Her husband walked in and leaned over the back of the couch to pet the cats before turning to her, "Have you seen my terrarium? The one on the bookshelf? I wanted to mist it." He wiggled the lime green spray bottle in his hand.

She tensed and pretended to concentrate on a game on her phone. In a flash, potential excuses entered her mind. He had a spotty memory, so she could claim he had gotten rid of it. Or she could blame the cats for breaking it. Or she could say she noticed mold engulfing the plants and threw it out. The first was risky, he might recognize being gaslit. The last would bring patronizing lectures and questions about what happened to the container itself. So, cats it was. Without looking up from her phone, she explained, "Oh, shoot, I'm sorry, the cats were being bonkers and knocked it off while you were out last night. The whole thing shattered and I had to toss it. I totally forgot to mention it." She tapped her temple for added effect, "Pregnancy brain!" The cats raised their heads but could offer no defense.

Her husband stood still for a moment, not believing her but not in the mood to interrogate her further and cause a fight, so he eked out, "Damn cats," and shuffled away.

That night, more nightmares scratched their way into her mind like pieces of shattered glass. Her eyes remained clamped shut as if stones sat on her eyelids, but her ears trembled at an unnatural, rhythmic sucking sound, as if someone approached, step by step, through muddy ground.

She burst into a sprint toward or away from some unseen monstrosity. She yelped as her bare feet caught on the razor-sharp ground. Jagged shards dug into her delicate skin and flayed it away down to the bone. A weight from outside this dream pressed up on her. The covers tugged a bit at the end of the bed, and she jerked awake, but realized in horror she had awoken long ago. She tried to wiggle her toes, but in their place found only searing pain. The covers sunk as the weighted thing now wetted them down. A syrupy goo soaked through and coated her legs, stomach and arms. A sickly, gamey odor like rotting, raw lamb filled the air. She reached to pull back the blanket but panicked as that tacky substance glued her arms to her body.

Nearby, ripping sounds followed by slurping and burbling pierced the silence. A sliver of moonlight cast a ghostly glow on an amorphous shape crouched on her husband's chest like a gargoyle. Bent forward, it bit down and pulled back a long piece of skin. It sliced it clean off and fashioned it to its own face-like surface. Her husband's teeth, visible now from a mouth that would never close again, grimaced at her. He groaned but the wide gash in his throat implied he was no longer really there. The thing flicked its head to her, and gurgled out, "Such nice lips," as her husband's blood gushed from its open maw. Her eyes growing so wide they hurt, she quivered in horror. She rocked back and forth, straining but failing to break her arms free. The creature slithered off of her husband and lurched toward her, settling next to her head. It stroked her hair, matting it down with its small, blood-soaked hands. "He said I get your eyes." With blade-like nails, it carved one out of her skull like a warm scoop in soft ice cream. She shrieked in agony. Its hands cupped its ears and it wailed like a barn owl an inch from her head. Her eardrums shattered and a warm liquid dribbled out and pooled onto the pillow. Her remaining eye beheld her lost one, now ensconced in this creature's large, monstrous head. A salty, gummy discharge leaked out of its remaining open eye socket and it buried itself in her chest and sucked its thumb. Her breathing crescendoed into hyperventilation; by contrast, the creature calmed itself down. It slid off her to resume its harvesting. It first scalped her husband, squishing the underside of his beautiful black hair onto its own formerly bald head. It then pulled out her nails one by one and shoved them into its own fingers. It grew accustomed to her screams, and after the fourth nail slid out of her body, she passed out. It continued taking parts of them until it grew into a larger, almost humanoid, form. Satisfied, it staggered in jerky movements toward the window and gazed, seemingly in wonder, at the night sky. She came to and wept, which recaptured its attention. Like a poorly controlled marionette, it stumbled over to her. "You said, get out." It drug its claws slowly, but deeply, through her belly, eviscerating her. Sinewy pieces of her or her husband spilled from its mouth as it spoke and slid down her collarbone. "Piece by piece, I did." She couldn't bear to look at it and turned her head away. It hissed and pounded her chest. "Fine, don't look!" and plucked out her other eye.

Dark Ramen

W.L. Lewis

I want noodles." Chiyo cupped her black-ink-stained hands, peering inside the old, kanji-decorated yellow machine. The round, red, laughing-faced logo of Big Daddy ramen stared back from the last pristine box in the city.

"We have to go, Chiyo! It's coming." Jin looked back down the alley. His calloused bare feet ignored the small rocks and bits of discarded trash. "I can hear the meat feet. Fuck."

Chiyo ignored the fear in his voice.

The sign read 100 yen, 500 if you wanted squid or chicken. Eating more squid, fresh or not, turned her stomach. Her mouth salivated at the thought of the cheap, freeze-dried, artificial chicken flavor. The chance of each bite hiding a pocket of dry, unmixed chicken powder that exploded across her tongue excited her.

Just once more, before she died, she didn't care anymore.

"Then go." Chiyo unslung her pack, digging in the secret pocket next to the wakizashi secured to the right side.

Her hand pushed past the Big Daddy machine map that had brought them here until her fingers touched the round coin—her last 500 yen.

The curved, short sword and coin were the last two things her father had given her after the horrors arrived. The coin was the first money he had earned after buying the fishing boat. The other was a fifteen-hundred-year-old family heirloom. The sword had been more useful until now.

Jin shook his head in frustration and moved away from the light of the rusted machine to peer down the dark alley.

Chiyo took a deep breath to shake off the unnerving anxiety growing inside her. The tiny hairs all over her body started to stand on end. It was just the ultra-low frequency emitted by the horrors—a way to flush out hiding animals and people. The thing was closer than she thought. She shivered at the coming sound of the meat puppets and their tapping feet.

Chiyo hefted the coin, examined the machine's lights to assure herself it was still working, and pushed the coin into the slot. The tumbling coin clattered and rattled through the box's innards.

The selection light remained dark.

Chiyo's forehead hit the window. She pounded on the shatterproof glass and rocked it onto two legs with a shove. As it slammed down on all fours, the coin return clanked.

The crackling speaker woke and said, "Step away. Any attempt to damage this unit will *static* use *static* force."

"Jesus! Shut that thing up," Jin whisper-yelled from the nearby shadows. "Fuck." He rubbed his muscled hands on his torn, black-stained jeans and re-gripped his four-bladed baseball bat.

"Run. Go," Chiyo demanded, watching him, and retrieved the coin from the small return box. She knew he wouldn't. The burly American needed people and liked people, unlike her.

They both froze as a loud bang echoed down the alleyway behind them. Jin hefted his bat, and Chiyo squinted into the black shadows between the two tall buildings. They both strained to hear the clickity-clack dance of the meat puppet's feet but only heard the occasional lapping of the nearby ocean against the seawall.

Silence consumed them.

Chiyo re-inserted the coin. The rust-tinged box responded this time. She chose ramen; add chicken. A quiet whirring noise emerged and ended with a clunk. The sound of water and the air began to smell of steam tinged with poultry.

"Seriously, what is your deal?" Jin asked.

Chiyo felt a murmur of a rumble through her feet and looked at the timer. She turned to face the alley and pulled the wakizashi from its sheath. "When my father would come back with his catch. I'd meet the boats. After he got paid, we would always stop at a Big Daddy's noodle box like this one."

The machine gurgled and buzzed at the mention.

"As I got older, I forgot that simple happiness. How to be happy. Now that he's gone. Now that those *things* took him, so are those moments. I want to feel a bit of that pure joy one more time." Chiyo stepped out of the machine's light. "It's here."

The digital read-out on the box was missing characters, but Chiyo thought they had about five minutes left. She pulled her backpack straps tight until she felt the ceramic plate press against her spine.

"Come on," Jin almost whined. "Let's get outta here."

She looked up into his bearded, square-jawed face, his chopped hair sticking out of his stars and stripes doo rag he always wore. Chiyo touched the scars around his left eye and stroked his cheek. She may have loved him at a different time. "I want my noodles."

"Fuck. It knows us by now. It's been stalking us for a week. Probably picked up an army by now." He looked back into the deepening dark. "Fuck it. I hate being alone." He drew the police revolver and checked the hammer was on the empty cylinder, followed by the two live rounds he had left. "You want this?"

Chiyo shook her head and walked down the alley toward the faint clickity-clack echoing between the buildings.

The Big Daddy noodle machine made a few beeping sounds from behind her. She checked to make sure it was still working.

The horror slid in complete silence down the side street and turned the corner into the alley. Two enormous tentacles pushed its five-meter core along the oozing slime wave it excreted in front. A putrid mix of rotted meat and decaying sea life preceded its black bulk. The smell had a distinct undertone of sulfurous gas. A mass of smaller tentacles stretched out from a hidden brain; at the end of each dangled a human body attached at the base of their skull.

The tentacles moved the meat puppets with spasmodic purpose. The shoe-clad feet flailed wildly in a macabre dance, skimming the ground and filling the air with a clickity-clack sound. They all breathed as one, creating a suss of death rattles.

"Chiyoooo," they whispered.

Chiyo swallowed hard at her name. She hesitated, unsure now. They had killed smaller horrors before, but this was almost two stories tall, and from every appendage dangled a living puppet gyrating and breathing. She stepped a few short paces backward and gripped the sword. Her heart fluttered in her chest for the first time. It could be killed if she could find the brain in the crush of bodies and tentacles.

The monster closed with a ponderous certainty. Death glided in silence, accompanied by skittering feet and breath from the grave.

Chiyo set her bare feet against the onslaught of slime that washed down the alley. The lukewarm fluid flowed over her ankles before it receded.

Jin leaped out of the shadows to her left, the bladed bat swinging for the fences. "Fuck you, squiddy!" A string of sickening, flesh-smashing thunks followed the scream.

Chiyo charged the puppets when their focus turned to Jin. She waded through the dangle of corpses that reminded her of meat-packing plants from the movies. The sword sliced through outstretched arms and opened abdomens, letting puppet entrails fall into the slime. She ducked, spun, and slashed, trying to sever the tentacles but only finding meat puppet parts. Blood gushed all over her as she fought toward the center.

The crush of tentacles pulled back to guard the brain.

The semi-alive corpses sometimes let out moans of pain. Their eyes would go wide with shock at being chopped into pieces before collapsing, limp on the end of the tentacle.

She heard Jin lost in the press of tentacles, trying to draw the thing's attention. A puppet slammed her hard, knocking Chiyo to the ground. Her nose and mouth filled with slime. She choked on the clear, thick, brine-flavored paste. A lifeless puppet fell next to her with a smack. Then another, and then one fell on her, pinning her legs.

The tentacle slammed into her exposed back. The ceramic armor plate held firm, but the thing probed for the soft spot at the base of her skull.

She got a foot on the body across her legs and sent the body skidding with a shove.

The tentacle pulled down her pack, exposing her neck.

She rolled onto her back, swinging the blade. The slice sailed through the squid's arm like butter. The black-ink blood flowed down across her forearm. A slime wave hit her again, and she knew the brain must be drawing closer. More bodies dangled overhead. The horror started dropping them on her.

Chiyo rolled to her knees in a ball as the bodies crashed into her. She held tight to the blade as more blows from body-free tentacles slammed into the ceramic plate. She tried to catch her breath under the onslaught, but the slime pooled higher around her. She felt the plate shatter and a tentacle wriggle inside her backpack. The pack jerked at the straps and pulled her upright. Air entered her lungs.

Jin grinned, wild-eyed, at her through a slime-encrusted beard. "We got her on the ropes!" He swung wildly, keeping the tentacles back.

Chiyo fought to free her legs. She caught a glimpse of the red timer—less than a minute. She had to let it go. "We have to run, Jin. Now!"

"I can see it! It's right there!" He swung hard at an incoming body, slicing it clean in half. "There are almost no puppets left! You're going to have those noodles!"

The horror drew a large breath and pulled the remaining dozen bodies in close to its center. It twisted a few bodies so their feet could rattle their song on nearby buildings.

Jin charged into the bulwark of tentacles. "Fuck you! Have some Louisville slugger, squiddy-bitch!"

"No!" Chiyo cried. She managed to stand and follow, but after a few feet, the wall of tentacles swallowed Jin.

His voice turned to screams.

Everything stopped moving.

Chiyo jumped at the gunshot. Then another. She stood amongst the clickity-clack of dancing feet.

The remaining meat puppets inhaled a sigh of relief all at once.

Her fear and anxiety grew into terror. It knew her now. It knew everything about her. The murmuring turned into a dreadful mix of harmonies that evoked every terrible memory she ever had. Every nightmare came to life.

The memory of Jin's soldier-cut hair and clean-shaven face beamed at her from the front row of her Japanese class, and cut through the despair. His terrible, Arkansas-tinged Japanese. The reserved but persistent pursuit of her. The nickname she gave him, Gaijin, shortened to Jin, which stuck, but he didn't care even after he knew what it meant. Their blossoming friendship turned toward something more in his bright blue eyes. Chiyo struggled between the pain of rejecting him and the desire to keep herself safe from feeling anything. The rise of the horrors spared her the obligation to say anything, and still Jin stuck by her.

It was too late to tell him she loved him.

The meat puppets formed a semicircle in front of her. A single tentacle extended forward. The blood and wounds were fresh, and the scarred face was familiar.

"I loved you," the Jin-puppet groaned. "I stayed for you."

Chiyo went slack. Her shoulders slumped, her head bowed, and tears ran down her face. She hadn't cried in so long. The wakizashi glinted as she flipped it into a reverse grip, a technique her father had taught her.

A set of smaller tentacles fitted Jin-puppet with shoes over his already bloody toenails. His feet danced across the slime-drenched street as he drew closer.

Chiyo steeled herself to meet his gaze. His face held pain and black hatred tinged with his love for her. A love she would never return, even though this could be her last chance. She backed away as the horror pressed forward until the face of the Jin-puppet was bathed in the jaundiced light of the Big Daddy noodle machine. A whiff of chicken steam reassured her.

The box responded with a beep and a satisfying clunk as the prepared noodle container fell into the dispenser.

Chiyo rocked the machine onto its back two feet. The speaker crackled to life, issuing its broken-static ultimatum.

Jin-puppet dangled in front of her, almost touching her nose. "Why? Why'd you let this happen?" The other meat puppets closed to hear the answer.

Chiyo fished behind her until her left hand fell on the freshly dispensed warm noodle box. An uncontrolled smile curled the edges of her mouth. She sat next to her father, short legs swinging, watching the sea birds as she ate her noodles. Her father had his arm around her, and he smelled of fish under a layer of soap. The ocean lapped against the sea wall.

"Love," Chiyo replied, pulling the container free and twisting, slashed upward, severing the tentacle at the base of Jin-puppet's skull.

Jin's body fell to the ground. Chiyo ducked as she shoulder-blocked the box, rocking it again.

The lights went red, and the facade of the Big Daddy noodle machine fell open. Two large caliber guns emerged and fired.

The horror flailed bodies under the raging bullets that turned the meat puppets into a bloody mist. The smells of primer and gunpowder filled the air.

The cacophony of noise made her hearing go blank, and then there was ringing. Chiyo could only huddle over Jin's body as hot brass fell on her exposed feet and calves; a few managed to land in her shirt. Abandoning her sword, she struggled to keep the sealed noodle container upright and cover Jin's still-twitching body.

When the firing ceased, she looked up in time to see the horror fling the remains of bodies in all directions as it fell backward. The guns retracted, and the box resumed glowing its friendly yellow.

Chiyo straddled Jin and checked for movement but found none. She reached behind his head, located the hard, nail-like protrusion, and pulled. It slipped out with a plop.

Jin shivered and inhaled. His body twitched and thrashed but then calmed. He still had a no-one's-home look in his eye. The container of noodles warmed her left hand. She leaned out, grabbed the wakizashi, and sheathed it.

Chiyo stood and searched through the carnage, wishing her ears would stop ringing. She found Jin's bat and staggered back to her companion. She put one of Jin's legs under her arm and, with the help of the slime, dragged him around the small vending building toward the sea wall. She propped him against the bench and flopped down next to him.

The container's lid opened with a pop. Steam rose as Chiyo unwrapped the short, make-shift plastic chopsticks.

Jin's foot twitched, and his breathing became more regular.

An explosion of unmixed chicken powder burst across her tongue. The firm noodles and reconstituted chicken were delicious. Chiyo closed her eyes and let the savory, over-salted memory of her father flow over her. A vague smell of soap floated on the scent of the sea.

"Dey good?" Jin slurred.

"Only because you're here."

One Night Stand

Caleb James K.

Amigos used to be one of the hottest gay bars in the Southside. Over the years though, it had developed a wicked smoker's cough and creaky joints. Now, you'd be more likely to catch the bouncer sleeping in his chair than checking IDs. The only time anyone under 35 entered through its swinging western doors was when the occasional group of belligerently drunk college girls needed a place to pee. But one step inside the pseudo saloon would be enough to turn them right back around to find the nearest alley to piss in. Sadly, the alley would probably be cleaner than Amigos' restrooms.

One muggy night in July, three young men ambled out of a nightclub called The Piston. On the main drag, the air tasted of sweat and ozone. Few people could be seen hanging out in front of the numerous bars and clubs; it was unusual for a Saturday night. The city was dozing and so were its inhabitants.

Traffic dawdled down the long stretch of road with what seemed like a series of infinite red lights. The few people out and about moved as if the ground was made of molasses. Even the sewer rats took their time rummaging through the overflowing dumpsters that lined the side streets.

"I can't believe the fucking AC's out. It's like a sauna in there," one of the young men said. His tight Gucci dress shirt was unbuttoned, exposing a smooth caramel torso lacking fat and muscle definition.

Another member of the trio, one sporting skintight pleather shorty-shorts and a black fishnet shirt, shook his head. "Did y'all see that fried meatball who tried grindin' on me? Like, stay in your lane, honey." He stomped the sidewalk with a matte black Doc Marten-adorned foot.

"Yeah, okay Addison," the third young man said. "Everyone's always trying to take a bite of that pancake you call an ass, huh?" Unlike the other two, he was modestly dressed in normal-fitting blue jeans and a white graphic tee shirt that was just tight enough to accentuate his athletic frame.

Addison clicked his tongue with a tsk tsk tsk. "Well, who spit in your latte, sugar?" He posed with a sassy hand on his hip.

"Seriously, Lee," the first young man said. "You've been pissy all night. What's wrong?"

Lee gritted his teeth. One thing he hated about being a gay man was the expectation of being open with his emotions. The last thing he ever wanted to do was share his feelings with a couple of drama queens like these two.

"It's just the humidity," he lied. "Let's go somewhere else."

The first young man shook his head and snapped his fingers. "No can do. Daddy's got a date?"

"Um, excuse me!" Addison cocked his head to the side. "This is news to me."

The young man bit his lip. "I kinda matched with this guy earlier and we've been texting all night. He wants me to come over." He couldn't hide his giddiness.

"Come over when?"

The young man's ivory-white smile lit up the dim street. "Now." He held up his phone and shook with excitement. "The Uber's on its way."

"Wow, okay. Fuck us then." Addison winked. "For real though, don't just stand there lookin' dumb. I wanna see this stud. Give up the goods." His eyes were fixated on the phone.

His friend blushed. "Okay." He tapped the dating app icon, and the screen lit up.

As the two giggled over the pictures, Lee grew impatient. A dull throbbing had set in behind his eyes and his mouth was sandpaper dry.

"Hey, I think I'm gonna call it a night. There's no action out here anyway."

"Boo, you suck," Addison mocked, barely looking up from his friend's phone. "Text me when you get home."

With that, Lee waved and headed down the street. The sound of his friends' feminine laughter faded away behind him. Why did he hang out with such immature people? All they ever talked about was sex and relationships. Surely there was more to life.

Continuing to walk, he pondered these thoughts for the next ten minutes until a blinking yellow sign caught his attention. "Amigos," he said to himself. Now that sounds like a place a guy could have a beer in peace.

***

While Lee sat at the bar nursing an overly bitter IPA, the onset of hunger pangs began to nag him. His headache had also gotten worse, and he wondered why he hadn't gone home instead of coming to this shitty dive bar. However, Amigos' air conditioner did work. Which beat sitting in his stuffy apartment with its one rickety ceiling fan.

The impatience he'd felt earlier toward his friends still lingered. It was as if he was waiting for something. Not company. He wasn't in the mood for that. Especially not the kind of company he'd find here: after scoping out the place, he was amazed and a little put off by the number of old, mustachioed gay men who kept checking him out. It would only be a matter of time before one hit on him.

"How about something a little stronger?"

As if on cue, Lee looked up from his corn stalk yellow beer to a handsome middle-aged man dressed in a suit much too nice for the establishment.

"What, like whiskey?" Lee said.

"Whatever you like." The man motioned toward the open stool next to him. Mind if I sit?"

"Uh, sure."

The man sat facing Lee. "Name's Harland." He extended his hand. Lee took it and was a bit taken aback by how much larger it was than his.

"Lee," he said somewhat sheepishly.

Deep crow's feet and a set of thick eyebrows complemented Harland's piercing blue eyes. A pinch of salt accentuated the pepper in his close-cropped beard adding to his distinguished appearance. The man looked as if he would be more at home standing in the front of an Ivy League classroom than hanging out in a cheap bar like Amigos.

"Never seen you in here before, Lee."

Lee smiled. He liked the sound of his name coming out of Harland's mouth.

"First time I've ever been here."

"Is that so? Shame you never got to experience the place in its glory days. It was quite the scene."

"I bet."

Harland smirked. His perfect teeth screamed veneers. "You were probably just a baby then. What are you now, 26? 27?"

For the first time in a long time, Lee felt like an awkward kid instead of a grown man. "24," he mumbled. "24 and a half, actually." He cringed before he even completed the sentence. He hoped his face wasn't as red as it felt.

"Mmm. I like 'em young," Harland joked. "So, how about that whiskey?"

Caught off guard, Lee stammered, "Oh I … I … I …" He paused so his mind could catch up to his mouth. "I'm more of a cranberry and vodka kinda guy."

"You like things a li'l sweet, huh?" Harland put his hand on Lee's knee and squeezed. "So do I."

With that, he stood up and walked behind the bar. Lee's eyes widened as his new acquaintance began fixing two drinks.

"What are you—" Lee stopped, stunned by Harland's boldness. "You can't do that."

Harland grinned ear-to-ear. "I can do whatever I want." He slid Lee's drink over. "I own the place."

"Oh."

"Now tell me," Harland walked back around the bar and sat down again, "why would a fine young thing like yourself want to drink alone in a place full of horny old men?"

"I uh, well. Just wanted a change of scenery."

It wasn't a lie, but it wasn't the whole truth either. If Lee was honest with himself, he didn't know why he came to Amigos. He probably passed at least 20 decent bars on his way here. And unlike Amigos, if he'd chosen one of those places, he wouldn't have stood out like a fresh trout among a bunch of hungry bears.

"Sometimes it's nice to change things up."

Harland was drinking whiskey neat. With each sip, he gave no impression that he felt its burn, but the alcohol vapors emanating from his glass betrayed the truth about the spirit's strength.

"Yeah, I guess."

"How's your drink?" Harland eyeballed Lee's untouched glass. Condensation streaked down its sides. "Hope I didn't make it too strong."

"Uh." Not wanting to be rude, Lee used the two cocktail straws to suck in a mouthful of the bright red liquid. It wasn't strong. If anything, it was too sweet. Almost medicinal. "It's great." He nodded, taking another long drink. "A lot better than that." He glanced at his half-finished beer.

"Never got the appeal of beer myself. Too much work to get the desired outcome," Harland laughed.

"True." Lee's pocket vibrated. Without thinking, He pulled his phone out. "Shit," he said to himself after reading a text message.

"Something wrong?"

"No. I just forgot to do something."

An awkward silence fell upon the two as Lee stared at his phone. Addison's sarcasm oozed from the screen. Despite his penchant for drama and overreacting, he was still one of Lee's best friends.

R U STILL ALIVE???

yea

sorry

lost track of time

BOIIII

Ur a hot mess

XXX

U home??

He didn't want to lie to Addison, but he couldn't tell him where he was either. That would only lead to unwanted drama. It would be best to tell him something came up and they could talk about it later. Addison was astute enough to get that kind of hint.

"Sorry about this. My friend gets worried when he doesn't know where I'm at."

"No problem," Harland gulped down the rest of his whiskey. "Will this friend of yours be joining us?" he said with a hint of irritation in his voice.

Lee chuckled anxiously. "No, no. I'm sure he's got better things to do. Let me just get rid of him really quick."

When he tried to reply, he found he couldn't focus; his vision was too blurry to make out the texts. Blinking several times, he came to the startling realization that he was hammered. It wasn't only his vision that was off kilter; his blood must've transmogrified into iron because his limbs had grown incredibly heavy. Within mere moments, keeping his head upright proved difficult. How could he have gotten so drunk off of one cocktail? Not even one cocktail. Half of a cocktail.

Country pop thumped through the speakers as the bar settled in for an ordinary night. Amigos' patrons mingled, laughed, danced, and drank. But at the corner of the bar, Lee swayed side-to-side, threatening to spill onto the grimy floor like the water from an old mop bucket.

"You feelin' alright, chief?" Harland said flatly.

Lee's response was a combination of slurred gibberish and slobbery nonsense. Nothing he said—or attempted to say—resembled any known language. From his perspective, the bar had transformed into a nauseous kaleidoscope.

"Come on, let's go somewhere a little quieter."

Even if Lee wanted to, he couldn't go anywhere; his legs were incapable of moving on their own. Yet he found he was suddenly moving all the same. A strange weightlessness had come over him, and though his feet were touching the ground, the softness of his steps proved he wasn't propelling himself forward. Someone was holding him up.

Sweet tobacco and whiskey wafted from the person helping him walk. With his head slumping to the left, Lee caught sight of an ear. Then darkness crept in from all sides. He was snoring before his head landed on Harland's shoulder.

***

Lee opened his eyes to an unfamiliar room. A soft country ballad played in the background as colorful LED lights rhythmically changed colors with the music. Lying on his back, he stared up at a dark skylight window. Clouds blocked out the stars.

When he tried sitting up, the clank of metal handcuffs tore at his wrists and ankles.

"Hey! What the fuck is this?" he shouted.

No response came. Other than a flat-screen TV on the wall and a weathered loveseat near the corner, Lee couldn't see much of the room. He was restrained to a bed—his limbs were handcuffed to odd-looking posts—but from what he could tell, this wasn't a room used for sleeping. The thought filled him with dread.

Though the temperature was warm, a chill ran over Lee's naked body. His mind raced with terrible thoughts. How did he end up here?

Remnants of his night came together like scattered puzzle pieces. He remembered watching his friends dance in the club. There was a point when he looked up at the cloudy sky hoping it would rain to alleviate the humidity. That was when he was walking somewhere, right? Yeah, he walked somewhere by himself. To a bar. And then he met someone. Who did he meet?

The outline of a face began to form in his mind, but then a shot of pain blew the image to tatters. What had been a mild headache earlier was now bordering on a full-blown migraine. This was almost immediately superseded by an insatiable hunger so powerful that he couldn't think about anything beyond eating. Like a rabid animal in a trap, Lee thrashed about, causing his constraints to clang.

"Finally, sleeping beauty's awake."

Hearing that voice put all the puzzle pieces into place. Lee remembered everything now: the bar, the drugged cocktail, Harland carrying him to an apartment above the bar. The revelation turned his stomach more than his hunger did.

Lee's wild eyes set upon Harland standing at the foot of the bed. The man was naked except for a black rubber ring affixed around his hard penis. He held a remote control.

"I like 'em awake. It's more fun when they struggle," he said, laughing as if he didn't have a care in the world.

"Let me go, you sick fuck!" Lee growled. Specks of white spittle shot out and dotted his lips and chin.

"You're a feisty one." Harland pressed a button on the remote and the two posts holding Lee's legs moved toward the headboard. This forced Lee's legs to spread wide at a vulnerable angle. "Don't worry, honey. You can scream all you want. The room is soundproof."

"I'll fucking kill you!"

"Now, now. You really should save your energy. After all, you're in for a long couple of days."

Harland set the remote on a dresser out of Lee's eyeline. Then he picked up and opened a bottle of lubricant, slathering his member generously with the jelly-like substance. Every move he made was meticulous as if he'd performed them many times before.

"Don't you worry, I'll be gentle, at first." Harland climbed onto the bed and got on top of Lee so they were face to face. "Don't want you bleeding just yet," he whispered into Lee's ear.

He kissed Lee's forehead which sent the young man into a rageful fit. This only increased Harland's arousal.

"I'm going to really, really enjoy this."

Despite all of the bucking and writhing, Harland slid a hand down Lee's muscular torso to his crotch and began probing with lube-slicked fingers.

"Fucking … Kill you …" Lee spat and sputtered. "Stop it, now! Or I'll —"

"Or you'll what?" Harland chuckled with a sinister grin plastered across his face. "How about you shut up and be a good little bitch."

Harland took a handful of Lee's hair and slammed the young man's head against the mattress. Then he used Lee's chest to push himself up onto his knees. The pressure forced a grunt from Lee who had become unusually still.

"Aww, don't give up already," Harland mocked. "We haven't even started yet."

With his hips pressed against Lee's hamstrings and buttocks, Harland thrust forward and put himself in position for penetration; the head of his throbbing penis pushed against Lee's anus. The middle-aged fiend's smile faded. His eyes narrowed like a tiger on the hunt and his muscles twitched animalistically. It was time.

Unbeknownst to both Harland and his soon-to-be victim, the clouds had cleared a few minutes previously and the full moon's light poured in through the skylight window. As soon as Harland had gotten up onto his knees, the pale moonlight washed over Lee's body and flooded his pupils until his eyes glowed like pools of molten gold.

Noticing this after the fact, Harland gasped. He'd never seen someone's eyes turn such a color before. If it was only the color that had changed, he might be able to dismiss it as a side effect from the drugs he'd slipped Lee earlier, but their shape had also changed; the young man's eyebrows had developed a pronounced slope while the eye sockets had seemed to space out more.

"What the fuck is this?" Harland said through gritted teeth.

Lee answered with guttural grunts that grew more bestial as his teeth lengthened into canine-like fangs. To fit the new teeth, his mouth audibly popped as it widened and expanded until it took on the shape of a snout.

"Oh my God!"

Harland recoiled from the horrifying transformation. In doing so, he lost his balance and grabbed onto the bedpost as he fell backward, but his hand was slippery with lube. Unable to catch himself, the back of his head bounced off of the lightly carpeted floor. The impact knocked him unconscious for a moment and when he came to, he was in a dizzy daze which made it impossible to stand.

Fur black as cast iron erupted from Lee's skin. His limbs cracked and twisted. The force from the change coupled with the broadening of his bones broke the metal handcuffs like they were made of cheap plastic. Dense muscle thick as corded rope ballooned and bulged over his entire body. The bed frame groaned beneath Lee's newfound weight; the pain from the transformation sent his giant claws ripping into the mattress.

Had he gone home when he'd parted from his friends, he could've hidden from the moon's cursed light. Now it was too late. Satiating his hunger was the only thing going through his animal brain.

***

Streaks of light danced in Harland's squinted eyes. It took several blinks and shakes of the head to clear his blurred vision. Waylon Jenning's voice, sounding dull and far away, slowly returned to normal as the song neared its end. Harland struggled to his feet where a shredded mattress greeted him.

"... the fuck ..."

Still woozy, he stared blankly at the broken handcuffs, unable to figure out what had happened. He ran a slick hand over a pronounced lump on the crown of his head. It was sticky with blood.

"Shit," he muttered, realizing his victim must've escaped and his whole house of cards was about to crash down around him.

Contemplating the consequences of his actions, he concocted a plan: he would call the cops, tell them he was assaulted during a lovers' quarrel, and pray his reputation as a business owner would sway them to his version of events. However, the idea of calling the police, with all those bodies buried in Amigos' basement, terrified him. If there was any kind of investigation, he would be screwed. Harland couldn't let that happen. He had to find Lee immediately and clean up this mess.

The first order of business was to get dressed. He kept a fresh change of clothes in the closet, but as he turned around, he was thrown violently onto the bed. The exposed springs stabbed his back and ripped a pathetic yelp from his mouth. Had he not been concussed, he might have noticed the hot breath on his neck while he was coming up with his dastardly plan. Not that noticing would have saved him from the beast now towering over him.

"No, please!"

The words were barely out of his mouth when the hulking monster sprung upon him. Its crushing weight shattered Harland's rib cage. Bone shards pierced his lungs and heart. Dark blood flowed from his mouth as he gasped for breath.

"Stop," he gurgled.

The snarling beast threw its massive head back and let out a howl that rumbled like a freight train. With a burst of speed, it dropped down and sank its fangs into Harland's shoulder, tearing a huge hunk of sinewy muscle from the bone. Harland's blood-choked scream was stifled by the creature's claw slashing across his face, tearing his jaw off with the sickening sounds of muscle, skin, and connective tissue ripping loose.

As Harland flailed—his large bloody tongue flopping about uncontrollably—the beast jumped back and took hold of the man's erection. Since the cock ring had kept it engorged throughout the mauling, Harland could do nothing but watch as his penis was snapped in half like a twig and devoured. A deep crimson streak spurted from the remaining stump sending the vile fiend into a seizure. If only death had come soon, but like the numbing lubricant Harland had slathered all over his member to keep from ejaculating too quickly, the beast made sure the torture lasted a long, long time.

***

Early dawn drove away the full moon, and with it came a flood of fresh sunlight that illuminated the horror beneath the skylight window. Gallons upon gallons Copious amounts of sticky blood coagulated on the ruined bed. In the middle, what was once a horny middle-aged bar owner was now nothing more than a turned-inside-out bag of meat. Conrad Twitty's familiar twang crooned from the blood-splattered speaker. All else was silent.

Down by the riverfront, Lee woke up, shivering with his naked body smelling of copper.

"Ah, not again," he said to himself.

He looked around, but the concrete walkway was devoid of people. Flickers of memory came to him, but they were more in the form of smells and flavors rather than full images. He remembered Harland's face and knew the man had taken his clothes and phone. Beyond that, he could only guess as to how the night had ended. Judging by his protruding belly, so full that it made him nauseous, he knew he must've had a good time, but he would have to reflect on the splendor of the feast later. Right now, he needed to get home before anyone saw him. He could lie about why he was naked to the cops, but the gore caked onto his skin was a different matter.

Realizing the easiest solution, though certainly not one he looked forward to, Lee climbed down the embankment to wash off in the cold river. It wasn't ideal, but this wasn't the first time he'd done it either. In fact, during the last full moon, he'd found himself sprinting along the riverfront in desperate need of shelter from the moon's wicked light. He wasn't able to avoid the change then, and by happenstance, his wolfish figure had stumbled upon an innocent man in the midst of a midnight stroll. There had been a lot of blood that night too, but the river water had washed away all evidence.

"I really need to get my shit together."

Taking a deep breath, he braced himself and then dropped into the river. He vowed to quit bar hopping then and there. It was the same vow he made and broke every single weekend.

Breaking News

Brian J. Smith

A blue background appears on screen with a large golden logo of the number 2 inside of a half circle. A chorus of boisterous synthesizer music blares from behind it as the logo glints like a chrome bumper. It fades away and a short curvy brunette in a lilac-colored business suit sitting behind a gray felt horseshoe-shaped desk appears. A small square appears in the left side of the screen depicting a cartoonish airplane with a bright orange flame beaming from its right wing above the words PLANE CRASH.

"We interrupt your nightly program for some breaking news," she says. "A cargo plane has crashed along Interstate Thirty-Three between Columbus and Lancaster. The highway patrol, state police and firefighters are already on the scene to . . ."

A live video of a large forest appears on the screen. In the distance, a large cargo plane lies in the middle of a large grassy meadow, its right wing lying twenty yards away, spewing thick ghosts of black smoke in the air. Inside of the smoke were smaller ghosts of red smoke.

The camera fades back to her. A solemn expression falls across her oval tan face.

"Assess the damage and ask all motorists to be patient and obey all traffic signs and please stay away from the area. There is new information at this time but when—"

The channel changes and a concerned voice speaks from behind a still photo of a tall, dark-haired Latino man in a black shirt and jeans that appears on the screen.

"...to us by a woman named Lita Nunez on the west side of Columbus. This video was taken twenty minutes ago by her husband Ricardo from inside of his home. His wife hasn't seen him since this morning and decided to send this video to us to explain the chaos now unfolding within our city. All of us here at Channel Fourteen suggests that everyone use extreme caution when documenting anything and that you stay off of the streets."

A small cookie-cutter neighborhood blooms across the screen, its bright yellow curbs stretching along rows of stucco bungalows and two story houses with thick iron bars across the windows. An old man with bedhead gray hair standing along the curb in a red plaid shirt and baggy jeans begins to twitch as if hit by an electrical charge. The pack of cigarettes in his right hand and the small metallic Zippo lighter falls from his grasp and plops onto the edge of the curb.

"What the (bleep) is going on here?" Nunez asks. "Ladies and gentlemen. My name is Ricardo Nunez, and I live on (bleep) street and this man just started having convulsions and I don't know if I should go out and help him or not."

He turns the cell phone around to face him and sighs.

"He's known for bumming money from people for cigarettes and booze and I told him to get the (bleep) out of here yesterday and I'm gonna have to tell him again."

He spins the camera back around to face his front door and opens it with his left hand. He steps outside, his shadow looming across the front porch and strides toward the top of his porch stairs. He holds the phone out in front of him and points his finger at the trembling old man; a large senior class ring gleams from his third finger on his left hand.

In the far-right corner of the screen, a light red mist floats across the air above the neighborhood. When he pulls the camera away from the old man to catch the mist, it disappears.

"Did you (bleep) see that? I did; it was like a red—"

A loud crunching sound cuts him off.

"What the (bleep) is that smell? It smells like peppermint and burnt anchovies."

He says, "Oh God what the hell is—"

He lifts his left hand toward the camera and winces in pain. His third and second fingers conjoin to form one thick extremity as his thumb folds in and presses against the middle of his palm. Beads of sweat dots his skin, burning away the flesh and hair along his forearm; blood pumps at the air and dribbles onto the porch.

He plops down on trembling knees as bits of flesh seep through the cracks in the wood and splatter onto the ground below. The phone falls from his grasp and leans against the white porch pillar on the left side and peers out at the neighborhood. He staggers down the stairs, his words purring behind lopsided lips, and across the street.

The old man sees him out of the corner of his eye and flinches. He spews a loud cry for help and runs down the street as Nunez staggers out of the camera shot.

The channel changes to another news station. A tall, broad-shouldered man with a clean-shaven head wearing a tan suit stands along the right shoulder of the highway. He grasps a large microphone with a bright blue wind muff in his right hand; his browns furrow as a concerned expressions falls across his face.

A long white banner unfurls across the bottom of the screen with the words PLANE CRASH in bold black print. The words fade for a split second only to be replaced by the name NATHAN BECKER below the word REPORTING and back to the previous.

"Good evening, folks. I'm Nathan Becker from Channel Four News reporting to you live from Interstate Thirty-Three outside of Columbus. A cargo plane has crashed into a field outside of the city as it was heading to a military base outside of Cleveland."

Traffic flies past, their engines buzzing like hornets. Air whirls around him and stirs his suit jacket.

He turns and motions toward the bright blue afternoon sky with his right finger. Red, white and blue lights pulsate in the distance, twinkling like Christmas lights. He turns back to the camera, his solemn expression looking more helpful and informative.

"We don't know what it was carrying at the time of the crash," he says. "A local hazmat team has been—"

"Oh God." A male voice says from behind the camera. "What is that?"

"What?"

"What is that fucking smell?"

"Doug," Nathan says. "I'll ask you to refrain from–oh God what the hell is that?"

"Oh no. I'm not."

"What's the matter, Doug?"

"I'm not feeling good," Doug says.

His voice sounds strained.

"Did you eat from that food truck again?" Nathan asks. "Oh God."

Becker's face crumples together as Doug lets off a loud, gut-wrenching heave that mingles with the sound of crunching bones and torn flesh that fills the background. The camera plummets toward the ground, distorting the footage into a swirl of distorted blue colors.

"I'm getting the fuck out of here."

The camera plops onto its side and catches Becker running down the highway, climbing into the news van and driving away. Two seconds later, a river of skin-colored ooze with bright red veins streaking across it seeps across the camera lens.

The channel changes again. A twenty-something black woman in a long-sleeved red skirt and yellow tee-shirt stares morosely at the camera. Her curly brown hair frames her round face; a thin golden chain dangles down from her neck.

"...not intended for young viewers. Again, the following footage was taken ten minutes ago by our field reporter Gus Lawson. Viewer discretion is advised."

A squat old man in a long-sleeved blue shirt and jeans stands next to a brick wall streaked with colorful graffiti shouldering the right side of a spacious gray parking lot. His kind, grandfatherly face does not accentuate his heavy morose lips. Thin shafts of sour yellow sunlight pours through the trees, spreading odd shadows across the lot and framing his narrow shoulders.

"Good evening, folks. I'm Gus Lawson with Channel Seven News. On today's segment I want to talk about how our state landmarks have been easily forgotten over the years. Right behind me here—"

He turns and points to the brick wall. More odd shadows bloom across the pavement and along the wall.

"This used to be a famous town landmark known as The Wilson Wall. If a town local dies their names are inscribed on a brick and placed inside of this wall but now that the wall was recently moved to the town square."

"This old wall has spent the last nine years being—"

There's a rustling in the trees, then a loud, phlegmy cough. Gus pauses, his brows furrowing with confusion and curiosity, and perks his ear to the wind.

"It must be a deer or something."

Before he can convince himself or anyone else of that, a tall figure emerges from the trees. To Gus' dismay, it isn't just any figure. It's an amorphous skin-colored blob with veins of blood streaking through it staggering toward him.

Its face slides down from its skull, pulling its brows over its eyes to obscure its vision. Its once thick forearms conjoin with the elbow and create a single limb. The left corner of its mouth sags toward the tip of its chin as its gelatinous chest rises and falls with each laboring breath.

"Helbhelbhelb," it says. "Helbhel—"

A loud panicked scream bursts from its trembling mouth in a chorus of incoherent stutters. It stumbles back, its hands shaking with horror, and loses its footing.

He plops down onto the pavement as the gelatinous figure leaps up on him and muffles his last dying scream. His left arm flies back as his right sleeve tears open, connecting it to the figure's hip with the sound of crunching bones and rending flesh. His face puckers into a pained expression as the figure's oozing skin conjoins with Gus' limbs and face, embracing him like a blanket of pink taffy.

The camera's LOW BATTERY signal appears on the screen and—

The channel changes to a curvaceous redhead in a green tee-shirt, jeans and white sneakers with bright pink stripes holding a gray microphone with a small black box three inches below the top. The word NEWS is stamped across the top above the number 9 in bright gray font. A tall cream-colored brick building with a flat-shingled roof inside of an L-shaped parking lot sits on the far-right side.

A bright cheerful smile spread across her face. A voice plays in the background, but no one can see who it is.

"…on the scene at Langston Elementary School. Janice, can you tell everyone about The Field Day activities the students will be taking part in today?

Her cheeks blushing, the reporter raises her microphone.

"I sure can. Today at Langston Elementary they have an exciting and active day planned for everyone here, including the students and faculty members."

The camera focuses on the far-left corner of a grassy meadow. Children donning shorts and brightly colored shirts and sneakers line up to wait their turn. On a pair of long gray Formica tables standing twenty yards away holds an array of sack lunches, a trio of red and yellow coolers and red Solo cups.

It pans back to the reporter and captures the smile on her face. A squat, broad-shouldered man with a halo of salt and pepper hair around his head approaches her with a lipless authoritative smile on his face. He wears a blue tee-shirt with the school's logo on the front, khaki shorts and white sneakers.

"I'm here with Principal Mark Geoffrey. Could you please tell everyone at home about why this Field Day means so much today?"

"Well," he says. "The school board and I have done our best to promote exercise and nutrition to the students of Langston Elementary School and—"

A loud scream cuts him off. He peers away from the camera and peers across the meadow. The trio of children scamper away from the refreshment table as a brown delivery truck speeds onto the property.

The screams increase as the teachers push the children out of harm's way. One of the children screams "holy shit!" from the crowd, oblivious to the teachers standing around. The delivery truck collides with the refreshment table and sends an explosion of damaged Solo cups and red punch flying through the air.

Two of the remaining coolers flip and tumble across the property. The truck rolls onto the parking lot, hits a concrete barrier hard enough to lift the passenger side from the ground and then slams itself back down. A peal of thunder explodes across the parking lot and thuds across the sky as the rear passenger tire ruptures.

It collides with the front of the building and screeches to a halt. Clumps of plaster and broken cream bricks clatter onto the front of the truck and tumble onto the pavement.

An oscillating wave of moans and groans erupts from the crowd as a cloud of dust emerges from the hole in the building. Principal Geoffrey hurries through the crowd, demands that everyone stay back and skulks toward the downed vehicle. The cameraman steps out from behind the reporter, walks around the left side of the crowd and follows him.

Geoffrey reaches the back of the truck and extends his left arm toward the crowd. Thick streams of smoke spew from the rear of the truck and dissipate in the air. When he sees the crowd is slowly approaching him from behind, he peers over his shoulder.

"I said get back. Everyone, stay back."

The truck shimmies as the rear doors fly open on old creaking hinges. A tall muscular man in a brown work shirt and matching shorts stumbles out of the truck. Small lucid beads of sweat pimples his brows as his skin slides from his bones, his hands shrinking into small stubs with exposed finger bones.

The skin above his right brow slumps over his eye as the left side of his mouth lolls toward his cheek, exposing two rows of blackened teeth and rotting gums. His right leg bends toward the left and writhes with every step he takes. Tiny lumps of skin and flesh sluice from his bones and drip onto the pavement like sizzling fat, spewing small ghosts of smoke into the air.

"Get inside," Geoffrey says. "Everyone get inside right—"

The melting man staggers across the lot, whips its arm back and smacks him across the face. Geoffrey reels back, barking a high-pitched shriek that is one part feminine and the other part painful. Small bubbles slide down his face, burning his cheeks and eyes to expose the network of veins, flesh and muscle beneath; a river of brownish yellow liquid pours down his legs and pools across the pavement.

Teachers and children scurry around the lot, their faces creasing with horror as loud panicked screams echo across the lot. The cameraman spins around and hurries across the meadow.

"Get over here," Janice says. "Get back over—"

The channel changes once more. A wide view of the city blooms across the screen as the edges of the buildings glint in the ochre-yellow sunlight. Another chorus of screams blare from the streets and tears the foundation of the sky wide open. The sound of twisting metal and broken glass mingles with the previous sound of screaming coming from all four corners of the city.

A ball of flame punches out the left side of an all-glass skyscraper and sprays a vicious mist of sharp glass that rains down onto the streets below. Thick plumes of black smoke billow across the air and spin inside the breeze in faint dark funnels.

There's a loud whump, whump, whump! in the background as a large banner appears on the bottom of the screen. The words EYE IN THE SKY appear in legible black font, shifts to the name OLIVER FINLEY and the word REPORTING LIVE. A sad male voice appears in the background amongst the overhead throbbing of the helicopter blades.

"This is Oliver Finley reporting live from The Channel 27 news chopper here in downtown Columbus and my God, ladies and gentleman," he says. "What seems like a beautiful day in a beautiful city has now turned into a nightmare straight out of the horror movies. It's just pure pandemonium down there. People are melting into pools of thick oozing skin and attacking others only to create—"

He sighs.

"I can't believe I'm saying this, but they're attacking others to make bigger blobs of themselves. It's as if they're multiplying by the minute. If you're out there, please get to your homes and lock the doors and don't let anyone in. Get to your families and stay inside of your homes until the proper authorities have arrived."

The helicopter shimmies to the left and then back again. A hand appears from the left corner of the camera and grasps onto a thick metal bar along the top of the door.

"What the hell are—"

The camera turns toward the right side of the cockpit. A loud shriek of horror blares out from behind it as a young man of medium height with short black hair slumps forward in his seat. His body convulses as his fingers curl into tight knuckled fists. His lips purse into a twisting red sneer.

His left knee tugs upward and connects with his hip through a small thread of muscle and sinew jutting from his stomach. Fractured bones and rending flesh fill the cockpit, igniting the reporter's terrified voice. The pilot slumps forward and leans against the controls.

The helicopter lurches and dives toward the ground. The reporter's hand tightens onto the holy-shit bar until his knuckles turn white and incoherent apologies spew from his trembling mouth.

"forthetimeiwentsarahohgodsarahhowcouldihavedonet hatto—"

It coasts through the space between a pair of red brick buildings. On the left shoulder, a pair of teenagers dash away from a gelatinous blob half dressed in what was once a crisp black policeman's uniform. On the right, a blonde woman in a floral print dress cradles a small child in her arms as a melting man in street clothes and a white apron staggers toward her with an insatiable appetite.

"sorrysorryimsorryimsorrypleasegoddon't—"

The sound of twisted metal muffles the man's dying scream. Gray static skitters across the screen like ants as if to signify the end of what no one had seen coming.

The end that most had predicted but never got right.

The Cost of Christmas

D.J. Tuskmor

There was an energy in the air that Friday afternoon at Our Lady of Mercy High School. The students dressed in reds and greens, creating a striking divergence from the regular stiff navy chinos and starched white polos required as the school's uniform. Among them, fifteen-year-old Mia twisted her knit reindeer scarf out of boredom. Beside her, the raucous laughter of Jake and Marcus echoed through the hallway, their voices rising above the excited chatter. Across the room, Leah sat at her desk, her eyes fixed on a dog-eared textbook, oblivious to the festive disruption around her. Snow fell in a gentle dance to the ground outside. Everyone eagerly expected the promise of freedom just one bell ring away, filling them with excitement.

Mr. Lucas, a tall thin man with a scoliosis hump at his shoulders, entered the classroom carrying an iced coffee. He paused, taking in the scene of unruliness playing out before him. Waiting, still unacknowledged, a picket fence grin shone beneath his goatee. Frustrated by the continued chatter, Mr. Lucas let loose a piercing whistle, slicing through the noise.

The space grew quiet as all focus turned towards him. The class, caught off-guard by the sudden need for concentration, quickly refocused. Mr. Lucas, his beady blue eyes bulging with excitement, scanned the room, ready to dive into the day's lesson.

Mr. Lucas clapped his hands together, commanding the undivided attention of everyone present. "Let's start with something fun." His voice lowered to draw them in. "Reflect on the possibility that Santa, the merry man in the red suit, shares similarities with Satan rather than Saint Nicholas."

Amusement and skepticism stirred among students, causing murmuring throughout the room.

"Consider this," Mr. Lucas said, striding to the board. He wrote 'Santa' and then, with a dramatic flourish, drew an arrow that moved the 'N' to the end, revealing 'Satan'. "Not simply an anagram, but a reflection of modern consumerism's true spirit." He turned to face the class, his eyes burning with fervor.

Leah raised her hand, her brow furrowed in confusion. "But isn't that just a coincidence, Mr. Lucas? How do moving letters prove anything?"

From the back, Marcus burst into laughter. "Next you'll have people wearing tin foil hats to block corporate brainwashing."

Mr. Lucas smiled at Marcus's jab, using it to strengthen his point. "Healthy skepticism is good, Marcus. But think about it—how much does society push us to spend every December? To worship material wealth?"

Mia, always empathetic, looked troubled by the conversation. "If consumerism is truly Satan's work, it's deeply ingrained in our culture. What can we actually do about it, Mr. Lucas?"

"The Santa you celebrate is nothing more than a corporate creation, designed to shift focus from the true essence of Christmas. This is pure idolatry, where material gains overshadow spiritual values," Mr. Lucas said, pacing the front of the room, his enthusiasm growing. "This Saturday, Christmas Eve, I propose we take a stand. Our purpose at the mall is to awaken, not to shop. To protest the idol that Santa has become."

Some students exchanged skeptical looks, while others, like Mia, caught up in Mr. Lucas's passion, nodded.

"I'm not just urging you to challenge the idea of Santa Claus," Mr. Lucas said, his voice rising with conviction. "I'm asking you to question what you believe in. Are we, as a society, going to continue allowing these corporately motivated 'Satanic' giants to dictate our principles? Will we show our true values?"

"How do you propose we protest? Teenagers handing out pamphlets may not be effective," Mia said.

"Wear comfortable shoes and meet me at the mall tomorrow at 10 AM by the main entrance," Mr. Lucas instructed.

"Sounds like trouble," Mia said under her breath, exchanging a glance with Marcus, who smirked in agreement.

"It's just a peaceful rally, designed to inform and enlighten," said Mr. Lucas.

He spent the rest of the period assuring them of their safety and the importance of their cause. As the bell rang and students filtered out, he raised his voice for one last instruction: "Tell your parents you're taking part in a religious awareness exercise."

***

In the bustling corridors of Mallard's Marsh Mall, Mr. Lucas and a small group of Our Lady of Mercy High School teenagers stood. They held signs that read 'Know the Real Meaning of Christmas!' and 'Santa = Satan'. Last-minute shoppers darted past, laden with glossy bags, throwing curious glances or outright scowls at the protestors.

Above the bustling crowd, the mall's elaborate Christmas decorations hung, swaying slightly from the ceiling. A concerned shopper glanced at the enormous banner Marcus and Jake were holding, muttering, "Seems risky to wave that around in such a crowded place, doesn't it?"

Mr. Lucas, his eyes fiery with conviction, paced back and forth, shouting slogans. "Wake up, people! Don't let consumerism steal your Christmas spirit!" His voice rose over the din of holiday music pouring from the mall's speaker system.

Marcus and Jake snickered each time someone glared at them. They seemed to relish the confrontation, waving the banner more vigorously. "Hey, ever wonder if those mall Santas are just Big Retail's little helpers in disguise?" Marcus yelled, a grin spreading across his face. A shopper shook her head in dismay as she covered her child's ears.

Nearby, Mia and Leah clutched their own signs, but their enthusiasm had waned. Looking for an escape, Mia's eyes darted around as more people whispered and pointed. "I don't know about this," she murmured to Leah, who nodded in agreement, her face pale.

"We're here to enlighten, not to frighten." Mr. Lucas raised the volume of his chanting in response to their discomfort. "Don't let greed bury the true spirit of the season!"

He paused, surveying the sea of distracted faces milling around the banners. Today, he thought, we tear down the facade of materialistic cravings to reveal the soul beneath. These decorations, this frantic shopping—nothing more than modern-day golden calves in a temple of excess.

His fervor did little to reassure Mia and Leah, who exchanged uneasy glances. Their commitment wavered under the weight of the growing hostility from the crowd. As another group of shoppers passed by, muttering disapproval, Leah stepped back, her resolve crumbling. "Maybe this was a mistake."

Despite the mounting unease, Mr. Lucas continued, undeterred. "Don't let them intimidate you! We are on the side of truth!" He brandished his sign as if it were a sword.

As the tension escalated, a security guard approached, his expression stern. "This is private property. If you refuse to quiet it down, you will be asked to leave."

The mall's festive atmosphere turned sour as the protest continued. Shoppers avoided the area near Mr. Lucas and his students, their expressions ranging from annoyance to anger.

Marcus, still riding the high of confrontation, waved the large banner more recklessly, absorbed in the moment's thrill. With a terrible misjudgment, the banner swung wide and collided with a decorative Christmas ornament hanging above the walkway. With a thunderous crash, a massive, glittering star shattered as it crashed into the ground.

The star's fall triggered a chain reaction reminiscent of a nightmare. Shards of the decoration scattered across the polished floor, skittering like ice.

A man, preoccupied with his phone, slipped on a shard and fell into the jagged sea of glass below. The gruesome sight of shards protruding from his limbs and torso drew gasps and cries from the onlookers. While attempting to free himself from the crystalline crucifix, another decoration, a faux icicle, detached and plummeted towards the crowd. It landed on the man's face with a sickening 'thunk'. Like a dropped pecan pie at a Christmas lunch, the contents of his skull painted the floor in a hot, sticky mess. The mall erupted into chaos, with people rushing to assist and others turning away, unable to witness the brutal scene.

Mr. Lucas, for a split second, stood frozen, his face a mask of shock. Then, as if awakening from a trance, his expression shifted to one of perverse satisfaction. His heart thudded with a grim thrill—this disaster, though unintended, was a spectacle more stirring than any sermon.

Mall staff rushed to the scene, pushing through the crowd. "Everyone back!"The security guard who had approached them earlier was now speaking into his radio, calling for emergency services.

Leah dropped her sign, her clenched fists covering her mouth in horror. Mia, tears streaming down her face, turned away, unable to watch. Marcus looked shell-shocked, realizing what his careless action had caused. He let go of the banner, his hands shaking.

"You all need to leave now! You're done here!" The security guard shouted at Mr. Lucas and the students; his voice barely audible over the cries of the crowd.

While being escorted out, Mr. Lucas's mind was already racing, not with concern, but with the twisted thought of how this disaster could further his cause. As they exited into the colder air of the evening, the flashing lights of emergency vehicles painted the scene in surreal, sweeping streaks of blue and red.

Mr. Lucas glanced back over his shoulder, his eyes lingering on the chaos unfolding behind him. Lips twisted; a grim smile emerged. He could almost hear the fervent discussions it would ignite, the moral outrage, the clattering of keyboards discussing every detail. This night would echo far beyond these mall walls.

Meanwhile, the other students were visibly disturbed. Leah's face was pale, her eyes wide with shock as she tried to process the events that had unfolded. Mia clutched her jacket around her, the icy dread snuffing out her usual warmth. Marcus walked with his head down, his earlier bravado now crushed under the weight of reality.

As they reached the parking lot, Mr. Lucas turned to them, his voice calm, almost detached. "Remember, this was an accident, a tragic one, yes, but it underscores the importance of our message. Today, the true cost of this holiday's excess is all too clear," he said, attempting to mold the horror into a teachable moment.

But his words seemed hollow, floating away with the winter wind. The group dispersed, each student engulfed in their thoughts, the bond of their shared cause now frayed by the grim reality of its consequences.

Left alone, Mr. Lucas walked to his car, the day's images replaying in his mind with macabre clarity. The night was far from over, and there was still more to be done. He started his vehicle and pulled out of the mall parking lot, the fading sirens in the background a stark contrast to the quiet satisfaction settling within him.

***

The neck of the bottle of Basil Hayden's clinked against the well-traveled crystal glass. Amber liquid began to splash as the cup reached two-thirds capacity. Mr. Lucas's hand was unsteady, his movements sloppy from the alcohol already coursing through his veins. He sat back heavily in his aged leather recliner; the room lit only by the flickering glow of the television screen.

On the news, the day's horrific events at the mall replayed in a continuous loop. The anchor's voice somber, detailing the chaos and the tragic death of the man impaled by glass. Each time the footage aired, Mr. Lucas's lips twisted into a grimace that was part smirk, part sneer.

It was the publicity he had never dared hope for, yet here it was, all laid out before a captive audience.

The wind howled outside, a bitter December gust that rattled the windows. Shadows crept along the edges of the room, where the light from the TV failed to reach.

Suddenly, a faint jingling sound cut through the monotony of the breeze—the delicate, unmistakable chime of sleigh bells. Mr. Lucas froze, his glass halfway to his lips. He squinted toward the fireplace, where the sounds seemed to grow louder, more insistent.

A cold draft swept down the chimney, carrying with it a whisper of laughter—a sound too merry for the solitary, somber setting. The room temperature dropped; his breath now visible in the air. He set his glass down, his intoxicated brain struggling to make sense of the sensory overload.

Before he could rise from his chair, a loud thump landed on the roof, followed by what sounded like several smaller thuds, scampering. Mr. Lucas's eyes widened as the reality of the situation dawned on him. The news droned on in the background, forgotten, as the jingling grew louder, closer—now right above him.

Then, silence—a heavy, oppressive silence that filled the room with dread. The next moments were surreal as the shadows seemed to coalesce into shapes, forming silhouettes of small, pointed hats and one much larger figure by the hearth.

Mr. Lucas, known for being talkative, suddenly lost his ability to speak. He couldn't divert his gaze from Santa Claus' shimmering eyes.

"Mr. Lucas," Santa boomed, his voice a chilling echo in the still room, "It seems you've been very naughty."

With a slow, deliberate movement, Santa reached into his sack and pulled out a climbing axe. Its handle was dark, weathered wood, carved with old Norse runes. The blade, gleaming steel with a wickedly serrated edge, caught the faint light. Beside him, figures emerged from the shadows, their gaunt faces framed by deep-set eyes and razor-sharp teeth—elves, but not as any child would imagine them.

Mr. Lucas, his senses heightened by fear, lurched from his chair. The heavy blanket of dread that filled the room seemed to weigh him down, yet survival instincts pushed him forward. With shaking legs, he stumbled towards the hallway that led to the stairs, his mind racing for a way out.

But as he rounded the corner, a tiny, grotesque figure blocked his path. It was an elf, its eyes gleaming with malice beneath the brim of a tattered cap. In its hand it clutched a candy cane. Not the small, sweet kind meant for stockings, but a large, sharpened one, twisted into a sinister point.

Mr. Lucas halted, gasping for breath, his eyes wide with horror. Before he could react, the elf lunged forward with surprising speed, thrusting the candy cane upward. The pointed end caught Mr. Lucas in the eye with a sickening, wet pop. Pain exploded through his skull, blinding and intense, as the candy cane ruptured his eyeball, sending a river of aqueous ichor and blood streaming down his face.

He screamed; a raw, guttural sound that filled the house. Clutching at his face, he stumbled backward, blinded and disoriented. With a wicked smile, the elf followed him, still grasping the candy cane. It scraped at the back of the eye socket, resembling a toddler trying to get the last bite of a Jello cup.

The room fell eerily silent; the shadows seeming to watch the unfolding spectacle. Overcome with panic, Mr. Lucas scrambled, desperate to escape. The hallway stretched impossibly long before him, his vision blurred by tears and blood, each step a struggle toward safety.

Behind him, the haunting jingle of bells and the heavy footsteps of Santa echoed, a chilling soundtrack to his torment. He realized that fleeing was impossible, trapped in his own home now transformed into a house of horrors.

Blinded, Mr. Lucas groped along the wall, his breaths ragged. The once-familiar hallway twisted into a labyrinthine trap. The soft, sinister padding of footsteps drew closer from behind.

Before he could react, a crushing blow landed across his back, knocking him to the ground. The air whooshed from his lungs as he hit the carpet, his face pressed against the rough fibers. The smell of iron and pine—the scent of his own blood and the Christmas tree in the next room—filled his nostrils.

As Mr. Lucas tried to push himself up, a sharp, excruciating pain exploded across his abdomen. He glanced down in horror to see a dark figure—another elf wielding a short, thin blade that appeared to be a toy maker's tool. With a precise and cruel gesture, the elf sliced through Mr. Lucas's belly with terrifying ease.

His intestines spilled out, slipping over each other like wet silk. The sight was horrifyingly surreal as his organs, gleaming under the dim light, slithered from the gaping wound and dangled over the sides of his torn shirt.

Yet the elf had unfinished tasks. Seizing an end of the intestine, it pulled, rapidly unraveling Mr. Lucas's viscera. With alarming speed, the elf draped the intestines along the banister, creating a grotesque parody of the festive garland Mr. Lucas had always refused to hang throughout the house.

Panic surged through Mr. Lucas's veins as he witnessed the horror. He tried desperately to pull back the slippery mass of intestines, his hands slick with blood, but the organs continued to bulge and spill beyond his grasp, impossible to contain.

Mr. Lucas lay gasping on the floor, his vision blurring. He could feel each shallow breath as a knife-edge, slicing through the agony. His thoughts spun chaotically as the elf that had eviscerated him stepped back.

But the nightmare wasn't over.

The soft, sinister padding of footsteps grew louder again, and another dark figure appeared. This one carried a sack, not filled with toys but with sharp, gleaming shards of Christmas ornaments, each piece as deadly as a razor. With a cruel chuckle, the elf began throwing the fragments at Mr. Lucas. The glass tore through his clothes and flesh, each impact cutting into him like a thousand tiny blades. His body jerked reflexively with each hit, trying to escape the pain, but there was no reprieve. Ribbons of skin and muscle were left exposed, glittering wetly in the faint light.

Blood pooled around him, mingling with the tinsel and broken ornaments, a macabre twist on holiday decorations. Mr. Lucas could only moan in helpless terror.

Then, through the haze of his agony, the figure of Santa Claus loomed into view. The traditional jolliness was absent; instead, his eyes burned with a cold, merciless light. In his hand, Santa clutched the climbing axe, its sawtooth blade gleaming ominously.

"Mr. Lucas," Santa's voice boomed, resonating through the gore-spattered living room. "You have only spread fear and misery. Now, you must face the consequences."

With calculated precision, Santa swung the axe down into the back of Mr. Lucas's ankles, sawing at and severing each Achilles' tendon with a sickening snap. The pain was explosive, unbearable, as Mr. Lucas felt his calf muscles roll up like window shades, the fibers tearing in agonizing rips. He screamed, a sound so raw and broken that it barely seemed human.

As Mr. Lucas squirmed, Santa circled him, his expression grim. "For too long, you've cloaked your malice in the guise of faith, harming others under the pretense of virtue," he said, his voice low and menacing. "Remember,

Mr. Lucas, while I am not Satan, I ensure that those who twist goodness for their own gain face their due punishment."

Santa picked up the bottle of whiskey that had been knocked over in the commotion. He poured the remaining bourbon liberally around Mr. Lucas, mingling it with the gore already pooling beneath him. Then, pulling a simple Christmas candle from his coat, he tossed it into the soaked mess. The flame caught instantly; the fire spreading hungrily across the concoction of alcohol and blood.

The heat seared Mr. Lucas's skin, the intense flames licking his flesh as the crackling of fire drowned out his screams. The room quickly filled with smoke, heavy with the acrid scent of cooking meat. As the fire engulfed him, his epidermis blistered, peeling back in horrific patterns that revealed the raw tissues underneath.

Santa and his elves watched as the blaze took hold, then they disappeared up the chimney, leaving behind the sounds of a house and a man consumed by flames.

***

On Christmas morning, each student who cheered at the rally found a piece of coal on their doorstep. It was a grim reminder, heavy and oddly shaped, smelling faintly of smoke and charred flesh. It came from a Santa who kept his list, knowing who was naughty and who was not.

Jamie Has a Plan

Terry Grimwood

Jamie has a plan and, to be honest, it's a good one. Okay, it is likely to get us killed, but at least Jamie's plan will wipe out the horde of dead-but-not-dead who are, at this very moment, converging on this building.

"It'll buy us enough time to escape deep into the countryside," Jamie says.

"Yes, it will," I answer. I doubt it though. What I really believe is that this is going to be our last stand.

The dead-not-dead are zombies. Of a kind which, I suppose, makes this whole mess a zombie apocalypse. If it is, one of the first things I discovered when it all kicked off was that the zombie lore you read in novels, see at the cinema and on *The Walking Dead*, is crap.

It started for us about half-an-hour before the coach arrived in the village. Nothing unusual about coach parties. Lessing is a chocolate box confection made up of a cosy, quaint pub, a friendly local shop and a collection of cottages, all constructed from the local stone. Some of the houses even have thatched roofs. The parish church is famous for something or other. Oh, yeah, I remember. John Wesely preached there back in seventeen-hundred-and-a-long-time-ago. I don't think his sermon went down very well, a bit too fire-and-brimstone for the local gentry, who didn't take kindly to some upstart casting doubt on their God-given moral and religious superiority.

Anyway, Sunday afternoon. Me and my mates were sitting outside The Crown enjoying yet another pint and trying to forget that tomorrow was Monday. Jamie was there, of course, and Anna (a trainee nurse, enjoying a rare weekend off), and Nina (degree in archaeology completed and off to work on a dig in Northern France in a couple of days). I'd been out with both Nina and Anna, on and off, over the years. Then there was Robbie, training to be a groundsman and gardener. Nice bloke. A gentle giant. And Simon, of course, who was employed as a bank clerk in the local town. I worked on a farm, much to my parents' disappointment. I had an A-Level or two, but preferred fields and fresh air to University and whatever office-bound purgatory would naturally follow.

We were all in our late teens/early twenties, not married, dating, breaking up, dating again and just enjoying a lull in our lives. A moment of peace before the storms of responsibility broke over our pretty little heads.

"I don't mind the job," Jamie said, as he often did. "It's just having to work with my bloody Dad…well, you know what I mean." I did, because his dad was a vicious bastard who had bullied Jamie into following the "family tradition" of working at the local quarry (where the stone came from for those cottages). "At least I've started working with the blaster."

The thud of controlled explosions was part of Lessing life. We ignored them. A distant boom, windows rattled, nothing more. A few of the townies who had moved out here once tried to get it stopped, but we'd laughed in their smug faces and usefully suggested places where they could file their petition. The quarry had been operating here long before any of the current generations of villagers were born and provided a fair amount of employment.

Anyway, that pre-coach half hour.

Anna noticed it first. "I've got no signal," she said, staring at her mobile phone.

"Me neither," said Robbie. He shook his phone then held it above his head as if to catch some stray data that might be wafted past by the breeze.

Unsettling, but we did live way out in the left armpit of nowhere, so internet and phone signals could be a bit unreliable at times. This wasn't a *bit unreliable*, however. It was as if the internet itself had failed. Suddenly we were cut off from the rest of the world, unable to receive and send all the bland, inane messages and pictures that made our lives so important and meaningful.

We muttered and swore and stabbed at those little screens like a family of chimpanzees trying to understand a crashed UFO. We weren't the only ones. I noticed others out there in that sunny summer beer garden poking and stabbing and shaking their heads.

Then the coach arrived.

It was one of those big bastards, with enormous wing mirrors that make it look like a giant insect. As I said, nothing unusual in that, except for the way it was being driven. It thundered round the bend at the far end of the main village street at around fifty miles-an-hour, took the corner too wide and scraped its gleaming white flank along the front of one of the cottages. The nearside mirror spun away. Sparks flew and metal screeched.

It then careered back into the middle of the road and hurtled towards us.

Towards *us*.

It's odd how you just sit there and watch as your doom races towards you.

Robbie moved first, and his yell of warning was enough to galvanise the rest of us into diving out of the coach's path. I went over the beer garden's low fence, slammed into the tarmac beyond and rolled just as the coach roared past. I felt its shockwave, the deafening snarl of its engine; I felt its heat. I smelled oil, petrol and the stink of its exhaust.

There was an explosion of shattered metal, masonry and glass. Then the long, mournful drone of a jammed vehicle horn.

I struggled to my feet in time to see that the coach had carved a path of mayhem through the beer garden and crashed into the front of The Crown. I saw broken wooden picnic tables, ripped and torn umbrellas. And bodies. The first dead bodies I'd ever seen. Like buses; you never see one and then several come along at once. The sheer horror of the accident didn't register straight away. I saw people, twisted and contorted. I saw blood. I saw streaks of pink gut splayed on the grass. I saw limbs that were at nauseating angles. I saw heads wrenched round to face in the wrong direction. I saw a severed arm, its hand with painted nails still curled about a bottle of Doombar.

I recognised Helena Millwood among the casualties. She worked from her home as an accountant. Her body was front down, her head, face up. Twin lines of blood were painted from her nostrils to her chin. Her eyes were wide and lifeless.

No time for shock or grief, however, because the first passengers were escaping from the coach. The door must have been jammed by the impact because they scrambled through the broken windows. There looked to be a fight going on inside, as bodies heaved. They clawed and shouted and swore.

Their desperation was understandable. I wanted to help them, but it was all too much, too wrong, for my mind to process. So, I just stood, frozen by the awfulness of it all. I wasn't alone, several others were strung out on either side of me. Silent and uncomprehending.

Then, as if things hadn't gone wrong enough already that afternoon, they went *very* wrong now.

Anna appeared and stumbled towards the beer garden casualties and escaping passengers. Driven by nurse's instinct, I suppose. Some of the passengers were heading our way now. They were a mess, bleeding, limbs broken and flapping as they scrambled out, dropped to the ground and struggled upright.

None of them appeared to be in pain, however, because all of them were grinning.

Grinning.

There was no mirth in that grin. Those that had eyes, and there were one or two that didn't, looked manic, crazed.

"It's all right," Anna called out to them. "I'm a nurse."

The closest of them broke into a run. Towards Anna. Towards us uninjured onlookers. They didn't look friendly.

I yelled a warning. Anna hesitated, then turned and fled. I saw the terror on her face. It was raw, primal. I ran towards her, to take her hand and pull her away from what had quickly turned into a mob of broken, ruined, monstrously injured human things. I was too slow. One of them, a tall, skinny specimen, grabbed her hair and yanked her back. His arm went about her neck. A large woman with only tufts of hair remaining on her mouldy-looking scalp joined in and forced Anna to the ground.

A moment later she disappeared under a mass of squirming, snuffling bodies. I heard a brief scream. Then no more because I fled. I propelled myself across the road and onto the village green with an energy that startled me. I heard my name and glanced back to see Robbie and Nina close behind. No sign of Jamie, though. My best mate, the brother I never had.

Whatever those dead-looking zombie-things were, they were fast.

Which exposes lie number one. Zombies don't shamble and stumble. They run. They sprint. Nothing will stop them.

I drove myself across the green towards the woods, not convinced I could outrun the bastards. Robbie was off to my right with Nina close behind. Jamie?! Where the hell was Jamie? And Simon?

I looked back. There were hundreds of them now. The fleetest of them were too close for comfort.

The church. Sanctuary, a sacred, holy place; that's where we needed to go. I yelled to Robbie and Nina and changed course. I glanced to my right and saw Nina go down as two of those dead-not-dead things overtook her and grabbed her. They fell upon her in a fury of tearing and punching and I saw blood, and wet, fleshy gobs of something else fly from the scrum. More of them closed on Robbie.

He put a spurt on and overtook me and was first to the churchyard gate. He did not wait, and I don't blame him. He powered up to the door and wrenched it open. I wasn't far behind him.

Then I saw Jamie.

He was running like a maniac across the village green, a horde of those bastards on his heels. He was fast. All those years fleeing his dad's fists, probably. On he came. I willed him to keep going. Come on, Jamie. You can do it.

His face was something I'll never forget. The terror and…exhilaration. A part of him was actually enjoying this! He kept coming. The dead-not-dead were a dark smudge behind him. They stank. Something I noticed for the first time as I stood in the church's open doorway. The ripe stench of them turned my stomach.

Robbie yelled at me to get inside and shut the door.

Jamie was my friend. There was no way I was going to abandon him.

A weapon.

There, in the graveyard. A pile of gardening tools, leaning against the flint wall of the church. Most of them were useless in the circumstances, but the spade, heavy and long handled, had potential. I rushed out and snatched it up in time for Jamie to make his final lunge for the church door and the first of the dead-not-dead to make a grab for him.

It was a man, balding, overweight. His business suit was filthy. His flesh white and mottled with purple. His eyes burned with hunger. I stepped into his path and swung the spade. It sliced through his rotten neck as easily as a knife through butter. His head flew away, that manic expression still in place.

Lie number two. Beheading is no more effective than standing on their toes. The overweight man's body kept coming. No reflex, this. No delayed nervous reaction. His body knew what it was doing and what it wanted.

Me.

Jamie was in the church now. His pleas for me to come inside melded with Robbie's.

The overweight man made a grab for me and only missed by inches, which was pretty impressive seeing that his head, and therefore his eyes, lay in the grass six feet away. I danced back then swung round and ran for the doorway. Robbie and Jamie yelled encouragement. The horde of dead-not-dead yelled insults and threats.

Then I was inside the church where, weakened by shock and exhaustion, I almost fell on my face.

There was a loud thud as Robbie and Jamie slammed the door shut.

And it was quiet. A cool quiet. A peace that I had never known before. The stained glass windows splintered the sunlight into shafts of blue, red and green which gave the place an ethereal beauty. There was comfort in the ancient pews, the cold stone floor, the centuries-old roof of dark beams, and the mingled perfumes of furniture polish and damp. I felt safe here.

It couldn't last, of course. Within moments, the dead-not-dead were pounding on the doors and demanding entrance and that we give up.

"There's nowhere to run, you warm-flesh bastards," a woman yelled. It could have been Anna; the voice, though roughened and brutalised by ruined vocal chords, was familiar.

"They have a point," Robbie said. He looked stricken. "If this is happening everywhere then…where can we go?"

"There's always hope," Jamie said. "We can hide deep in the countryside, make our way up to Scotland or somewhere. Live off the land, find others like us."

"A good idea, Jamie." The new speaker walked towards us down the aisle. The local vicar, Martin Miles, impressive in his full vestments. "The only problem we have is that we have to get out of the church, not an easy task because we appear to be surrounded."

"They can't come in, can they?" Robbie said. There was hopefulness in his voice. Almost childlike. "I mean, this is a holy place…isn't it?"

"I wouldn't count on it. I don't think they're particularly religious," I said. "Did anyone see what happened to Simon?"

"I think they got him." Jamie said. The sentence echoed starkly through the empty cavern that was the church. If he was right, that meant that there were only three of the gang left alive. Three quarters of an hour ago we were sitting around enjoying a pint. Now half of us were dead, whatever that meant in this new normal.

I was startled by a sudden, loud bang. The church door shook under the impact. A moment later one of the windows shattered into a waterfall of coloured glass. I saw a silhouette in the arched space. It looked like Simon. I experienced a moment of hope, then reality closed it down. The Simon who stared down at me from the broken window was not the Simon I knew and loved.

And how the hell had he got up there anyway?

Something revved outside, an engine, rough and powerful. A moment later the door crashed inwards, punched off its hinges by a metal battering ram. The bastards had commandeered a tractor. So much for the mindless, all-we-want-to-do-is-eat-brains crap we had been fed all our lives. These zombies had thought this through and were working together to get at their prey.

They'd arrived in the village by coach for God's sake. How much more organised could they have been?

A movement caught my eye, and I turned to see Simon slither through the broken window and take a headlong dive into the church. He slammed into a pew with an awful thud and crunch, then rolled and leapt to his feet.

Meanwhile, the tractor reversed out to allow the dead-not-dead horde into the church. It took a moment for me to understand that we were finished.

A mass of stinking, rotting flesh boiled in through the broken doorway. More thudded into the pews from the broken upper window. I backed away towards the nave. Nauseated by the sight of some familiar faces in the vanguard of the undead. Nina. Oh God, Nina was there. So was Sarah Mason, the determinedly unmarried forty-something who was the object of every village male's fantasy at some time or other. Richard Evans was there too; eighty-odd, gnarled and tough, and John and Jayne Peck, the village shopkeepers.

Infection and transformation from living-living to living-dead was obviously a quick process. No time for a courageous, self-sacrificing plea of "I've been bitten. Kill me now before it's too late." One nip from those mouldering yellow teeth and you were a fully paid-up member.

I realised that I still held the spade in my hands. At least one of us had a weapon.

"Back, in the name of God, get back." Robbie pushed past me, carrying a silver cross he must have taken from the altar. He held the cross high and for a moment he was magnificent, brave, big and strong.

The horde attacked.

Robbie was overwhelmed and down in seconds. So much for crosses, silver or otherwise.

I saw Sarah Mason rear out of the melee; Robbie's heart clenched in her fist. Blood ran down her wrist. She brought it to her lips and licked it.

We ran, Reverend Miles in the lead. His vestment billowed behind him like a superhero's cloak. I brought up the rear, swinging the spade in an effort to keep the horde back. It seemed to be working but I knew it wouldn't last. Jamie leapt up onto the altar and snatched up one of the big silver candlesticks. I saw him raise it then hurl it at the giant stained glass window that dominated the nave.

There wasn't so much a rain as a blizzard of glass. It seemed to dissolve, then explode outwards. He stood and yelled at us to hurry.

Reverend Miles grabbed my arm and urged me up onto the altar. I scrambled onto the shiny wood. I glanced back and saw Miles turn to face the horde. He lifted his hands and intoned the Lord's Prayer. He was heroic, impressive, like Charlton Heston as Moses when he parted the Red Sea.

But only for a moment.

I was sure that one of those who fell upon him was Anna. I didn't stay to make sure.

I crashed through the bracken and dodged trees. I leapt fallen tree trunks and stumbled and tripped over other obstacles hidden in the undergrowth. Somehow, I had made it out of the churchyard and into the woods. For all their seeming intelligence, the dead-not-dead had not thought to completely surround the church but concentrated their forces on the door. Which meant that when I dropped, heavily onto the grass beyond the nave end of the church, there was no enemy in sight.

I'd lost the spade. I didn't feel much like a macho resistance fighter anyway, more like a scared little boy running away from the bogeyman, or men, or men and women.

They were behind me somewhere, but, thankfully, I seemed to have lost them, for now. Perhaps the woods confused them...

Jamie jinked and weaved ahead of me. He didn't look back, as if he wasn't interested in saving anyone else's skin but his own. I didn't blame him. The time had come for the captain to admit that it was every man for himself. Or person. We're supposed to say person these days –

These days? Surely no one cared, *these days*.

The woods ended.

At the wire fence around the quarry. It was ten-feet high and topped with barbed wire. Beyond was an almost sheer drop into the great crater from which the local stone was mined. The crater was huge. There was a collection of buildings on the far side, huddled in the shadow of a giant science fiction complex of gantries, pipes and industrial elevators that looked like a fairground ride from hell. Lorries and pick-up trucks were parked by the buildings. A steep road gave access and exit to the quarry.

"Fuck, fuck, fuck." There was panic in Jamie's voice. He was already running along the fence, and I followed. The pit was probably about a half-mile in circumference. The going was not easy for most of it as the woods had been allowed to grow right up to the perimeter fence. I understood his despair. We were finished.

I began to wonder what it would be like to be dead-not-dead. Would it be so bad?

"Found it." Jamie had come to a halt. He was laughing with relief, by the sound of it. Although I wasn't so sure about the intensity of his mirth.

"Found what?" I yelled breathlessly as I caught up.

"An emergency gate." It was clasped in place by a giant combination-padlock. "There's a few dotted around the fence, in case we have to make a run for it."

"But it's locked. I thought emergency exits should be - "

"That's the company all over. They think health and safety doesn't apply to them," Jamie said. "Now, shut up and let me open this lock."

"You know the combination?"

"I think so…" He frowned and slowly turned each wheel until he was satisfied that he had the right number aligned with the marker.

I began to lose hope. Why was he taking so long, and what was that noise? Voices? Bodies crashing through the woods?

And then the lock fell open. We both stood and stared at it like two idiots. I regained my senses first, slammed open the latch and opened the gate.

"Wait," I said as Jamie made to go. "Why are we going down there? We haven't thought this through. We'll be trapped."

"I have a plan," Jamie said, then quickly relocked the gate from the inside and lead the way down the zig-zag of precarious-looking metal steps that led to the quarry floor.

It required concentration and an iron nerve. The staircase clanged and shook and seemed to go for ever. I looked over my shoulder constantly, expecting to see the horde emerge from the wood at any moment and tear after us in pursuit. But so far so good.

Resisting the temptation of a papal kneel-and-kiss once we reached the dusty floor of the quarry, I followed Jamie in a tired jog towards the complex. The going was rough and treacherous with loose soil and stones. It was dry and hot, and we kicked up a lot of dust in our wake.

Another backwards glance.

Movement, up there to my left. Bloody hell. The vanguard of the dead-not-dead swarmed up the fence then scrambled over the coiled barbed-wire, apparently unheeding of whatever injuries it inflicted on their rotten flesh.

A loud clang jerked me back to the job in hand. Jamie had reached the buildings and was at the door of a squat, concrete blockhouse. He had found a pickaxe and was using it to attack the lock. I tore my gaze from the oncoming zombies and cast around for a tool of my own. I spotted a sledgehammer in the back of one of the pick-up trucks parked nearby.

Although *nearby* would take me a few yards back in the direction of the first of our attackers. I had to risk it. Jamie needed help and I needed a weapon. I ran for it. Sarah Mason appeared and weaved towards me through the parked vehicles. Her hair was sticky with blood. There was more of it smeared over her bright yellow sundress. Bizarrely, horribly, Robbie's heart was still clenched in her fist.

We met head-on at the pick-up truck. Desperation made me do it. Fear, adrenaline, whatever drives you to perform acts of heroism and madness. In those final seconds before impact, I put my head down and rammed it into her abdomen. Something gave way, horribly. My momentum carried me forwards, and her backwards, then down onto the ground.

She shrieked and lashed out as I rolled free. As I scrambled to my feet she sat up and hurled Robbie's heart at my head. It hit me with an awful, soft thud.

And stayed there.

It clung on.

Robbie's heart, trailing blood vessels, torn from his chest. It quivered then forced one of those arteries into my ear while others tangled themselves in my hair. The world became a muffled, wet, hell of thick blood and pulsing softness. I grabbed at the thing, tugged and yanked, all the time yelling and even screaming in fear, revulsion and anger.

Another vein fumbled its way into my mouth.

I bit down, hard, then managed to tear the monstrosity free. A handful (or was it vein-full) of my hair was ripped out with it. There was a brief, fiery pain deep in my ear. As I threw it to the ground I saw Sarah coming in for a renewed assault. I lunged for the truck and scrambled for the hammer. In one motion, made graceful by my animal terror, I hefted it into my hands and spun about, arcing the lump of iron at the hammer's business end into Sarah's head.

I didn't stop to examine my handiwork. I was aware of an explosion of red and grey, but I was already running for the blockhouse and no longer interested in the village femme fatale.

Jamie was still working at the blockhouse door with his pickaxe. I shoved him aside and brought the sledgehammer down on the lock, which disintegrated. The door swung open.

We were inside in a moment. I made to close it.

"No, no, leave it open. I have a plan."

"A plan?"

"Yeah. I need to set up the ANFO."

"Ann-what?"

"Ammonium nitrate and fuel oil." Jamie sounded a little exasperated by my ignorance. "A-N-F-O. We use it for blasting. Ninety-four percent ammonium nitrate and six percent fuel oil." He pointed to a huge metal cupboard that took up one wall of the small blockhouse. "Open that, will you."

I did so, without thinking. It took two blows from my trusty sledgehammer for the door to swing open and reveal.

Explosives.

Shelves of the stuff, contained as granules in plastic bags like fertiliser or chicken feed.

"Bloody hell, Jamie, you could have told me."

"Stop worrying. It's safe without blasting caps - which are in here." He managed to open a second cupboard with the pickaxe. "I'll deal with them if you run this wire outside. Through that back door there. Take it as far as you can, then connect it to this." He handed me a cable drum and a brick-sized, plastic box. It boasted two terminals, a key slot similar to a car ignition and a red button. "Here." He threw me the key. "For fuck's sake don't unlock the safety until I tell you."

I did as I was told, carefully allowing the twisted, two-core cable to unwind from the drum as I went. I was glad to be outside again.

Which is where I am, right now, crouched at the foot of the quarry wall, about ten yards from the back of the block house. Jamie is still in there doing whatever he needs to do to make his plan come together. I can see the dead-not-dead as they move in on the building. None of them seem to have thought of coming for me around the blockhouse. I guess they smell Jamie in there and that trumps tactics and strategy. Perhaps they don't know I'm here. I'm on my belly, keeping to the shadow cast by the quarry wall. They'll find me soon enough once they've finished with my mate in there. Come on. This is unbearable. Surely, he should have finished fitting, or setting, or whatever, the blasting caps by now.

The box. I haven't connected the wires. I was so relieved to out of there that I forgot. I move carefully, slowly. I still have my sledgehammer but I won't last long if the dead-not-dead attack en masse. I untwist and part the two wires and bite the insulation off each one. My hands are so sweaty I can barely get a grip on the detonator terminals. I fumble and struggle. All the while glancing at the blockhouse.

Shouts. Sounds of a struggle.

Christ, no.

A final turn. Detonator connected and ready. I push the key into the slot.

Come on Jamie. Please.

The first of the dead-not-dead must be at the door now. Inside, even. Perhaps he's done for. Perhaps he's already one of them.

How long do I wait? How long do I delay?

I count down from ten.

…Nine…Eight…Seven…

The door bursts open and Jamie surges towards me.

I turn the key. Detonator set.

He's still too close to the block house.

Which is full of zombies. clawing each other, all struggling to get through the back door at once. The sickly-sweet stink of rotting flesh billows out. My stomach contracts, but I manage to fight back my rising nausea. I see terror on Jamie's face. He shouts. I can't hear above the thunder of my heartbeat, but the message is clear.

"Now!" he says. "Now! Now!"

The first of the dead-not-dead erupt from the blockhouse's back door. The Reverend Miles, Anna, Robbie with a bloody hole in his chest.

I stab the red button.

There is a moment when everything is silent. Even the horde of dead-not-dead inside and outside the blockhouse seem frozen and quiet.

Then the world ends in a roar, and everything disintegrates and disappears in a cloud of smoke as an army of heavyweight boxing champions pummel me to the ground and crack my ribs and scream into my ears.

There is dust and a torrent of debris, then things that are wet and that splatter and burst. A red rain pours out of the smoke. Gobs of stuff arrive; sacs of gore, writhing intestines, an eye, a hand. Then a scorched, blackened skeleton staggers out of the inferno and collapses into a pile of bones that rattle and clatter on the ground, driven by whatever grotesque energy it is that fires these things.

And that is where the plan breaks down.

As the smoke and dust clear enough for us to see the pile of guts and offal that covers the rubble of the blockhouse, what should have been obvious comes back to bite us in the arse. The energy that drives the dead-not-dead does not require a complete body. In fact, it doesn't require a body at all. A steaming red-black sludge is spreading outwards from the blast centre. It quivers and bubbles and boils. Intestines swim through the mess like serpents, hearts beat and pulse and propel themselves forwards like grotesque jellyfish or hop like hellish frogs, hands scuttle like blood-soaked spiders. The sludge itself, the soup of blood and liquified organic tissue rushes towards us, like a huge blanket of gore. It is both foul and cloyingly sweet.

Jamie is face down. He's moving, struggling up onto his hands and knees. I should go help him, but the gore is already lapping at his legs. Human organs slither and scuttle over his back. I retreat until I feel the wall of the quarry behind me. I spin about and try to climb. It's impossible. All I can hear is the ringing in my ears. I cough on the dust. It's hard to see now, because a gritty, impenetrable fog is swirling out of the ruins.

Figures emerge from the mist, indistinct at first, but I know who and what they are. I am too battered and exhausted to run any further or attempt to fight my way out.

"Okay," I say. "I give up. I'll join you. Just make it quick." At least I have friends among their number.

I drop to my knees in the mess and something wet, cold and stinking clambers up my back. The first of the dead-not-dead emerge from the fog. And right now, in this last, brief moment of real life, I see my mistake. It's clear, in their eyes, that they are not interested in recruitment right now.

They are hungry.

Coffin Creeper

Dave Davis

Blondes were always my preferred companion, but beggars can't be choosers. It's all the same when you're cummin', as they say. Mainly, I just wanted a compliant partner to satisfy my urges. All that bitchin' and complainin' was a total turn off, so naturally, I just found more agreeable specimens. I could only take so much of them screwin' up their face and barkin' at me, *not like that, don't touch my tits, not in that hole, my jaw hurts!* All I needed was a fuck-bag, and so what if they came in a body bag.

I stumbled across this most amicable situation accidentally, like most grandiose discoveries. During some rambunctious body rockin' with a local prostitute, the whore just up and died during the middle of the festivities. Guess her chemical compulsion finally got the best of her. Well, I wasn't about to be deprived of my expensive exploits, so I just said *what the heck*, and finished myself off with the limp corpse. I had to admit, to my pleasant surprise (pun intended), it was pretty good! Actually, even better than tolerating the self-powered version. The epiphany hit me; I could have my cake and eat it too. I didn't have to put up with all the trouble and expense of engaging with attitudinal, demanding live cunts. But acquiring the complacent ones would require a new approach. Looked to me like coffin coitus was the best option.

It wasn't hard to make friends with the local cemetery owner. He had a huge hankerin' for beer and indulged that thirst nightly at the local waterin' hole. After many long nights chuggin' drafts with him at the dimly lit ice house, I broached the vile subject. I figured I had nothin' to lose, other than a drinkin' acquaintance, if I somehow disgusted him with my inquest. He merely chuckled at the idea briefly, then went straight to discussing the collaboration. Apparently, Mr. Flowers had been harnessing some depraved fetishes of his own. That night, since we were sharing secrets, he confided in me with tales of BDSM. He, of course, required animated constituents for this sort of fulfillment, but relayed that there was no way he could judge me for my interests from where he was sitting. In fact, my request didn't offend him in the least. That old coot made it plain for me to understand that he was particularly glad I had the gumption to suggest bringing some excitement into his mostly mundane existence, barring the floggings and strap-on dildo cornholings, of course. All he asked in return for access to the ripest buried cadavers of my choosing was that he be permitted some voyeurism, and some contribution to his nightly bar tab. So, my rampant escapades began.

I'll never forget the first, and best exploit at the macabre bordello. Brimming with anticipation, I could feel my neurons firing on all cylinders as we turned off the dark farm-to-market road, lined densely with a copse of tall pines, to pass under the archway delineating the Cherry Hill Cemetery. Equipped with our flashlights and shovels, Mr.

Flowers led me to a secluded region of the grave plots, where fresh dirt lay plain to see as we approached the offering my deviant sidekick had designated for me. Admiring the epitaph, *Monique Berrymore*, my willing unit began to engorge and pulsate.

"According to the headstone, this chick was only thirty years old. What, did she get eaten up with cancer or something?"

Mr. Flowers imparted, "Nope, poor bitch offed herself with sleeping pills. Depression or some shit, I believe. I usually don't take too much interest in the deceased that I traffic in, but once I got a look at this one, I knew you'd be all over it!"

"Aw, hell! She oughta be in decent shape then."

I felt like a kid digging for the prize in a Cracker Jack box; the excitement overflowing to the bursting point. The zeal I was reveling in was only further heightened by the inward acknowledgment that an ensured explosion of my loins was imminent. The strawberry blonde was tantalizing upon exposure; her serene display, so inviting. I could delay no longer. My trusty fixed blade knife greedily bisected her burial garments. Then I pounced on her, wasting no time plunging my aching cock within her decomposing twat. The pre-cum, which I couldn't suppress, negated any need for lube, due to my prolonged overarousal during the excavation process. Like a pubescent schoolboy, a torrential eruption vacated my shaft, in a fraction of the time I would have preferred. Though this was my shortest stint to be had at the horror whorehouse, it remained the most gratifying of all. No one could ever deprive me of the dreams and memories replaying that event in my mind. And no one could ever change the fact that although Monique couldn't moan, I was her first postmortem fuck.

The interludes between my fucking corpses seemed interminable. My new addiction consumed my entire existence. The desire to expand my graveyard girl gallery was all encompassing. Daydreams of diddling the decomposed, and fondling the festering fairer sex, occupied my mind. Running a gauntlet of open casket orgies was now my perpetual pursuit.

"What took you so long, Flowers? I've been dying for some coffin cooter!"

"Shit man, you just got some cold fur burger a couple of nights ago. I'm runnin' outta fresh deliveries lately. You're gonna end up havin' ta settle for some spoiled meat."

"That's alright; a little bit of decay just makes 'em slicker 'n softer. It's gonna be light soon. What was the hold up?"

"Had a little trouble with the hemorrhoids if ya must know! My new dominatrix surprised me with her latest accessory. Damn near made my eyes pop out… he he."

"Speakin' of, I hope you brought the polaroid with ya, I'm hankerin' for some skullduggery tonight, if you know what I mean…har har har."

My ninth corpse conquest spurred me to seeking the greater latitudes awarded within the realm of necrophilia. Although the more conventional sex acts performed with the previous partners were satisfactory, I couldn't resist seizing the opportunities awarded by my docile, unknowing, albeit non-permissive supplicants. Anticipating the progression to skull fucking, I had brung along a table spoon, for expedient clearance of the orbital glory (or should I say gory) hole. Well acclimated to the morbid sex scene, the miasma exuding from the more matured fuck buddy didn't bother me in the least. By this point, my decadence had instilled a delight with decay. I wouldn't pass on a gangrenous gash. In fact, the gelatinous ichor involved with this novel enterprise didn't disappoint, as the excitement ensured ejaculation exceedingly well. I guess we had plenty of time for this excursion after all. From that point on, my gluttonous greed for the grotesque knew no bounds: erotic evisceration, synchronized fellatio flaying; you name it. The polaroids granted me ongoing satisfaction from my dastardly deeds, as the visitations were necessarily too brief. Even with the low probability of discovery due to the cemetery's isolated geography, I had no intention of letting my favorite pastime be stripped from me. My ghastly activities would go on.

As I passed beneath the green glowing neon sign (The Drip) demarcating our humble haunt, my eyes adjusted to the typical dark ambience of the saloon, finding Mr. Flowers observing my approach with anticipation. An atypical demeanor exuded from him, accompanied by a disturbed visage.

"We got a problem…"

I stared at him. "Oh, what's that?"

Avoiding the bar keep's gaze, he waited until the server moved away from our proximity, after depositing our usual, unwavering choice mugs of draft lager, before continuing. "Well, ya know them polaroids you're so keen on…? I inadvertently left one in my coat pocket after one of your flings. It musta got hung up when I was handing the batch off to you after we cleared out that night.

"Anyways, while I was in the bathroom after getting roughed up by my mistress yesterday, she noticed a corner of the photograph protruding from my jacket and took a gander to satisfy her curiosity. Now the bitch is demanding we take her with us on the next rendezvous, otherwise she'll turn us in to the sheriff's department!"

Aghast, I said, "You gotta be fuckin' kiddin' me!"

Obviously, I had no problem with an audience during my putrid porno performances; however, this indiscretion had me fuming. I was more concerned with the potential for my carnal circus coming to a close. Mr. Flowers had drawn on about his favorite torturous fetish dispenser while shooting the shit over many beers, many a night. And, I knew she was a kinky slut. But this just didn't sit right with me. For all I knew, she was aiming to collect more damning evidence, and then really put the squeeze on us. She probably had dollar signs in her eyes, with him owning his own business and all. Blackmail could be her motive. Maybe turning a buck one whipping at a time was getting to be too much for her, especially with the chance for riding the gravy train just falling into her lap like that.

If we just dismissed her threats, and tried to call her bluff, even an anonymous tip to the police from her could lead to my residence being searched. No way was I going to destroy the incriminating evidence revealed within my treasured polaroid collection of necrotic flesh frolics. And worse than that, the county could arrange to have the cemetery delights exhumed, in search of burial desecration, or traces of DNA to compare with the accused perpetrators she fingers.

After reflecting on this inwardly, I decided to ease my vulgar companion's mind. Upon plastering a calm expression and cool grin on my face, I leaned in with, "Looks like your girl wants to be dished out some discomfort of her own…Well, let's give it to her!"

The necrodemons must have been smiling upon me. While perusing the obituaries for candidates, for the group carcass cramming outing, a specimen was presented to me that would suffice for my intended plot. Especially since the recently deceased's grave plot happened to be positioned within the Cherry Hill Cemetery. *Tabitha Torn, 52, survived by unknown next of kin.* Apparently, the woman had arranged a living will, directing her remaining bank funds to provide for her burial. The county officials arranged it with Mr. Flowers, as she had no family to speak of. There were rumors that she had relocated and changed her name; an outcast, or the like.

Mr. Flowers, during one of his alcohol fueled story times at the dive bar, revealed that Luna the dominatrix was an undocumented immigrant from Romania. We did not know her real name, only her occupational alias. Nor did we know what made her choose to relocate overseas under the radar. Maybe she found herself enveloped in the sex worker community due to an inability to join the formal corporate work force without legal identification. Or perhaps she gravitated to the lust brigade organically, as a natural fit; a volitional undertaking; a desire to assume that role; a delight in donning latex and doling out deviant decadence; a satisfaction with the sensual slave vocation. It mattered little to me.

Cherry Hill Cemetery beckoned its pleasure patrons, like the inviting beacon of lights outside a peep show, with a full moon reflecting off the headstones, illuminating our path to the newly buried Tabitha's gravesite. Our practiced craft allowed expeditious preparation of the gruesome playground, with polished strokes of our shovels and crowbars.

While positioning myself in preparatory posture for the ghoulish display, juxtaposed to Ms. Torn's previously functioning pelvis, I motioned to Luna. "Come on down here an' enjoy the action a little closer. Why don't you take the photos for me?"

She readily snatched the camera from my cohort, then slid down the excavated dirt wall to join me for a close-up of the proceedings. I drew my faithful blade and readied it for the stiff's disrobing. Luna peered through the camera's view portal, but the only flash that occurred came from the brutal crowbar swing that pummeled the apex of her skull. An eruption of laughter escaped my mouth upon beholding the burst of crimson which coincided with the precision driven splintering skull crack. Her stupefied blood streaming face further enhanced my delight. Mr. Flowers had sent her crumbling to the dirt before she could take a single snap shot.

That night, I added a thirty-five-year-old brunette Romanian notch to my belt. I didn't have to settle for the over the hill, already undergoing putrefaction ugly hag that was the original tenant of the grave. The dominatrix would soon be roommates with her. The European's petite, fit, curvaceous physique was a sumptuous trade-off for the bag of worms, and even more delectable, since she was the most fresh, unanimated cum bucket I had the pleasure of slapping skin with since I stumbled upon the glorious enterprise of necrophilia.

"I still cain't believe you didn't wanna have her before we eliminated her!" Flowers said, as we made the relatively short drive back down the farm-to-market road, heading back into town.

"You know me… At least you got to switch roles with her for a change."

"Yeah, that was kinda fun! But dammit ta hell, I lost my favorite dildo slingin' whip wielder!"

"Sorry 'bout that bro. But hey, dominatrixes are a dime a dozen. On the contrary, the bevy of placid porn playmates is priceless to me."

"Well, you got a point there…" Flowers said. "It's gonna cost ya a few more beers though, and then some, haaaa!"

My headstone was simply inscribed with, *Mr. Creeper*. Curiosity about my absence within The Drip patronage was easily quelched with Mr. Flowers' explanation that I had 'moved out of town.' This was easily digested by the care-free, drunkard clientele, as I was an assumed drifter anyhow, having appeared amongst their ranks only months ago, relocated from a far-off region, which I had lied to them about my true origination. The same inherent apathy, ambient in that environment, ensured no concern, the evening that Mr. Flowers escorted me, under impaired ambulation, with assistance to his truck, after the barbiturates he slipped into my beer, while I went to relieve myself in the pisser, took effect. Just another case of 'one too many,' on a regularly occurring booze binge. He knew that I had presented myself under a false name. And, he knew about the dead hooker I left in my hotel room, to so hastily go on the lamb. I didn't have to share all of my secrets with Mr. Flowers; as I came to find out, he surely didn't reciprocate. A player should always hold their cards close to their vest. It appears that he didn't actually 'accidentally' leave that polaroid (the one that his other murder victim supposedly discovered) in his coat pocket, either. Because, not only did he switch roles, from masochist to sadist, from recipient to inflictor, when he brandished the crowbar to dispense pain onto Luna; in my case, the loss of posthumous virginity was delivered rectally, by a three-hundred-pound undertaker. Looks like I'll never have to give up my frequenting of the Cherry Hill Cemetery, after all.

The Grind

Paul Allih

F rank watched organs and de-boned hunks of meat fall from the hatch above, slopping into the jaws of the MC1200. His phone vibrated in his pocket, but he ignored the alert, keeping his focus on the product as it hit the blades of the meat grinder.

The MC1200 was the oldest machine at Keller Foods, and all the machinery was pretty damn old. Aged by more than a decade of use, the MC1200 was a mammoth rectangle of heavy metals. It had three rows of jagged blades on top and several rows of smaller blades in its belly. The proteins were broken down and made into a smooth, creamy paste that would be formed into patties for Keller Food's Salisbury Steak Family Meal.

The gears strained to take down the meat. Lungs, intestines, and fatty cuts compounded in the steel teeth, seemingly too much for the ancient grinder to take all at once. This was a common occurrence ever since Keller Foods signed a contract with a national grocer a few months back. No upgrades were made to the equipment, the workload was increased, and the employees were left to deal with the repercussions. More meat going through the antiques at Keller meant more breakdowns. But Frank could only do his job. Frank stood by on his platform, ready to grab his rake and assist the old girl as she started to fuss.

After some whining, the MC1200 finally worked through the obstruction. While the blades tore the pieces into bits, Frank took out his phone from the back of his Wranglers and glanced at the screen. It was a text from Danni, his wife of seventeen years. "Are you still meeting up with your friends?"

"I already answered that," Frank huffed beneath the humming gears.

Danni asked if he was going out that evening three times before he left the house that morning. Mere hours ago, he told her he was going to Freddy's Hideaway with Kyle, Steve, and Thomas.

Frank looked out for Mr. Hernandez as his thumbs quickly hammered out, "Yes, after work."

He hit send and shoved the phone back into his pocket. Within seconds, his phone was shaking with another text alert. Frank pulled out his phone and held it low as he read, "What time are you meeting them?"

The screech of the metal hatch above his head took his attention. A bigger load than the last descended. Cartilage, ligaments, and big slabs of muscle and fatty hunks rained into the moving blades. The meat was brown, and the gristle was almost yellow. The sour odors wafted around Frank as the fibers were ripped apart and shredded. But he'd grown used to the smell. If he was being honest, there was a certain sweetness in the aroma that he found appealing.

Before the MC1200 could finish the previous load, another shipment arrived on its heels. Guts; a massive dump of slimy, squirmy guts. They looked like a giant glob of dead snakes, cold and intertwined. The entrails hit with a thud and the MC1200 tried to take them all in at once, seizing with a loud whine, as if it was crying out for help.

Frank pocketed his phone and grabbed his rake.

"Alright Hun, let me get you freed up," Frank said, speaking to the machine like a nurturing parent.

Frank leaned over the railing of the platform with his rake held out. The stink of old copper and feces loomed in the air. After almost seventeen years of dealing with open guts, the smell didn't affect him anymore. He used the forks on the rake to pull back the intestines, untangling them from one another, making it easier for the MC1200 to grind them down.

Mr. Hernandez came from around the corner and shouted up at him. "Hey Frank, hurry up and get that damn thing going again!"

"Yeah, yeah," Frank said under his breath.

Mr. Hernandez hustled away, hollering at Carlo on the de-boner. Ignoring the commotion, Frank continued to ease the guts into the MC1200. The moist bits slapped and smacked together. Blood was squeezed out as the pieces were reduced, and the juices lubricated the steel.

"There you go, girl," Frank subtly cheered, as the machine purred along.

Frank took out his phone.

Mr. Hernandez hollered up to him, "How's she doing?"

Startled, Frank quickly shoved his phone back into his pocket.

"How's she doing?" Hernandez repeated, louder while stepping up closer.

For a moment, Frank thought Mr. Hernandez was talking about his wife. Looking at his supervisor's face, he realized he was talking about the machine. "Oh, yeah, she's grinding along fine now."

"Great, stay on top of it!"

Frank's phone vibrated again. He watched Hernandez walk away and took out his device. It was a text from his friend, Kyle. "Can't make it for drinks, give the boys my regards."

Kyle had been Frank's best friend since sixth grade. They'd been through a lot together, up to and including Trish Cassidy, the smasher of wills and the breaker of hearts. After high school, they enrolled at the community college together. Frank dropped out after Danni announced she was pregnant while Kyle earned his BA in business management, taking a cushy office gig after he graduated.

Kyle thought Frank was crazy for leaving college to work in a slaughterhouse. Then again, Kyle would never have fathered a child. He did what he wanted, who he wanted, when he wanted, which was why Kyle's sporty black Mercedes had been parked in Frank's driveway while he was at work the past few weeks. The neighbor across the street tipped Frank off. She was a retired private investigator who had nothing better to do than observe and report.

Frank didn't want to believe it, but then he found a condom wrapper on the floor under his and his wife's bed. He didn't need to wear a condom with Danni because he had a vasectomy. She insisted that he get one after Sean was born. It was painful, and his scrotum became infected. He developed sperm granulomas; his testicles were covered with milky cysts. But she asked, and he delivered. He'd do anything for her.

Frank took an early lunch one day and drove by the house. Kyle's Benz was in the driveway. Frank parked a couple of addresses down and snuck around to the back of the house where his and Danni's bedroom was located. He peered into the window across from their bed. Between a gap in the curtain, he caught a glimpse of his wife pressed up against the headboard with his best friend between her open thighs. Sheets cast off, naked, him on top of her, thrusting.

Now they were messaging Frank, duping him into the

scheming of their next rendezvous. Sean was at a friend's binging a new video game and Frank would be at the bar with Thomas and Steve, giving Danni and Kyle a quiet night of adultery.

He thought about calling them out on their not-so-subtle sneaking around, but he couldn't do it. Frank wasn't the confrontational type. No matter how many times she stabbed him in the heart, Frank could never retaliate.

Disgusted, Frank swiped away his former friend's message and texted his son. "Sean, I hope you're having fun. Enjoy it. Love you always."

He turned off his phone and shoved it into his pocket as a fresh batch of flesh dropped from the hatch. Lungs, livers, jaws, and innards. The meat was grayish in color and moist with sweat, and there was a lot of it. It plopped into the MC1200, slapping and smacking, chunks mashing together in the rows of rolling blades. Frank sucked in a deep breath of copper and oiled steel, and he wondered what it was going to feel like when he *fell* in.

Frank had considered it for a while, but he made up his mind last week. He was going to have a nasty accident at work by falling into the MC1200, and his son would reap the rewards of his tragic demise.

He had it all planned out.

Frank bought a life insurance policy ten years ago when an operator at the plant in Massachusetts ended up on the wrong side of a de-boner. Frank changed Sean to the sole beneficiary, and the one-hundred-thousand-dollar payout would be given to him when he turned eighteen.

Danni would most certainly sue Keller Foods for a litany of safety violations, such as shoving rakes into an active meat grinder to keep production moving. He hated her for ripping his heart out, but she was Sean's mother, and she was entitled to whatever a jury saw fit.

Frank got them a small house in an okay neighborhood

and was able to put food on the table. Sean was older, and he needed to go to a good college where his intelligence could blossom, and he could realize his dreams. That wasn't going to happen with Frank working at Keller Foods.

Most of all, he couldn't stop seeing his wife fucking his best friend. The image was burned into his mind. Kyle's hairy ass, thrusting and pounding, Danni's ankles pinned behind her ears, eyes rolled into the back of her head while she made sounds that he only wished he could drive her to make.

Mr. Hernandez walked up the stairs to the platform and said, "Hey Frank, check this out. Last night, I found out that my wife spent three hundred dollars on shoes."

"Is that right?"

"Yeah, three hundred on a pair of pumps."

"That seems like a lot."

"Yeah!"

Frank couldn't care less. He didn't know how he was supposed to go into the grinder with Hernandez unburdening himself. His nerve was wearing off and his edge was fading. Death by small talk, and his mother swore it couldn't happen.

Mr. Hernandez questioned, "How much does your wife spend on Amazon?"

"Danni isn't much of a shopper."

"Yeah?"

"She gets off in other ways…"

Hernandez looked at him curiously, unsure of where he was going with his words.

"She's been liking my friend's cock a lot."

Hernandez laughed. But Frank didn't laugh.

Hernandez stopped laughing. "Bro, are you serious?"

"Dead serious," Frank said, straight faced.

"Your wife's doing your friend?"

"Best friend."

"Oh, man, I'm sorry!"

"It's not your fault."

"What are you going to do?"

Frank shrugged. "What can I do?"

"I guess you could leave."

"I'm working on that."

"Oh, do you know where you're going?"

"Not sure yet."

Another load came through. Another big one. Hunks and chunks, strewn with entrails. Slimy and pale, almost grey, the heavy bits flopped against the steel. The product became twisted up together, and the blades came to a halt.

"It's just too much at one time," Frank said, shaking his head. "One can only take so much, you know, and shit keeps coming and coming, and then, you can't take anymore!"

"Yeah, I know. Let me get that for you," Hernandez said, picking up the rake that was leaning up against the railing.

Frank was reminded about the alterations he made to the company rake a week ago. He straightened its curled fingers with a pair of pliers and a blow torch. That way, if he were to lose his nerve, the machine would get him anyway. He couldn't let his customizations possibly take the life of someone else.

"No, let me do it!" Frank said, countering his supervisor.

Mr. Hernandez ignored Frank while looking his way. Blindly shoving the rake at the meat pile below, he talked at Frank about Danni's infidelity like he had been watching too much Dr. Phil. Frank's eyes were focused on the forks as they bobbed towards the budging blades. He kept trying to warn his supervisor, but the man kept going on until Frank had to shove Hernandez out of the way and take the rake from his grasp.

"What the hell?!" Hernandez spouted as Frank knocked him to the side.

The blades started hitting the rake and pulling Frank over the railing. The rake flew, hitting Hernandez across the head and knocking him out.

Frank tumbled downwards. His eyes widened as he descended heels first into the bloodied steel teeth of the MC1200. His heart stopped for a moment, and he couldn't exhale. Frank had a sudden change of heart; he wanted to live. He prayed for something miraculous to happen, like the MC1200 suddenly shutting down or an angel whisking him to safety.

Reality struck fast.

Frank touched down, the blades sliced through the soles of his boots, then ripped into the soles of his feet. The sudden burst of pain swallowed his being as the blood began to spray and splatter. He'd never felt anything so excruciating as the MC1200 popped his toes off of his feet, shredded the meat, and broke the tiny bones into splinters.

This wasn't the plan.

The plan was to go in headfirst. His skull would have been crushed and his brain turned to slaw before he would have felt an ounce of pain. But there he was, experiencing every awful sensation the MC1200's blades had to offer. Frank's feet were decimated, and next were the ankles. The joints were rolled and crushed in the gears, taking him down like all the other aged product at Keller Foods.

Screaming and flailing, Frank cried out to Hernandez, but Hernandez was still out cold. Almost everyone on the floor was probably listening to music or podcasts through their ear buds. They weren't supposed to, but they did it anyway, and Mr. Hernandez was enough of a sucker to turn a blind eye. As long as the machines were running, that's all that mattered, and machines were indeed running.

The MC1200 worked past Frank's ankles and down to

the shins. His fibulas cracked and his tibias snapped while his muscular calves were diced into hamburger-like pulp. Frank begged for it to jam up and end his agony. The one time he wanted the machine to stop, it seemed to run like new. The damn thing was destined to kill him.

Short of breath, his heart thudded against his chest, and Frank started blacking out. Between flutters of light and dark, he saw his kneecaps explode under the pressure of the gears. Blood and shards of bone and ribbons of skin cascaded all around. Faint from the unending affliction, the smell of his own meat and the stink of his open bones made him vomit. Bile and his breakfast burrito from earlier that morning burst from his mouth and his nostrils in a hot froth of burning acids.

Once he upchucked everything in his digestive tract, he screamed as loud as he could. Frank's shrieks stripped his throat raw as they echoed through the plant, but the anguish only escalated. His thighs were hacked apart, the meat gouged and tenderized, tendons torn asunder. The femoral arteries were eviscerated; blood swooshed and splashed while his femurs cracked and split apart.

Frank was barely conscious when his genitals were torn away and ground up. Shrapnel from his femurs was pushed into his pelvis before shattering it, taking him down to the stomach. Frank's guts unspooled and his lower intestine became wrapped up in the lower gears. The MC1200 seized and bellowed in distress, finally having enough.

Coming to, Hernandez pulled himself up from the platform to find Frank sticking out of the MC1200. All the blood and human debris forced him to look away. "Frank, hold on, man, I gotta shut it down!"

Hernandez raced down the stairs of the platform and around to the base of the machine and slammed the big red emergency shutdown button with his palm. The MC1200 powered down and Hernandez rushed back up the stairs. He looked down on Frank, mangled from the waist down and twitching in a chunky bath of red.

George came from the patty press and Carlo rushed from the de-boner. Hernandez patted himself down, frantically searching for his cell phone before realizing he didn't have it on him. Protocol.

"Someone call an ambulance!" Hernandez shouted to the men behind him.

"I don't have my phone," George hollered back, hesitating to step any closer.

"I'll go get mine," Carlo said, jetting to the lockers.

Hernandez turned back to Frank, "Don't worry, we're getting you help!"

There was no helping him. The tears and the abject terror on Hernandez's face told him as much. Frank was numb and his vision was fading.

"Hold on, Frank," Hernandez said. "You saved my life, Man! Thank you, Frank. You're a hero!"

The word *hero* stuck out in Frank's brain. Sean would be proud, he thought with his last stream of consciousness. A smile formed on his bloody lips, stretching wide and freezing in place.

OTHER HELLBOUND BOOKS
www.hellboundbooks.com

Anthology of Splatterpunk: Vol 1

splat·ter·punk
noun
informal
noun: splatterpunk

Definition: "A literary genre characterized by graphically described scenes of an extremely gory nature."

HellBound Books are incredibly proud to present to you horror most raw and visceral, two-dozen suitably graphic, horrific tales of terror designed to churn the stomach and curdle the blood.

This superlative tome is an absolute must for fans of Richard Laymon, Clive Barker, Monica J. O'Rourke, Matt Shaw, Wrath James White and Jack Ketchum – all put to paper by some of the brightest new stars writing in the genre today.

Featuring stories by: Nick Clements, Carlton Herzog, NJ Gallegos, Scotty Milder, Steve Stark, Frederick Pangbourne, Cristalena Fury, Amber Willis, Kenneth Amenn, Erica Summers, Allie Guilderson, Cory Andrews, Andrew P. Weston, Shula Link, Carlton Herzog, DW Milton, Brent Bosworth, JD Fuller, Robert Allen Lupton, C.M. Noel, Julian Grant, Jay Sykes, Phil Williams, and the incomparable James H Longmore.

Satan Rides Your Daughter Again

Welcome to the second volume of HellBound's satanic-themed anthology, our homage to all things Old Nick and those who worship him and his demonic underlings!

From a poor woman suffering at the hands of witch finders, the building of an infamous Bunny Ranch and absolute living Hell that is high school, to encounters with angels, Hades' pit, the quest for a hellishly good chili, and so much more in between, Satan Rides Your Daughter Again is packed with devilishly good tales to torment your soul with a taste of the fire and brimstone underworld that roils below us…

Featuring some of the very best independent horror authors committing words to paper today: R.D. Tyler, Dan Bolden, K A Douglas, Dylan Bosworth, Conor O'Brian Barnes, Dan Muenzer, Josh Darling, Barend Nieuwstraten III, Matthew Fryer, Kevin L. Kennel, J Louis Messina, Terry Grimwood, James Musgrave, Donn L. Hess, Shannon Lawrence, Chase Hughes, KT Bartlett, Sarah Goodman, Mariah Southworth, and Terry Campbell.

Anthology of Horror

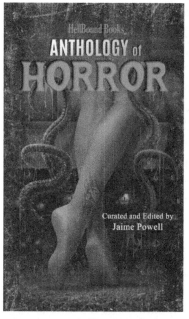

hor·ror
/ˈhôrər/

A literary or film genre concerned with arousing feelings of horror.

Rest assured, HellBound Books knows what scares you!

Skulking around in the deepest, thickest, darkest shadows of our authors' imaginations lies a whole host of terrifying tales to scare you witless and stir your greatest fears and, dear reader, we have compiled twenty-one such short stories for that specific purpose within the beautifully crafted pages of this very tome!

So, dig in – we dare you – and do remember to leave a light on…

Featuring short tales of terror from: Cory Andrews, Kathrin Classen, William Presley, John Schlimm. K.L. Lord, Jane Nightshade, K. John O'Leary, Dante Bilec, D. H. Parish, Whitney McShan, Keiran Meeks, Josh Darling, Paul Lonardo, Martyn Lawrence, Eric J. Juneau, Terry Campbell, Brett King, Sophia Cauduro, Christina Meeks, Kody Greene, and HellBound Books' very own James H Longmore.

The First Time I saw Her

Anna and her mother are on the run after a tragedy shatters their world. A stranger has offered them protection in a private community hidden deep in the woods, and Anna and her mother have no choice but to abandon their life and belongings to take refuge until they can figure out their next move.

But the woman who helped them may not be what she seems, and the safe-haven community has its own secrets ... and its own dangers.

Anna is no ordinary girl, though. She can perceive things others cannot, impossible things. Now thrust into an unfamiliar setting with horrors unfolding all around her, Anna must figure out what she is and what she is capable of before she loses what little she has left of her life.

THE FIRST TIME I SAW HER is the first installment in the folk horror Gossamer and Pitch Trilogy, a series about love and hate, witches and demons, and the sheer veil between life and death.

The Gentleman's Choice

"A clever twist on the age-old adage, Art imitates reality, drives this terrifying possibility into the deepest places of your imagination." Andrew Neiderman, author of *The Devil's Advocate* and the V.C. Andrews novels.

A sleazy internet dating show blamed for a viewer's death, a host with a dark, secret past, and a killer with a sadistic grudge…

Someone is kidnapping and murdering previous contestants from the popular streaming show *The Gentleman's Choice* – a strictly adult hybrid of *The Bachelor and Love Island.* Private Investigator, Vanessa Young, is hired by a victim's family to infiltrate the show as a contestant to expose and capture the killer.
Vanessa and Cole Gianni, the show's charismatic star, begin to fall romantically for each other, until Vanessa's plan goes terribly awry when they're drugged and taken to a remote location to take part in their captor's own brutal, ultimately fatal, version of *The Gentleman's Choice.* With the clock ticking toward their fateful final night, Vanessa and Cole are forced into a battle of wills to survive their tormentor and escape with their lives before it's too late…

HellBound Books Publishing

**A HellBound Books® Publishing LLC
Publication**

www.hellboundbooks.com

Made in the USA
Middletown, DE
13 June 2025

76955629R00188